WILD JUSTICE

To Robin & Peter,
Wonderful friends

Arthur Haberman

LEAPING LION BOOKS

Copyright page

Wild Justice by Arthur Haberman

Published by

Leaping Lion Books
4700 Keele Street
Toronto, ON
Canada M3J 1P3

www.yorku.ca/llbooks

Copyright © 2018 by Arthur Haberman

All rights reserved. No part of this book may be reproduced in any form or by any electronic or mechanical means, without permission in writing from the publisher, except by a reviewer, who may quote brief passages in a review.

This is a work of fiction. The names, characters, businesses, places, events and incidents in this novel are either the product of the author's imagination or are used in a fictitious manner. No identification with actual persons (living or dead), organizations, corporations or events is intended or should be inferred.

For permissions, contact

Michael O'Connor, oconnorm@yorku.ca

Cover design and back cover blurb by

Farheen Abbas
Christopher Lai
Michelle Mogilner
Nixon St. Nicolous
Zara Snitman
John Wilson
Nicole Wyile

Issued in print and electronic formats.
ISBN 978-1-988170-14-5
eBook ISBN 978-1-988170-13-8

Book Design by Stephanie Wilcox & James Zhan

To Jake and Kyle

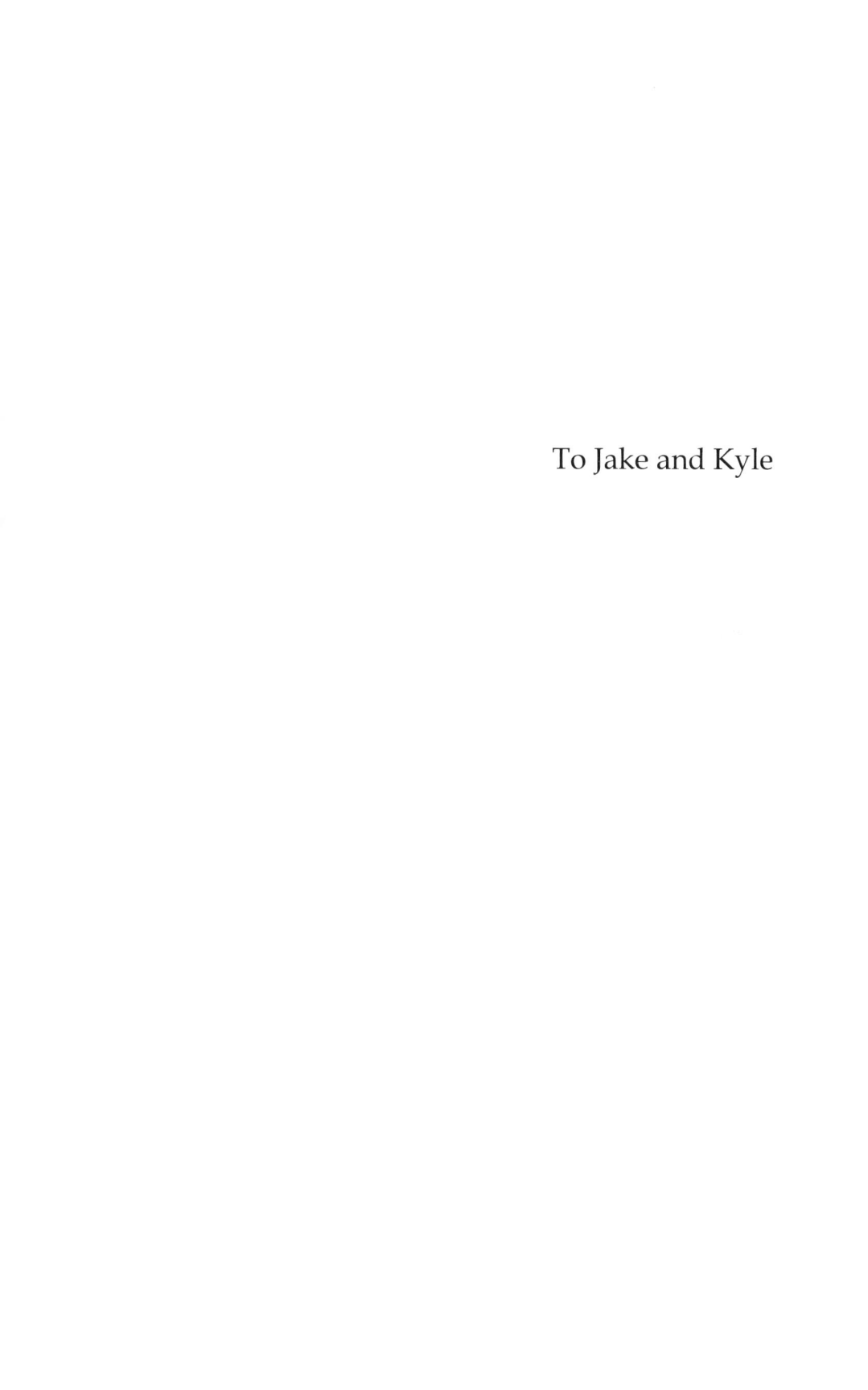

> "Revenge is a kind of wild justice."
> Francis Bacon

WILD JUSTICE

PART I

I

Detective Sergeant Daniel Miller, of the Toronto Police Homicide Squad, rose especially early on the anniversary of his father's death. Danny was not an observant Jew. As he put it, he was not very good with the first four of the Ten Commandments, though he thought he did pretty well with the last six. The fifth, honour thy father and thy mother, mattered to him. He didn't attend synagogue regularly, but he did so to say Kaddish for his parents. There wasn't much he could do for them now, beyond this. Last night he went to a service near his office. This morning and afternoon he would go to the Kollel to fulfil the duty of *yahrzeit*.

Danny parked his car on a side street near the Kollel on Bathurst, below Wilson, put on a fedora, what he called his shul hat, and entered. It was the same Kollel where his father learned the Torah and other sacred texts. From the outside it looked like an ordinary storefront. Inside, there was a large room that doubled as a synagogue, with a small ark in front, along with a lectern, tables and a library. When appropriate, those who were studying, a few strays who liked to hang out, and anyone else who cared to come, made up the ten-person quorum required for a *minyan* three times a day.

The class at the Kollel, led by Danny's childhood friend, Aaron

Goldstein, was wrapping up before the service started. When Danny entered, Aaron, now also known as Rav Aharon Goldstein, nodded to him and came over to greet him before the service. "I assume you haven't seen the light and are coming to join us regularly," Aaron joked.

"No, Aaron. You know why I'm here. This is a good place to have a conversation with my father."

"A fine man. He taught me a lot. You do him honour to remember him in this way."

"I'm pleased you approve of a few things in my life."

"You know I don't judge you. I just wish you would find some peace with the tradition and with Hashem."

"Ah, Aaron. God and I don't get along very well. As you know, I have a very Jewish position on Him. I don't believe he exists and I argue with him regularly."

Aaron sighed, though he had a small smile at the edges of his mouth. "Anyway, let's pray to the God you don't think exists and honour your father."

"Good idea."

II

After the service, while Danny was driving downtown to 52 Division on Dundas, he thought about his father's life, and how his own life had turned out differently from what had been expected of him. As a forty-two-year-old cop, he had long ago given up on the idea that life was predictable and he often thought about how taking a particular path could lead to the unexpected in the labyrinth of being.

This morning was almost certain to bring something unexpected, for he was to be assigned a new partner, probably a young detective constable. His previous partner, Joe Gleason, had recently retired after thirty years on the force, the last five with Danny. The two had gotten along, but they never became friends. Joe was a plodder, which was good for Danny, who could be a little wild sometimes, as his superiors put it. It had been a respectful professional relationship, though sometimes boring.

At six feet, Danny was an imposing figure. His body was reasonably fit, his shoulders wide, and his waist was not much larger than his narrow hips. He had full black hair, parted on the right side. His beard was heavy, so that by five in the afternoon there was stubble on his chin and cheeks. He had expressive grey eyes, his most arresting facial feature. His mother used to say he had an animated face and he never looked the same from one photograph to the next. People could often read his feelings on his face—not a good quality in a cop, and one he worked hard to control.

When Danny arrived at 52 Division, he had fifteen minutes before going to the office of his superior, Inspector Sydney McIntyre, and he spent it pushing around some of the excessive paper on his desk. At nine, he crossed the corridor, knocked on McIntyre's door, and walked in. As always when he entered her office, his eyes were first directed to the large window facing north onto Dundas Street, allowing natural light to flood into the large room. The window looked out at the activity on the street, at the busy lives of those they were sworn to serve and protect, uniting the street life with the police station. As he turned to face McIntyre he realized there were, in fact, two women in the room.

Sydney McIntyre was in her early fifties, and she wore her age well. She was, as always, dressed in a tailored suit with a tasteful blouse. She had salt and pepper hair, an oval face, with lively green eyes, and a tough chin. Her face was unusual and not quite symmetrical. Though she could not be called pretty in any conventional way, hers was a face of character. Danny worked in an unconventional way, which sometimes annoyed her, but they had worked together for the last five years and they liked and respected each other.

"Detective Sergeant Daniel Miller," McIntyre said, "let me introduce you to our new colleague, Detective Constable Nadiri Rahimi."

Nadiri stood to meet Danny and they shook hands before sitting down in the two chairs facing the Inspector. Danny smiled to himself, affirming one of the things he liked best about his city and his country. Here was a Jewish sergeant being paired with a constable, likely from the Middle East, to help keep the streets safe in what had been, when he was born, a very Anglo city. He noticed Nadiri was dressed similarly to McIntyre, but with more colour and flair. He estimated she was about five feet seven inches and in her early thirties. She was slim, with a dark complexion. She had black hair, a stud in her left lobe and several others in the arc of her ear above it. Her eyes were dark, nearly black with a touch of grey, and her face was alive and interesting.

McIntyre continued, "I've been talking with Nadiri about our work and our procedures. She's been on the force for several years and only last week moved into the detective squad. Nadiri is anxious to get going, which is a good thing, but she agrees she needs to look, listen and learn in the meanwhile. So, I'd like you and Nadiri to work together."

Danny turned to the younger woman and said, "My pleasure. Let's give it a try and get to know each other as the next few months unfold. Delighted to have you here."

"Thanks, sir," Nadiri said. "I really hope I can help both you and the Inspector." Her voice was pleasant, and she had a mild accent, which Danny could not quite identify. Her manner was at once respectful and watchful.

"Where were you before?" Danny asked.

"In 42 Division, in Scarborough," she said. "I've seen everything from schoolyard fights to domestic violence to gangland murder. I've worked with neighbourhoods and schools where there are fifty languages spoken in the homes, none of them English. I know that area backwards, but I'm excited to be downtown."

III

He left the Centre for Addiction and Mental Health, on Queen Street West, feeling impotent and angry. He took the streetcar to work in the stockroom of a large store near Kensington Market.

He had just met, as he did twice a week, with his psychiatrist at CAMH. Nothing was sorted out. He was told his problems were of his own making, even though they could be traced firmly to events some twenty-five years ago.

He was told his nightmares, his delusions, his inability to find joy or relate to others, would not be resolved unless he transformed his life. The doctor had taken some positive initiative instead of listening quietly, as usual. "Yes," the doctor had said. "We know what happened to you when you were in your teens is the source of your unhappiness. At this point, if you want life to change, you need to actively develop a program."

What could he do? What could a thirty-seven-year-old university dropout and recovering cocaine addict do? He wanted to rerun his life, to go back to age twelve and make another movie, or to slide into another script.

He thought about acting out against the men he blamed for his trauma, but how? He had little money, and he had alienated himself from his family years ago. His current solitary life, in a cramped rented apartment at King and Dufferin, was intolerable.

He did have one thought, one possible avenue to redemption. What gnawed most at his soul all these years later was that those who committed those unspeakable acts against him when he was twelve, thirteen and fourteen, had simply gone on with their lives. There was no fairness in that fact—he suffered and they prospered.

Perhaps they should suffer too.
Perhaps that would release him from his demons.
He would act, though he knew not how.

IV

Danny's home, near the Danforth, was a small house originally, on a lot only eighteen feet wide, though the previous owners had added to the back to enlarge the kitchen and living area. The couple that sold it to Danny lived there for twenty years, and Danny found the place very comforting. When he arrived home around seven that evening, he found there was a noise from the back that could only be caused by one person—his son, Avi.

"Hello," he shouted as he entered.

"Hi, Dad," Avi said. "Jordan and I are in the kitchen."

Danny found Avi and his friend, Jordan, sitting at the table eating leftover chicken and salad from the fridge. The two fourteen-year-olds had empty soup bowls on the side.

Avi hugged his father and Danny kissed him on his head, realizing the boy would soon be too tall for him to do that easily.

"A good batch of soup, Dad," Avi reported. When Avi was a little boy, he loved matzo ball soup, part of the DNA of many Jewish children. After the divorce, Danny made certain to always have some in the fridge, both for himself and in case Avi came over. The first thing the boy did when he entered Danny's house was go to the fridge and scavenge for food for his unfathomably huge appetite. Danny varied the recipe every so often, trying to make the perfect chicken soup, and perfect floating matzo balls. He had yet to reach his goal, and Avi was his best taster and critic.

"Thanks. I used a different oil for the matzo balls. Still, I'll keep going until it's worthy of the soup gods. What brings you guys here?"

"We had a basketball game at the Eastminster Church and we were hungry."

"Good reasons. I'll join you. How'd the game go?"

"We lost by a few points. St. Joseph's has a good team. But now we're third in the league."

"Not bad. Good enough to make the playoffs," Danny observed. "Do you want to sleep over?"

"I don't think so. We have to be in school early tomorrow."

"Homework?"

Jordan replied, "We did it, Mr. Miller. Thanks for supper."

As Danny ate, the three of them talked about school, what was happening in the next week, and about the Maple Leafs, whose fortunes seemed to be finally changing after years of mediocrity.

"How are the bad guys?" Avi asked.

"Still there," Danny replied. "But in hand. There's some stuff, but nothing like the mess that exists in some cities in the States. We try hard to keep it civilized."

"Mom says you guys are good at catching murderers and robbers, but a lot of white-collar criminals don't get the punishment they deserve."

"Your mom is probably right. We need to have the same standards for everybody. Even under the law, rich people are privileged. What do you think?"

Jordan entered the conversation. "I think a banker or politician who cheats is just as bad as an ordinary person who robs the corner store. A gonif is a gonif, no matter what clothes he wears."

"I agree." Danny was pleased to have this conversation with these youngsters who were in the process of developing their sense of social justice. "Do you talk about these kinds of things in school?"

"When we study the Torah, or in Talmud class, we have lots of discussions about what is correct and about what is just," Avi said.

"And we sometimes have arguments about the behaviour of Israel or Canada," Jordan added. "Just bring up the issue of the Israeli settlements, or Canada's the military involvement in the Middle East, and you'll get lots of opinions."

"That's good," Danny said. "We all need to talk about what's right."

Abruptly, Avi asked, "Can we use your computer?"

"Sure." Danny naively thought they would be doing some schoolwork, but the two boys became absorbed in a video game for the next half hour. Danny marvelled at how the boys could be simultaneously very mature and little kids at this stage of their lives.

"We have to go," Avi said at eight-thirty.

"Do you want a ride home?" Danny asked.

"Come on, Dad. We use the TTC all the time now."

"OK. But call your mom to let her know you're on your way."

"No need, Dad. I'm on a nine-thirty curfew today."

After the boys had left, Danny cleaned up and put on some music, Mozart's *22nd Piano Concerto*. He reflected that the only thing he experienced that was more beautiful than Mozart was Avi.

V

In the first two weeks of their partnership, Danny and Nadiri investigated an assortment of violent crime, which is what the homicide squad did when it was not busy with murders. Danny first had Nadiri read a bunch of files to familiarize her with what they would be doing. After looking at a case, Nadiri would discuss it with Danny. She asked good questions, some about procedure, some about how and why decisions were made, and some about handling the incident and the people involved. After the first week, Danny pushed her a bit by asking how she might have done things differently.

Danny was impressed with Nadiri's intelligence, though not surprised after he discovered from her personnel file that she was among the first of her entering class to make it to detective. She was clearly a very determined person.

On the street, they handled several cases together, including two domestic violence incidents that ended with people hospitalized, a street fight near the Junction in which knives were used and an armed robbery where private citizens were injured.

Nadiri was deferential, letting Danny decide how to handle a case, and how to interrogate witnesses and criminals. She was watchful, and rarely asked questions without getting a signal from Danny that she could enter the conversation.

The two of them, without discussing it, went slow. They realized it would be better if they just worked together as professionals first and let their personal relationship develop on its own.

They did exchange some personal history in their conversations in the car and in the office. Danny discovered the source of Nadiri's unusual mild accent. She was born in Iran and left that country with her family to avoid the violence and arbitrariness of life that occurred after the fall of the Shah. The family immigrated first to Germany, where her father, a pharmacist, found work, and they lived there for three years. Then, at the age of nine, Nadiri and her family moved to Canada. Her first languages were Farsi and German, though Danny said he thought her English was at least as good as his.

Nadiri said that she and her family regarded themselves as Persians, different from those in the Middle East who think of their ethnicity as Arab. Though Islam is a religious force for Persians, their customs go further back to Zoroastrianism and other ancient beliefs. Danny told her it sounded as complicated as trying to sort out what it meant to be Jewish. Still, he said, "I understand the desire to be ethnic and cultural, even if you're not religious." Nadiri smiled and reminded him that the oldest Jewish communities in the Middle East had probably been those in Iran.

They also had in common degrees from the University of Toronto. His degree was in political science and her degree was in sociology. They left the rest to be uncovered as the partnership matured.

Danny liked that Nadiri knew how to drive in the city, and she was happy to do so. He didn't mind driving, but he liked to use the time to reflect on what was happening in their cases rather than navigating the crowded streets.

After two weeks, he was not surprised to get a call at home from Sydney McIntyre. It was a mid-November eve, a Thursday, which was witnessing the first hesitant snowflakes of the season. She assigned him a homicide that had occurred in an apartment near Yonge and Sheppard.

He called Nadiri, gave her the address, and jumped into his car. He tried to clear his mind and anticipate nothing. He wanted his perceptions to be fresh when he arrived.

The murder was in one of the many high-rise buildings on Kenneth Avenue, part of a corridor of condos built in the last twenty years around that area. What had once been a quiet suburban area had been transformed by the growth of the city, and the determination of a major local politician, into a monopoly set of large buildings, housing middle class families and others. What had been a residential neighbourhood was now a centre of commerce with its own theatre and even a concert hall. The area attracted many Torontonians of East Asian origin. Some of the best Japanese and Korean food in the city could be found on streets named Greenfield and Doris.

The building was three blocks north of Sheppard, and it was already cordoned off by yellow tape and two squad cars when Danny arrived. Danny parked and walked a few yards to duck under the tape. With his identification in hand, he went over to the uniformed officer at the entrance to introduce himself.

"Hello, sir. I'm John Karsch, from thirty-two Division. The body's on fourteen and my partner's at the door. We confirmed the body was dead, but touched nothing."

"Forensics?"

"They're on their way. Another detective is upstairs as well."

"Thanks, Constable. You did the right thing."

Danny took the elevator to the fourteenth floor and found the scene. Nadiri was outside the apartment waiting for him.

"What do we know?" Danny asked.

"Not much. I checked with the concierge and the apartment is owned by a man named James Frawley who was living alone. The concierge said he thought he was a teacher."

They both put on white slippers over their shoes and white gloves on their hands. Danny knew this was an important moment. What he would absorb here—both consciously and unconsciously—would be crucial as the investigation unfolded.

They entered a small foyer leading to a large living room, furnished with simple furniture—a couch, a coffee table and two chairs. There were several bookcases filled with many books. A small CD player was on a table next to the couch and a shelf next to it was full of CDs.

Seven Christian crosses in different styles were spread out on the grey walls as one would display works of art. Danny recognized some of them—an ordinary cross in the shape of a lower-case T, a cross of Lorraine, associated with De Gaulle and France, and an Irish cross. He would have to look up the others.

The body was in the middle of the room, next to the coffee table. Pieces of a simple wooden chair were near the body. Danny and Nadiri went over to it, and Danny leaned over to check for the pulse, though he was certain this man was gone.

"OK," Danny said, "What do we have? Let's talk about it. I'll start. A male, in his forties, with his head bashed in, probably done with one or more pieces of the chair beside him. Death probably came from the blows on the head. His clothes are simple—pants, shirt, socks, no shoes."

"What about his hands and fingers?"

"You're ahead of me. You tell me."

"Some of the fingers are broken."

They both looked carefully. "Almost certainly," Danny said. "Anything else?"

"I wish I could tell you who the killer is, but I'm not that smart."

"I want to keep an open mind, but it's worth thinking about whether or not this was sudden, planned, organized, spontaneous, whatever."

"My guess would be it was sudden and unplanned," Nadiri said.

"Why?"

"Because of the murder weapon, assuming it was the chair. I don't know why the murderer was let in, but he didn't bring a weapon. Of course, one of the first things we were taught at OPC was it could appear to be one thing and yet, in fact, be another. And a clever murderer could make it look sudden and unplanned."

"Good thinking. Let's just say it appears spontaneous and leave it at that."

There was noise in the corridor and both the forensic pathologist and his team entered. The leader was a small, stocky, middle-aged man with a belly and an Irish accent. "Ah, Danny, what do we have?"

Danny didn't smile, but he was glad Dr. Hugh O'Brien was on the case. They knew one another from two earlier cases and Danny had quickly come to understand O'Brien was a very able doctor, a decent person and a man of good humour. "Dr. O'Brien, this is my new partner, Detective Constable Nadiri Rahimi."

O'Brien smiled. "Good to meet you, even under such circumstances."

"We don't have much," Danny said. "We just arrived five minutes ago. He's dead, his head's bashed in, and some of his fingers are broken. Nothing you won't know in half a minute. Probably one James Frawley. What I suggest we do is leave the body to you and have a look around the place while the forensics team does their thing."

"Good," O'Brien replied. He thought well enough of Danny not to caution him to leave things untouched for the moment.

Danny and Nadiri began exploring the rest of the apartment. Danny explained the procedure to Nadiri. "This is just to get a feel for the place. Later, we can go through papers and anything else we want to examine."

They walked through a white galley kitchen. A frying pan and teakettle were on the stove and a clock was on the wall. The kitchen led to a simple bathroom with a tub, a shower and standard toiletries.

The master bedroom had a lot of bookshelves as well. The room was large enough to hold a queen-size bed, yet there was no bed at all. Instead, on the floor there was a simple sheet with blankets, neatly folded, with a small towel in place of a pillow. Some books and magazines were on the floor next to the sleeping area. Danny took time to look at the titles in the bookcases.

On one of the bookshelves was a wallet, a set of keys, and some change. Danny peered into the wallet and determined the victim was indeed James Frawley.

A second bedroom held more bookshelves, and a desk with a computer and a small television set, the kind one usually put on a kitchen counter.

They had done all they could for now. Danny asked Nadiri to check on Frawley, specifically to find out if he was a teacher and, if so, where. He went outside, found a tiny park a block away, sat on a bench and let his mind roam.

Nadiri came out ten minutes later and sat beside him. "No form," she said. "No record at all. Frawley works for the Toronto Catholic District School Board. I don't know what he teaches, but he's listed as being at Pius XI High School."

"So," Danny said, "knowing what we know from the last hour or so, what do we make of James Frawley? What would you make of this person if you read about his apartment in a Margaret Atwood novel? I know this may be a question I'm asking too soon—cops learn everyone has secrets and, as you said earlier, appearance often conceals reality rather than reveal it. Still, let's hypothesize."

Nadiri was silent for half a minute and then answered, "The bed and the crosses are unusual. Clearly a religious person. Catholic, obsessive, a bachelor living alone, likes things simple, reads a lot."

Danny said, "His books are mainly on theology or the history of the Church. He seems to have a fondness for British mysteries, especially Agatha Christie, Reginald Hill and P. D. James. He also has books on geometry, mathematics and physics, which he might have taught."

"Do you think he sleeps on the floor because he's a masochist with a bad back?"

"No," Danny said, "I think he sleeps on the floor because he's a masochist with a bad conscience."

"What do you mean?"

"His lifestyle is more like that of a secular monk than an ordinary citizen. By choice. Maybe we should stop here before we build a castle in the sky without enough supporting structure. Let's go back. O'Brien and his people should be finished with their work and we can poke around some more."

They re-entered the building and went up to the fourteenth floor just as O'Brien was leaving.

"Danny and Nadiri," he said, "goodnight to you and good hunting. The crew will be finished in about fifteen minutes."

"Anything we should know?" Danny asked.

"Time of death is probably last night. I'll get it fixed better at the autopsy." He paused, wrinkling his brow. "I'll add this. He had interesting undergarments. Made of some coarse material, probably animal hair. Not comfortable at all."

While waiting to enter the apartment, Danny called McIntyre to inform her of what was happening. Before he could ask for support, McIntyre told him she was assigning two constables to him. The constables would first ask around the building to see if anyone had witnessed anything unusual.

Danny then walked to the bedroom and found more sets of rough underwear like the ones O'Brien had mentioned were worn by Frawley. In a closet much too big for Frawley's minimalist wardrobe, there were several small whips and one instrument that looked like something out of a medieval torturer's armoury.

Danny and Nadiri learned Frawley was a neat and orderly person. He kept personal files for his taxes, insurance and such matters. Some pictures revealed he had a family somewhere, either a sister or brother who had children. They found out it was a brother, and got his address and phone number from a handwritten address book. It was one o'clock in the morning. McIntyre agreed they should inform his brother first thing in the morning.

"Let's end it here, for now, and get a few hours of sleep," Danny said. "His brother lives in Thornhill. I'll pick you up at seven-thirty and we can go to their place to inform them. I'll be calling a team meeting at eleven and we'll try to move quickly. At the moment, nothing is obvious. There was a murder, but no robbery, and nothing to indicate a motive."

VI

They rode in the morning from Nadiri's apartment to the address in Thornhill. It was a well-kept, modest suburban home in a solid middle-class development.

There is no good way of informing people that a family member has been murdered. And there is no accounting for the responses, despite what many fictional detectives make of a twitch of an eyebrow or a sob. People respond in different ways to tragedy.

Paul Frawley and his wife Edith were at home at eight o'clock in the morning, when Danny and Nadiri arrived, as were their two teenaged children. They were very surprised to see the police, though they invited them in and offered coffee and tea.

Danny got straight to it. "I have bad news, Mr. Frawley. Your brother James is dead. He was found murdered last night in his apartment."

Frawley and his wife were distraught, but collected. They paused to absorb the news and then asked for details. Danny gave them as much detail as he could and asked Frawley to attend the autopsy that afternoon, to identify the body.

"Your brother was a teacher in a separate high school?" Danny asked, as a way of getting conversation going, though he was unsure if

Frawley was up to it. Frawley was subdued, but he answered.

"Yes. He taught mathematics and physics, though sometimes he also met with students for religious exercises or special study."

"He was a religious man?"

"He was a very devoted Catholic. He was a bachelor and much of his life was centered on the Church and its activities."

"Did you see him regularly?"

"Oh, yes. He came here for dinner every other week or so. We're Catholic. Not regular churchgoers, but we had a good relationship with James. We sometimes found it hard to find things to talk about, but the Church and education gave us something. I can't tell you we were close, but we were family. James was the younger one and our lives took different paths."

Danny decided that was enough for the time being. He was grateful to Frawley for his candour at a difficult time. He stood, as did Nadiri, and said, "I'll see you this afternoon. If you don't mind, Mr. and Mrs. Frawley, I'd like to continue this conversation at a more appropriate time."

In the car on the way to the station, Nadiri said, "Unless every instinct of mine is wrong, I don't think they're in the mix."

"Neither do I," Danny replied. "They seem like solid citizens, decent people. Let's see."

The meeting, held at eleven, gathered what would be their team, at least at the beginning of the investigation. In addition to Danny and Nadiri, there were two constables assigned to the case. One, Taegan Green, Danny knew. He was on his way up in the force and was gaining a variety of experience before getting a permanent assignment. He was from Jamaica, and he was watchful, bright and tech-savvy. Danny didn't know him well, but so far he liked what he saw.

Sydney McIntyre, who sat in on the occasional team meeting to get a feel for a new case, introduced the other constable, Connor Swift. He was tall, something of the map of Ireland on his face, and respectful. Danny believed he might be the son of Charlie Swift, a bit of a wild card as a cop, though devoted to the force, and part of a family whose roots in the force would now go back at least three generations.

The two constables were not yet finished questioning people in the building, but reported no one they had interviewed had anything unusual or valuable to offer.

"What about the concierge?" Danny asked. "Or, really, the concierges."

"I saw two of them," Green reported. "One last night and the main guy this morning. Both don't think anything odd had occurred in the last twenty-four hours. They have cleaning people coming to apartments, a few elderly owners have day help, and there are deliveries where many packages are left at the desk."

"Do the concierges leave their posts?" Nadiri asked.

"Yes. Actually, they don't seem very attentive. They don't behave like cops on watch. It's fairly casual. The night person makes some rounds. The day person meets with the manager in the office sometimes."

"Any cameras?"

"Yep. The door is always on-camera, along with the pool and exercise area. But there are no recordings. They watch but don't tape."

"Well, keep going," Danny said.

Danny then summed up what was known and concluded, "We have a bare bones case. So far, there's no clear sense Frawley had enemies, even though his private behaviour was unusual. He was very religious, very Catholic, very much into that community, but that's no cause for murder."

"What about the weird underwear and the whips?" Connor asked. "Anything sexual there?"

"I have an idea, but I need to know more. I need to talk with his priest and the people at Pius XI School. I think that will yield more information about them." Danny looked at McIntyre. She indicated she had no questions or comments.

"Let's get on with it. We need more information. You guys get on with the interviews. Interview other people in the building, other concierges if there are any, cleaning staff, the manager. Nadiri and I will pursue Frawley's life and attend the autopsy at three this afternoon."

Danny had set up a meeting with the principal at one o'clock. He would go from there to the autopsy. As they got into the car with Nadiri driving, Danny asked, "Lunch?"

"Do we have time?"

"We meet the principal, Barry Greene, at one o'clock. Given we've had little sleep and probably not much else besides coffee, we should probably eat."

This was the first meal they would have together, and the matter of food had never arisen in their many casual conversations.

"Well," Nadiri said, "both our traditions have rules about food. Let's figure out where we can eat."

"And what," Danny added. "I'll start. I can go anywhere. I don't keep to all the rules about kosher food, though there are some things I just don't eat. But I can find something to eat in almost any diner or restaurant." He smiled. "Like many non-observant Jews in my tribe, I have a fondness for both kosher deli and Chinese food."

Nadiri exhaled. "Well, we're both in trouble with God. I more or less eat anything, too. I love Iranian food, and there are now some good places in ethnic neighbourhoods, but a hamburger or a sandwich is fine for me." They decided on the Avenue Road Diner, at Davenport. Danny had a tuna-fish sandwich and Nadiri had her cheeseburger, loaded with the works.

They arrived on time at the school and were ushered into the office by the principal. After the introductions Greene asked, "What brings you here?"

"We have bad news. Your teacher, James Frawley, is dead. He was murdered yesterday."

Greene gulped, and his body shook a bit. "I knew something was wrong. James was regular, he was devoted to the school. We called several times today, but no one answered. Any details about the funeral? A number of us, staff and students, will want to pay our respects."

"Not yet," Danny said. "The family was only informed this morning. You can get in touch with them. Tell us about James Frawley. Right now, there is very little for us to go on."

"He was something of a solitary person," Greene replied. "Still, he was valued for his devotion to the Church, to the school, and to our students. He had a few colleagues he spoke with regularly, though I don't know whether any of them were friends. He was sometimes more demanding of students than we like, but good students see him … saw him … as an interesting eccentric. A good mind. Very spiritual. He didn't coach sports teams, he probably knew nothing about sports. But he did work with the debating team and with a student club that met weekly to discuss religious texts. Frankly, I wouldn't want a whole staff of James' type, but one or two are good for a separate school."

"Was he involved in any controversies?" Nadiri asked. "Would he have any enemies? Did he support the teachers' union or anything that might cause someone to be angry with him?"

"The only controversies he cared about were those related to theology. He was very, very traditional. But that kind of thing doesn't result in the kind of anger you're talking about. The days when people killed each another over issues about whether we should pray in Latin or English are long gone. I don't think he had enemies, though there were some people who viewed him as belonging to an earlier age. As for the union, James stayed away from it. He made it very plain he thought teaching was a calling, not a job. The closest to controversy he came, as far as I know, was during the lead-up to the last teacher job action. 'St. Francis wouldn't take job action,' he said at one contentious meeting. And he voted against it as part of a small minority. But once a work action is over, people who were seemingly divided usually move on."

"Do you know if he was a member of a particular club or any organizations outside of the school?" Danny asked.

Greene fidgeted. There was silence for several seconds. Danny signalled to Nadiri not to interrupt the silence and then said, "This is a murder, Mr. Greene. We're not gossiping."

"My best guess, though it never came up openly," stumbled Greene, "is he did belong to a Catholic society." After more silence, Greene said, "Opus Dei."

"I've heard of it," Danny said. "But I really don't know much about it other than that it's a place where people of deep religious beliefs, mostly traditional, find themselves comfortable."

Greene said, "It's very controversial, though it's a recognized society responsible to the Holy Father in Rome. There are lots of rumours about it because it operates somewhat secretly. I'm not the best one to tell you about it. If you want to know more, speak to the person in charge of the Toronto branch."

"And that person is?"

"Father Clarence Burke. You can get in touch via the archdiocese office."

The discussion continued, though neither Danny nor Nadiri learned much else. Danny ended the meeting at about two o'clock. Nadiri stayed at the school to see several teachers who knew Frawley while he moved on to the autopsy. Before leaving, Danny called the archdiocese office and arranged to speak with Father Burke the next morning.

The autopsy revealed Frawley was indeed killed by blows to the head with pieces of the chair, between eighteen and twenty-four hours before he was found. Danny spent more time with Frawley's brother, who had come to identify the body, than he did with O'Brien.

VII

By the time Danny was finished at the morgue, it was five o'clock on a Friday evening, which meant he would be going to his sister and brother-in-law's home for Shabbat dinner. He called Nadiri to check in and they agreed to meet the next morning for coffee before going to speak with Father Burke.

This was Avi's week to join Danny for dinner at the home of his aunt, uncle and cousins, not far from Glencairn and Bathurst.

Danny's sister Ruth, who was older by four years, took him under her wing, especially after the death of their parents and then his divorce. She didn't always approve of her little brother, but she loved him unconditionally. Danny was often annoyed by Ruth's opinions, even her meddling, though he would never accuse her of that. He was grateful for her warmth and affection, bestowed not only on him, but on Avi as well.

On the way to Ruth's, Danny stopped at a kosher bakery to purchase some Danishes and cakes as a sweet offering for the Sabbath. He parked two blocks from the house and reached into the glove compartment to take out his kippah, which he put on his head. He walked over, thinking about the peaceful shift from work to Sabbath, even though he would be working in the morning. Though he rarely took advantage of it, Danny believed the invention of the Sabbath was one of the most civilized contributions of his people to the good of the world.

He entered the house—he and Avi were the only non-residents who had keys—and called out to announce himself.

Ruth was in the kitchen, putting together the last pieces of the Sabbath meal. Danny kissed his sister on the cheek and sat comfortably at a small breakfast table while she cooked and organized the food.

Ruth had black curly hair, though Danny suspected it was now dyed, given that their mother's hair had gone grey in her late thirties. She was a handsome woman, neither tall nor short, and she was getting a bit thick in her middle age. Her hazel eyes looked intelligent and she had an appealing sense of whimsy. She radiated warmth and was always a comforting person to be around.

"Avi is here already," she said. "He's downstairs with Leo doing whatever they do on the technology they love so much. He's looking good. What's new with you?"

"Not much. The usual stuff, chasing after the bad guys. I do have a new partner, a very pleasant and very bright young woman."

Ruth raised an eyebrow and made a gesture with her left hand. "No," Danny said. "There is no possibility of romance. First, it's simply unprofessional. My job is to mentor her and to help her grow as a cop. She has an interesting background. Iranian, though Persian rather than Islamic. She also lived in Germany as a child, before coming to Canada."

"They used to say 'only in America,'" Ruth said. "But America is a different place now. Now, your partnership is an 'only in Toronto.'"

"It's healthy."

"I agree. Do you want a nosh before dinner?"

"Sure. Who could resist a nosh from you?"

Ruth smiled and served him a small plate of chopped liver with some crackers as a taste of what was to come. Bringing it to the table, she put it down and gave him a kiss on his head as she did so.

Friday Shabbat dinner at Ruth and Irwin Feldman's house could mean anywhere from six people—the Feldmans, their children, Danny, and Avi—to fifteen or so—friends or visitors to Toronto who were invited to share the meal. This evening, there were eight people. Ruth and Irwin's neighbours, Malcolm Grossman, a pediatrician at SickKids and the former president of the Feldmans' synagogue, and his wife Jean, completed the table.

Ruth's husband, Irwin Feldman, was a lawyer. He specialized in corporate law at Sachs LLP, a major firm with offices on Bay Street. He had a granite-like face, though Ruth or the children could occasionally break through and get a smile from him. He and Ruth were very active both in their synagogue and in charitable endeavours, making them respected and well-connected in the Jewish community. Irwin disapproved of Danny's profession, but he was wise enough to temper his feelings in the interests of keeping peace with Ruth.

The two Feldman children, Deborah and Leo, were older than Avi.

Deborah, twenty-one, was at York University, majoring in history with the intention of following in her father's footsteps and going to law school. Leo, nineteen, was at Ryerson University, taking courses in computer technology that ranged from programming to animation to music production. Leo was still deciding what he would do after graduating, though he had announced to his parents his intention of going to Israel when he graduated and entering the Israeli armed forces for three years. Both Deborah and Leo treated Avi like a younger brother and looked after him as best they could.

The eight of them gathered at the table in a ritual thousands of years old. They held hands and sang a few tunes to welcome the Sabbath. Then, Irwin said the Sabbath blessing over wine and asked Malcolm to say the blessing over the bread.

Dinner was relaxed and lengthy. The conversation ranged from the politics of Canada and Israel to hopes for the Maple Leafs and the Raptors.

At the other end of the table, Irwin and Malcolm got especially agitated over an issue in their local Orthodox synagogue. The synagogue was large, with roughly eight hundred families. On the spectrum of Jewish practice, it was modern Orthodox rather than hard-hat Orthodox. The building was being renovated, which was causing anger and distress among the members. The issue was what to do about the tradition that men and women sit separately and a barrier, a *mechitza*, is placed between them. In old-time synagogues there was a balcony, so men sat below and women sat above. However, their synagogue had no balcony, so men sat in front and women sat behind. There was a symbolic barrier, about waist high. Some members were now demanding the barrier be higher, according to the dictates of the very orthodox, so men and women would not see one another. The two men were upset at the idea of this change, done by fiat by the rabbi and the board, believing it would alienate many. The counter-argument proposed by the rabbi and the board involved attracting more people and conforming to the new standards of the ultra-orthodox community. Malcolm, with white hair and a kind face, asked Danny what he thought about it. Irwin winced when Malcolm brought Danny into this discussion.

"First, let's note it's not only Islam and Christianity that have gender issues. We're dealing with a larger problem. My sense is your shul provides an important niche. Why change into something people can experience in many other places? You might lose your voice."

For once, Irwin was happy with Danny. "Well said, Danny. I wish you could tell that to those fools who think they are holier than everybody else."

Deborah broke into the discussion. "What does any of this have to do with the mission of Judaism, with tikkun olam, with trying to heal the world? Why are we wasting our time with this stuff when people who need help are suffering? Why are Catholics worried about women having power in the Church when they tell us their job is to take care of the poor?"

Irwin answered, "It's important to argue about where people sit. It's been a matter of concern for thousands of years. You can't just abandon tradition that easily."

Avi, for the first time, summoned the courage to enter this kind of conversation. "Dr. Grossman, you told me you remember when there were quotas on how many Jews and how many Blacks could enter medical school. That, too, was a tradition, but who can defend it? Some traditions are unjust."

Leo added, "After all, slavery was also a tradition. It still exists in some places. Not only were we slaves in Egypt, but we had slaves in ancient times. Tradition is fine, but we live in a world where human rights matter."

"You're dealing with important matters," Irwin said. "Change is fine, but do it carefully."

Avi spoke again. "Maybe we're asking the wrong questions."

"What do you mean?" Danny asked.

"In our Talmud class, Rabbi Telson stressed the importance of questions. He said the answers we get are determined by the questions we ask. He talked about how some questions can limit thinking and put you in a box. The example he gave, Dad, is what you did when I was younger. You'd ask me if I wanted to go for a walk or to play ball, as if those were the only options."

"What are the right questions?" Danny asked.

"I think the right questions are about how we should be Jewish, how we should behave. I know how we pray is important. Maybe why we pray is also important."

Danny was proud of his son. 'He's a thinker,' he thought, and then he smiled inwardly. He realized Avi would be giving him trouble, the kind of trouble he didn't mind at all. Maybe there was hope for the Jewish future after all, he thought, something that worried all members of the tribe.

They moved on to less contentious matters over tea and dessert. The evening ended at ten and Danny said goodbye to all, including Avi, who, as he did every other week, was spending the Sabbath with his aunt, uncle and cousins.

VIII

Nadiri picked up Danny at eight-thirty the next morning, before going to see Father Burke. Danny invited her into the house for coffee and a Danish he bought at the kosher bakery the day before.

"Nice house," Nadiri said, sitting in the kitchen. "Cozy and pleasant. I like that your skylight lets in lots of natural light."

"Thanks. I've been happy here. It suits me. What did you find yesterday at the school?"

"I spoke with several teachers and Frawley's department head. I didn't learn much more. Frawley was respected, though I don't think everyone liked him. He was a loner. He ate his lunch at his desk. They all spoke about his deep religious beliefs. He was, if there is such a term, very Catholic. Capital C."

"Who were his friends, or at least close colleagues?"

"As far as I could tell, Frawley didn't have close friends like that, at least not at the school. He was described politely as a good teacher, though rigid and eccentric. He was devoted to his students, and his religious attitude was something people respected, but didn't warm to. Not a single person indicated they knew of anyone who wished him harm. Some people told me he was a pain in the ass sometimes, especially to the union types, but you don't bash someone's head in because they're a pain in the ass. Especially someone who was devoted to the mission of the school, even if he was a little overzealous. I wrote a report on the interviews and put it in the file."

"I hope Clarence Burke can help us," Danny said. "Frawley is turning out to be enigmatic."

They finished their coffee and Danish and Danny rose to put the dishes in the sink. "You know," he said, "we may be asking the wrong questions."

"What do you mean?"

"I'm not as clear as I would like to be yet, but my son gave me an idea yesterday, in the context of something else. Maybe we're limiting our investigation by limiting our perspective. I'm not certain. I need to do some thinking."

"How old is your son?"

"He's fourteen. His name's Avi. And he's a wonderful guy, biased as I am. Sometimes I think we should just turn the world over to young people like him. We certainly haven't done a decent job of it. At least we males."

Nadiri smiled. "Don't worry. We women wouldn't cull all of you. There are still some nice guys around, undoubtedly including your Avi."

"Do you have a family?" Danny asked as he was washing the dishes.

"Yes, a close one. I don't live far from my parents. I have an older sister and younger brother. My parents think I should still be living with them, since I'm an unmarried female. I like living near them, though I would go crazy living with them. I also have three nieces and nephews, with a fourth one on the way."

"So, the middle kid is the rebel?"

"If you call being a cop and preserving law and order rebellious."

"You know what I mean," Danny said. "It's interesting that both our traditional families regard us, upstanding citizens both, as rebels. Neither of us is following the script."

"I never thought of it that way. Still, my family matters to me more than anything even if I'm considered by them to be somewhat weird."

"Weird is fine. Just ask Avi. Let's go talk to Father Burke."

They were to meet Clarence Burke at the University of Toronto's Ernescliff College. Nadiri navigated across the Danforth, over the bridge above the Don Valley and into downtown. She turned left at St. George and parked near the Robarts Library.

Burke was waiting for them as they entered the college and he led them to a small neat office on the first floor. He was a handsome man with a mane of neatly groomed white hair. He looked like the Hollywood version of a vicar in *Mrs. Miniver*.

"Thanks for meeting with us so quickly," Danny said. "We appreciate your cooperation. I assume you know why we're here?"

"I was very sad to learn about what happened to James Frawley. How can I help you?"

"We need to learn as much as we can about Mr. Frawley. That's one of the ways we can hope to solve the murder. There are indications he was a member of Opus Dei."

"We usually don't reveal our membership but, yes, James was part of our group. Let me say that he was a devoted Catholic and someone whose life led him to Opus Dei to bear witness to his beliefs in his everyday life. He was a good person."

"He doesn't seem to have had a lot of friends. Even his relationship with his brother and his brother's family doesn't seem close. Was his social life mainly in your organization?"

"Probably. We meet regularly for various activities that are part of our devotion and our discipline. James attended many sessions here and elsewhere. In some cases, members live in group homes. James did so for a time, but found himself uncomfortable, so he moved to the condo where, according to the news reports, you found him. He was a solitary type."

Nadiri signalled to Danny that she wanted to ask something. "You're a controversial group, sometimes said to be secret, sometimes thought to be even conspiratorial. Could James's activities have resulted in some people wanting to do him harm?"

Danny liked the intervention but wanted to temper the question. He added, "We're not interested in making judgments about theology or belief. We respect that. But we do need to ask some delicate questions to get a better understanding of what we are dealing with."

Burke answered, "No offence taken. Since Dan Brown's *The Da Vinci Code*, we've been in needless controversy. I've spent the last decade or so explaining we're not some underground revolutionary organization. We're a small group by the standards of the Church. We have eighty-five thousand members worldwide in a Church with over a billion souls. Most of our members are lay people who see their lives as holy and want to live ordinary lives in a way that values what is sacred, and in devotion to the teachings of Christ. There's nothing I know about James Frawley's life or activities that could shed any light on the murder. He was certainly deeply connected to our mission. His teaching was more to him than just a job. He tried to live in the tradition of our faith."

"Let me push further into his personality, rather than into your group," Danny said. "Do you know if he was celibate? It's my understanding that some Opus Dei members, though they may be laypeople, do take on celibacy as part of their devotion."

"I appreciate that both of you have done your homework. Yes, some of our laypeople take a vow of celibacy."

He stopped. There was silence for several seconds, broken by Danny. "Father, were you his confessor?"

After a brief pause, Burke said, "Yes."

"I'm not asking you to violate your seal of the confessional. I would never do that. But we need to know as much as you can tell us about James."

"I appreciate that, Detective, and I appreciate your sensitivity. Yes, James did take a vow of celibacy. It wasn't a secret between us. Others in the group knew."

"There's one other place we need to go," Nadiri said, looking at Danny. "Mr. Frawley was wearing unusual undergarments."

At this, Burke, who was very poker-faced, blinked and tilted his head slightly.

"They were made of coarse material, probably animal hair," Nadiri continued. "He had a drawer full of these garments in his bedroom. I don't want to assume anything, but in my small research into Opus Dei yesterday, I found there was mention of self-mortification."

"There's nothing kinky about this. Some of our members want to remind themselves of the pain experienced by Our Saviour. This is a devotional act, albeit an extreme one, to help fulfill our mission of living a holy life in the world."

"Is there anything else you can tell us?" Danny asked.

"I don't think so. The fact that James lived according to our beliefs is no secret. That it had anything to do with the horrible thing that was done to him seems to me to be remote."

Danny stood up and extended his hand. "Thanks Father," he said, with a firm handshake. "We may need to talk with you again as we proceed."

"Anytime. Losing James is something we all regret deeply."

Danny and Nadiri walked silently back to the car.

IX

He left CAMH feeling better than he had in many years. His doctor had told him that he saw real progress and his mood was much more positive. He was handling his life in a more mature manner.

That was because he had acted. He had finally returned some of the hurt he had been dealing with all these years. He had even tried to have a small social life. He joined the bowling league at his workplace. He asked his supervisor about ways to get ahead, even how to get a small promotion. He started taking walks in the city. He found The Beach very comforting. He made a resolution to get out of his house, even if that meant just spending time in a public library. He wondered if he could acquire some skills, or some credentials, by taking courses online or pursuing continuing education.

At last, he believed he didn't always have to have this terrible cloud over his head. He could lift his head high and find a better life.

He knew he wasn't yet finished with the important work of making those who had destroyed his life suffer. There were still two others he wanted to get revenge on. And this, above all, gave him purpose.

He would be patient. He would find where the next one lived and worked. He would follow him. He would taste redemption.

X

On Sunday morning, Danny followed his decade-old routine. He got up early and went to the Miles Nadal Jewish Community Centre, at Bloor and Spadina, to play squash with his old group of friends. There were ten of them, though on any given Sunday roughly eight showed up. They played round robin. Then they gathered in the sauna for a shvitz, followed by a shower, and coffee and bagels in the cafeteria.

The squash group included some wealthy men and those of modest means, from members of the Order of Canada to ordinary citizens, and from distinguished medical men to a detective. It was, on the court and nude in the shvitz, the essence of democratic social life. The person most loved by all of them was the modest owner of a corner store—Jacob

Schmuelovitz—an immigrant from Ukraine. He had been in Canada for twenty years and was as gentle a soul as Danny had ever met, with a presence that he thought made Jacob a warm person to be around.

Danny's partner and opponent this Sunday was Mike Ryan, who he had known since they were boys living on the same block.

For Danny, squash was an activity with psychological value. Hitting the ball hard and being intense for forty minutes was an outlet for stress. Squash became a lot more fun, he reflected, than sitting in a chair in a psychiatrist's office for the same amount of time. Moreover, he would never forget the words of his former wife, Rachel, when he went to get his squash bag some twelve years ago. At that time, the two were quarrelling silently and wondering about their marriage. "Make believe I'm the ball," she had said as he went out the door.

Danny and Mike had an intense match, Danny winning eleven to seven in the fifth game. As they went to the locker room, Danny asked, "Do you have a few minutes after coffee?"

"Sure" Mike said. "Anything serious?"

"Nothing personal, Mike. Just a small question related to your Catholic life."

When the whole group finished schmoozing in the cafeteria, Mike and Danny got together in a quiet corner.

"What's up?" Mike asked.

An odd question. What do you know about Opus Dei?"

Mike was a regular churchgoer, usually to the Saturday night mass, so he could play squash and socialize with his friends on Sunday mornings. Danny and Mike had gone to different schools; Mike went to St. Michael's College, the elite private Catholic high school in the city. He was, Danny knew, an active lay member of the Catholic community. He also contributed his skills *pro bono* as a lawyer to several Catholic service organizations.

"What gets you involved with Opus Dei?"

"It's come up in my work, and I'm puzzled by the reluctance people have to talk about it."

"I don't know a lot. I can tell you it's controversial, because it seems to operate as a separate group outside the regular Church channels. People in Opus Dei are responsible to Opus Dei, not to their bishop or parish priest."

"So?"

"There's a sense they have their own agenda. Some of them regard themselves as better Catholics than the rest of us. They're very observant, very traditional, very close to one another. Some people see them as infiltrating institutions, especially schools, as a means of furthering their agenda."

"What's their agenda?"

"There are a few ways of looking at it. On the face of it, they want to live their lives in a Catholic manner, which means their whole lives, not just their lives in church. Maybe you can liken them to certain Orthodox Jews or fundamentalist Muslims who want their whole lives governed by the religious codes."

"A throwback?"

"Maybe. I don't know enough about the history. You and I acknowledge we live in a civil society. Your work upholds the civil laws. They regard the modern world as we live it to be … I don't know what word to use, but the formal word is profane. It's unholy. It's to be made holy by applying religious law to everything in their everyday lives."

"What are the other ways of looking at it?"

"Well, they're associated with right-wing politics, especially in Europe and Latin America. Some say they're undemocratic. They value family, tradition, devotion. Things that on the surface appear to be normal, but in this case they're associated with the agendas of some extremist groups. They don't support women's rights, Vatican II, new liturgy, things like that. And there are those who think they're in a conspiracy to slowly take over the Church. Of course, Pope Francis is not their favourite leader."

"Are they violent?"

"No. At least not that I know of. They are very disciplined. People in the movement are expected to follow the rule of obedience. But they're not violent."

"Perhaps only to themselves, to their own flesh."

"You've heard about self-mortification, then? They see it as a holy act, helping them to come closer to Our Saviour." Mike looked directly at Danny, "Does this help?"

"It fits with what I've learned from talking to a few others and researching online. And it gives me a better insight. Thanks."

"So," Mike said with a smile, "have I solved a murder or two?"

Danny laughed. "You've helped. We'll see where it goes. Thanks for your candour, Mike. I'll treat this as a privileged conversation, counsellor."

XI

On Monday morning, Danny and Nadiri had their team meeting with everyone, including the two constables, Taegan Green and Connor Swift, and Sydney McIntyre.

Danny started. "I don't know how much further we've gotten since Friday. I now know more about Opus Dei than I knew before. Probably more than I'd care to know if this murder hadn't occurred, but I don't know that we're any closer to identifying the killer. He had the means and the opportunity, but what was the motive? Can we go around and talk about what we think? I'm willing to consider any way of going forward. Nadiri?"

"Opus Dei is interesting and it's controversial. It's also secret, which appeals to people like us who like looking in dark corners. Maybe it has a lot to do with James Frawley and nothing to do with the murder."

"Keep going," Danny said.

"Well, I don't think it was random, that some stranger entered his apartment and killed him. I still think Frawley was killed by someone who had a grievance. What was the grievance? I don't know. Maybe it lies in his past, or even in his school. Maybe we should look into someplace other than Opus Dei.

"Any thoughts, Taegan?" Danny asked.

"You've said it before. No one stole anything. It was Frawley they were after."

"Connor, do you think they went there wanting to kill Frawley? I don't want to put you on the spot," Danny continued. "This is a question for all of us."

"This is my first murder, sir. I have no sense of what usually happens. I'd say the person went to the apartment to do something to Frawley, maybe not to kill him. But it happened. If they went to kill him, they would have had another weapon. Maybe they went to the apartment not knowing what they would do other than confront Frawley and hurt him in some way."

"Ma'am, do you have any comments?"

"Yes. First, I think all of you have combined your efforts to go as far as you could have gone. Good work, even if it is unsatisfying because we seem no closer to a resolution. I agree that Frawley was singled out. We have a mysterious killer on our hands."

Nadiri said, "Sir, I recall you said your son gave you some insight. That perhaps we're asking the wrong questions. Maybe the solution lies in Frawley's history, not in his life as he lives it now. Maybe we have to find out something secret in the past."

"Makes sense," Danny replied. "I think it's time to dig up what lies in Frawley's past, if anything. I'll take that on. In the meanwhile, let's keep asking around the school and around the Church. I don't want anyone to think we're giving up."

Danny spent the next two days trying to build up a personal history for James Frawley. Frawley, according to his brother, had an ordinary childhood with the exception that he became absorbed by his religion at an early age. He was an altar boy and he sang in the choir of his parish church. He went to separate school, considered becoming a priest, then became a teacher. He went to camp in the summers where he was involved in some inter-faith groups, and was befriended by several priests. Danny couldn't find any serious female relationships, though he occasionally dated in high school and university. He got his Bachelor of Science degree, then his Bachelor of Education and his teaching certificate. He became more active in his local church, in Catholic study groups, and he joined Opus Dei. Somewhere in his late twenties, he made Opus Dei the centre of his life. He took a vow of chastity, furthered local projects, and continued teaching. He didn't have very close friends, though he was friendly with several other Opus Dei members. He was intelligent and solitary. He knew his science, math and theology. Probably not lonely if he was wedded to the Church and to his God.

A very dull life, Danny concluded, that of a secular monk. Danny was reminded of a Russian story he read many years ago in a history course about a superfluous man. His frustration continued.

XII

On Wednesday evening, as he did regularly, Danny went to the Royal Conservatory of Music on Bloor Street. He was a member of a local chamber orchestra, a group of thirty amateur musicians who practiced weekly. At the end of the school year, in June, the group gave a public concert. Several members were associated with the Conservatory as teachers and got permission to use the space.

Danny played the violin. He resisted calling himself a violinist, since he remained an amateur. He thought of himself acceptable, but not excellent. His chair in the violin section was in the last row, and he often wondered whether he might have to leave the group as their talent grew, which would upset him greatly. He took much pleasure in the music and in the activity.

This evening they were going through Vivaldi's *Sinfonia in C Major*, (RV 112), working on the piece for several weeks before they moved on to a new work.

Some members of the group were music teachers who had formal training. Some were immigrants, mainly from Russia and Ukraine. Others were Toronto born and bred. Their ages ranged from people in their late twenties to their sixties. Several were friends. What they all enjoyed was the magic that resulted from communicating with each other via sound and blending all their contributions to find a voice together. Danny believed you could talk about music, but it had a purity and language when played that could never be captured in words.

There was an outstanding chamber orchestra in the city, called Tafelmusik. This group, without a name other than the Bloor Street Chamber Group, took them as their model, knowing they were several steps below.

The group was now led by Gabriella Agostini who was in her mid-thirties. She, too, played the violin, far better than Danny did, though it was not her first instrument. She taught at the boys' school associated with St. Michael's Roman Catholic Cathedral Basilica. St. Michael's Choir School was one of the elite boys' choirs in the world and one of only six pontifical choir schools. She also conducted the youth orchestra of the Conservatory. Agostini had been the major flautist for the group. She moved up to be its leader only two years ago, when the long-serving, well-known Andrei Sokolski stepped down because of illness.

Gabriella obtained a sound from orchestra in a way that was different from how Andrei did. His style was stronger and a bit heavier than hers, which was sweeter and had greater clarity. Danny often thought about how different conductors could obtain such different sounds and interpretations from the same musicians.

Danny's partner in the back row was the charming Olga Nevsky. She was in her sixties, elegant, formal and a European *grande dame* of sorts. As the session neared its end, the two of them turned to one another to nod and smile while playing. The music was beautiful. This was what they came to create.

Danny had asked Gabriella to stay for a few minutes afterwards. He had three things he wanted to speak to her about, though he didn't know if he would have the courage to say the third.

"Good session," he said, as they sat in the first row of seats.

"Yes. Everyone really loves this stuff, and it shows. I only hope people aren't finding me too demanding or too different from Andrei."

"You have nothing to worry about. You're our leader and we're a happy bunch."

Gabriella smiled. She was a southern Italian beauty, not only with black hair, but also with a skin colour that reflected her ancestral roots in the Mezzogiorno, closer to Africa than to middle Europe. Her eyes were also black, with some light sparkles here and there. She had a Roman nose and a full mouth. There was a firmness about her, a sense she could be tough if necessary, which Danny thought probably stood her well at the boys' school and in the youth orchestra.

"Thanks," she said. "I admire Andrei so much I fear being compared to him."

"No one compares you to him. We like your sound and ideas. We also like that you're more open to interpretation than Andrei was."

"That helps. What did you want to speak about?"

"A couple of things, some not related to what we're doing here. First, if you worry about your conducting, then I worry about my playing. I know I'm not the best violinist in the group. In fact, I know virtually every other violinist is better than I am. That doesn't trouble me personally. But I thought I'd give you a chance to fire me by offering to leave if you don't think I'm up to scratch. I would miss it after these ten years, but I don't want to hold back the group. So, if you want me to fall out of the last row, I'll do so."

"Danny, it's sweet of you to do this. You're thoughtful, but it's unnecessary. You're doing fine. You contribute a lot to the group. Your sound is especially fine for a conductor like me. Stay where you are and keep playing."

"Seriously? I really have doubts."

"You're wrong. You do your job well. I would probably tell you to practice more if you can. Please stay. You help make the group what it is."

"You're kind. Thanks. Anyway, if you think at any time I'm dragging down the group, you must let me know."

"I will. Now let's get off that subject."

"Good. My second question. Do you or people you associate with at the school and the Cathedral, know anything about Opus Dei? … This has to do with a case I'm investigating."

"Oh. I was wondering where that came from. I know very little. I know it exists. I also know it's not my kind of Catholicism at all. I stand at the other, social justice end of the spectrum."

"Do you have anyone in mind I could ask?"

"Father Collelo, the rector of the Cathedral, knows everybody. You could try talking to him."

"Thanks. I might do so. I'm on a case in which Opus Dei pops up, but I don't know how important it will be in solving it."

Danny was quiet. He wondered whether to bid Gabriella goodnight. She broke the silence. "Is there anything else?"

"There is. I might as well get on with it."

"Yes?"

Danny came close to blushing for the first time in a long while. "Would you join me at the opera a week from Saturday? I have tickets to *The Magic Flute*."

Gabriella's eyes and mouth smiled.

"Danny, are you asking me out on a date?"

"Yes. I'm awkward. I don't know how to do this anymore."

"Let me think about it. I'll let you know in a few days. Give me your number and I'll call."

"Sounds good. I think we'd both enjoy the Mozart."

"Of course. I'm not used to this either. And I'm sure you have baggage, as do I. Let me think about it."

They rose together and exchanged goodnights, both a bit flustered.

XIII

Nadiri spent her Wednesday evening on Kenneth Avenue. She arrived at five in the afternoon, when the shifts at the desk changed, so she could talk to the two concierges in addition to any of the cleaning staff who were still around.

She had gone to 42 Division in Scarborough the previous evening, to discuss the case with her mentor there, Sergeant Beverly Smithfield. For once, Nadiri didn't follow Smithfield's advice, which was to take everything to her superior in charge of the case. Danny was someone for whom Smithfield had great respect.

"You're lucky to be paired with Miller," Smithfield said. "Don't go off on your own." She went back to Kenneth on her own time to duplicate the work done by Taegan and Connor, in case something was missed.

Nadiri had about two hours before she was to go to her parents' house for a family meal to celebrate her brother's birthday.

She spoke to both concierges. The evening concierge, Winsome Robinson, seemed to be someone who might have more information than was revealed earlier.

"Do you remember anything about that night?" Nadiri asked.

Winsome, fifty and impatient, told the younger woman, "I spoke to the officer. I told him everything."

"Tell me again. You might remember something new."

"There was nothing strange. People go in and out. Deliveries are made to the desk. I don't treat everyone who comes in as if they are criminals."

"Who came in that night?"

"People who live here. Relatives and friends. Delivery guys."

"No one else?"

"Maybe. I go on rounds about seven o'clock. That takes ten minutes."

"If I sent a sketch artist to you, could you tell me what the delivery guy looked like?"

"He looked like a delivery guy. He had a brown uniform and carried two packages."

"Maybe an artist will help you to remember."

"You're pushing me too far. You think I did it, right?"

Nadiri winced. "No. We just need to catch the guy that did."

"Go catch him, sister. Leave me alone."

"We won't leave you alone until we catch him."

Winsome sighed. "You're wasting your time, girl. Go do something useful."

"Don't tell me how to do my job. We'll get him."

"Sure. And I'm going to win the lottery."

Nadiri questioned others, but found nothing new.

The next day she told Danny, "I think the concierge, Winsome Robinson, might remember something if we had a sketch artist work with her."

"Why do you think that?"

"I saw her yesterday and I get a sense she knows more than she is aware of."

Danny was silent for several seconds. Then he said, "Where did you see her?"

"At Kenneth. I went to the building on my own time. I thought I might uncover something that was missed."

"Who asked you to go?"

"No one. I went on my own. I wanted to check again."

"Excuse me? Did you think that Taegan and Connor didn't do their job?"

"I thought I might find something."

Danny sat up straight. "OK. Before we talk about Winsome Robinson, we need to talk about protocols."

"What do you mean?" Nadiri asked.

"We all work as a team. I don't expect Taegan or Connor to get involved in something without clearing it with me. The same holds for every member of the team."

"I just thought I might find something if I double-checked."

"If you had asked me, I probably would have agreed after we discussed what the purpose of your visit would have been. But you can't go off on your own. How would you feel if I sent Taegan or Connor to check on something that you did?"

"I wasn't checking on Taegan or Connor. I just thought …"

Danny interrupted, "Sorry. I understand your devotion to duty and your eagerness to solve the murder. However, I don't understand how you feel you can do whatever you decide without clearance from your superior. What's next? Are you going to talk to the priest at the cathedral without letting me know? I can't have people on the team who don't work with others. We work together. No surprises."

Nadiri remembered the advice given to her by Beverly Smithfield. 'How stupid can you be, Nadiri?' she thought. Her body language changed as she slumped and moved about in the chair, hoping to disappear.

"You're right, sir. I won't try to defend what I did. I just hoped I could make a breakthrough. It was bad judgment. It won't happen again."

"It can't happen again, Nadiri. Do you understand? You've been doing very well. Don't wreck your chance."

"Yes, sir. I get it. It was a dumb thing to do."

Danny changed course. "Maybe it wasn't a dumb thing to do. It was wrong to do it on your own. Now, why do you think Robinson can help us?"

"I pushed her, and I think she might remember something if we can jog her memory."

"Nadiri, I want you to think about how you questioned her. After that, if you still think she can help further, then we'll talk. Now let's get back to business and decide where we go from here. I'll see you in an hour."

"Yes, sir." Nadiri left, feeling she had just done the stupidest thing in her life since she destroyed her sister's doll in a fit of anger when she was six years old.

XIV

That evening, Nadiri went to her sister's house for dinner, something she often did. While she lived in a Western mode, her sister's family kept some of the traditional customs from their homeland. Nadiri stopped on the way to the house to get small presents for her young niece and nephew.

She dressed conservatively She was wearing a skirt and blouse with a shawl. Her sister Afari, and her brother-in-law Farid, had changed as a result of living in Toronto. They did things together, rather than separately by gender. Not all Iranian families were even this modern. However, they were very Iranian in separating their public and private lives. Family was the centre, and it was in family that one could be authentic.

They loved traditional foods, as did Nadiri, who looked forward not only to talking with her elder sister, but to Afari's cooking. The table was formally set, with only a fork and a spoon. Tonight, they had *taftoon*, a Persian wholemeal flat bread, Persian rice, a chicken dish with turmeric and saffron, and halva served with a topping of pistachios and almonds for dessert.

During dinner, Nadiri recounted to Afari and Farid the events leading to Danny, to whom she always referred as Sergeant Miller, letting her know she had made several mistakes. Afari was the one who Nadiri had looked to for advice for most of her life, an elder sister who took her place in the family very seriously and conscientiously.

"Your enthusiasm sometimes gets you into trouble," Afari said. "You need to think carefully before you act."

"Yes, but I don't want to play it safe all the time by doing nothing."

Farid entered the exchange. "It sounds as if Detective Miller was right to be concerned. But he was calm, wasn't he?"

"Very calm, but very firm. I sense he's a good person, but there are lines that can't be crossed."

"Well," Afari replied, "we too have lines. Maybe he's not so different from us."

Farid said, "I wonder if your partnership is the first one in the force of two people with origins in the Middle East. His people and ours have similar customs. For example, they live two lives as do we. They behave one way in public, but they have their own customs, prayers and food at home."

"I never thought of it that way," Nadiri said. "Perhaps he understands me better than most people."

"He sounds like a decent person," Afari said. "I think he would like to help you. He responded in a very friendly way. Learn from your mistake. But don't repeat it. Be enthusiastic, even bold, but do so in the bubble of the team."

"Good advice, Afari. Thank you both."

They finished the meal with a customary prayer, thanking Allah for their good fortune. Nadiri ended the evening playing a board game with her niece and nephew. She went home feeling better than when the evening began.

XV

The case went nowhere in the following week. Danny spoke to Father Collelo at the Cathedral and several others in Frawley's school. Nadiri sometimes went with him and also went on her own to interview people who seemed like they might yield some useful information. By mid-week, McIntyre assigned Taegan and Connor to other cases.

It seemed like the perfect crime, though Danny didn't believe there was such a thing as a perfect crime. He spent a lot of time awake and had a hard time trying to sleep at night. He kept imagining what might have happened and trying to find a new way into the case.

The only positive thing that did happen to him was that Gabriella called him. She said she would be pleased to join him at the opera next Saturday. Danny asked if he could pick her up at her condo. Instead, she suggested they meet in the lobby of The Four Seasons Centre for the Performing Arts at University and Queen.

They met at seven o'clock and chatted about the chamber group and the opera. Both were very familiar with the Mozart opera and found themselves wondering about how it would be interpreted. Danny recalled he long ago saw a version of *The Magic Flute* that had been set, bizarrely, in Weimar Germany, and turned into an allegory about the impending doom of Nazi Germany.

"Did it work?" Gabriella asked.

"Of course not," Danny said. "It ruined the evening—the attempt to make it something by Alban Berg went totally awry."

They were companionable before the curtain and they had the same kind of anticipation when the first notes of the overture were played. They talked during the break about the performances, the beauty of the music, and the unusual "folk opera" they were attending, a prelude to modern musical theatre. Both bumped into acquaintances at the intermission and there was pleasant chitchat.

When it was over, they agreed to get a coffee. There was a coffee shop nearby and they found a small table in a quiet corner of the café.

"Thanks, Danny," Gabriella said as they got settled. "That was fun. It's nice attending it with someone who obviously loves the music."

"My son Avi calls me a Mozarthead. There are Deadheads, he tells me, but I'm the only Mozarthead he knows."

"You're certainly not the only Mozarthead, in this town or in the world. He's one of my heroes. I think if I were to be branded, I'd be a Bachhead."

"That's pretty clear to all of us in the group. But maybe we could do the overture to *The Magic Flute* or to one of Mozart's other operas some year?"

"Why not? I often wonder if we should listen just to the music of an opera sometimes. Whether the music conveys all that is necessary. I bet *The Magic Flute* qualifies as one of those pieces where the music does it all. Opera without words."

"Not hard. There's a lot of programmed music. Beethoven's *Pastoral Symphony*. Tchaikovsky's *1812 Overture*. It would work."

"Can I ask you a question you don't have to answer if you don't want to?" Gabriella said as she played with the cup of her latte.

"Sure."

"Why did you become a cop? You have an unusual set of characteristics. Not many Jews enter the police force. And not many police officers are Mozartheads and play the violin for a hobby."

"If you had asked me why I became a cop just after I entered the force, I probably would have given you a different answer. I've thought about it in retrospect, though I've never discussed these thoughts with anyone, and I've come to a different conclusion."

"I don't want to intrude. You don't need to answer."

"No. I'd like to try to talk about it, though I may not be as clear as I'd like to be because I've never fully articulated it. I became a cop because I wanted to do something that was useful to the community. That's easy. But I also became a cop because I wanted to go my own way, because it was not 'a Jewish thing' to do. It was a way of telling my family and community I was going my own way."

"A rebel?" Gabriella asked.

"You're hardly a rebel while upholding law and order. But, yes, it was—how do I say it—rebellious in the sense it was unusual and left me to my own devices. In a way, it was weird. I believed in most of the values of my parents and the Jewish tradition. I still do, but I didn't like how the community demanded you live a certain way. It was claustrophobic. So, instead of becoming a lawyer, I became a cop. Much less prestigious—and much less money earned—but it seemed to suit me."

"Did your family respond?"

"Oh, yes. They were upset. It's like a nice Jewish boy telling his parents, who aspired for him to be a doctor, that he wanted to become a nurse. But it's part of a larger picture. I didn't like the script that was written for me. I wanted to live differently, more openly, more freely. This caused big issues to rise. Not only was I a cop, but I stopped fully observing the Sabbath. I occasionally ate forbidden foods. I played the violin in a group led by Catholics. And so on. I'm still suspect. My brother-in-law, who's a nice guy, a lawyer and an observant Jew, puts up with me—after all, I am hardly a criminal and I am reasonably cultured and polite—but he doesn't approve of my life."

"Any larger consequences?"

"You're a good interviewer. You could be a cop. Let's say it contributed to my divorce, though I don't want to talk about that now. My former wife is seen by our families and the community as normal. I'm the strange one."

Turning the conversation around, Danny continued, "And you? Why is a gorgeous, intelligent, nice Catholic girl like you still single? You must have had a hundred marriage proposals."

"Hardly a hundred, but several. I finally said yes to one. It didn't work out. I should tell you more of my story in exchange for your openness. Not now, though. Another time."

"That's fine. Now let me tell you why I think the director blew it tonight in his portrayal of Sarastro. A missed opportunity."

They went back to discussing the opera and music for a time.

Then Danny asked, "Can I drive you home? I parked three blocks away."

"You don't have to, Danny."

"I want to. Besides, one of the traditional values I still buy is the importance of being a gentleman. It's old-fashioned, maybe a little too old-fashioned by today's standards, but I'd feel better if I saw you home. Maybe it's the cop in me." He added, with a smile, "If your feminist heart tells you this is silly, let me say that, if you had the car, I'd let you drive me home."

"You win. Take me home, Danny."

Gabriella's condominium turned out to be not very far from Danny's house. She lived in an apartment on the edge of Rosedale, near the Castle Frank subway station, a long walk from Danny's place on the Danforth.

"Not even out of my way," Danny said, as he pulled up in front of the building. They grasped one another's hands awkwardly and had what might be described as a half hug before Gabriella exited the car. Danny smiled all the way home.

PART II

I

The next week for Danny and Nadiri was a continuation of the frustration from the previous week. They felt they were getting nowhere, and there was nowhere to go. On Thursday, they met with Sydney McIntyre and reported their disappointment.

"It sounds as if you've gone everywhere," McIntyre said. "I really don't have any suggestions. I do have a proposal, though it's not something I often do."

She surveyed their faces, as the two waited for her to go on. "I think you need a rest from the case. This is one of those cases that needs to sit in your unconscious. I'm not saying you'll wake up at two in the morning one night with the solution. But I think, at the moment, there's nowhere to go."

"What are you suggesting, ma'am?" Danny asked.

"I'm going to assign you another case when one comes up that suits your team. Then you'll be working on both. I think continuing full-time on the Frawley case will not get us anywhere."

"Are you telling us we failed? This has never happened to me. I want to keep working on the Frawley case."

"Don't make it personal, Danny. You'll solve the Frawley case. You just won't solve it right now. I'd like to solve it today, but it will have to be solved later. I know this is unusual. I'm asking you to consider my suggestion. Moreover, I can't justify two people working on something for months when there's no sign of progress. I'm asking you to give this a try."

Danny swallowed. He liked McIntyre and he trusted her. Finally, he said, "I'm reluctant. Let's try this and see if somehow we can solve two cases at once."

"Thanks, Danny. I'll let the two of you know when a new case comes up. In the meanwhile, I'd advise you to take the afternoon off. I know you two have been working hard."

II

He was enjoying life these days far more than any time since he was a child. He loved The Beach and thought he might look for an apartment near enough to take regular walks on the boardwalk. His work was better and his boss gave him some praise instead of just ignoring his existence. His bowling was lousy, but his companions made fun of his bowling, not of him.

Above all, he and his psychiatrist began thinking of his future. He would enrol in some online courses, maybe in technology. He would acquire some skills, which would help him get a better job. And he was beginning to get some measure of self-worth after all these years of wanting to dissolve or disappear.

What he liked most was the hunt. He realized in some inner part of his being that the anticipation was at least half the pleasure of redemption. So, this time he managed to be patient. For now, he knew where his quarry lived and worked, and he had some sense of his rhythm and activities. He would learn more. He thoroughly enjoyed knowing he would take revenge, knowing what his quarry did not know. He liked the feeling of control. He knew the future. His tormentor only thought he had a future.

III

Two days later, Danny was in the office when he got a call from McIntyre. "There's a new case. I think you and Nadiri should be on it. See Hugh O'Brien at the morgue. He knows you're coming. We'll talk about it later today."

When Danny and Nadiri arrived, O'Brien was cleaning up an autopsy.

"Good afternoon to you both," O'Brien said. "We have an unpleasant one. Let's go to the office."

When they were settled, O'Brien continued, "A young woman is dead. Twenty years old. Her name is Halima Nizamani. She was found on the rocks below the Scarborough Bluffs. At first, the officers in charge regarded it as a suicide, since they see several of those at The Bluffs each year."

"You have suspicions?" asked Danny.

"No, Danny, I have certainty. It wasn't a suicide. The poor young woman was choked to death. Then she was thrown down The Bluffs to make it appear as a suicide."

"Was she killed at The Bluffs?"

"I don't know. I don't think so. All traces of fingerprints are gone. This makes me believe she was killed elsewhere. Then the murderer cleaned up, put on gloves if he didn't have gloves on when he killed her, took her to the bluffs and threw her down. I can't tell you whether the murder was premeditated, but I'm quite certain that, in disposing of the body, her killer was determined to hide the murder. There is also a knapsack belonging to Ms. Nizamani, which was left at the top of the Bluffs. I'll leave that to you."

"Hugh, I understand an autopsy in cases of apparent suicide is a regular procedure."

"Yes. The families don't like it, understandably. And in ninety percent of the cases nothing untoward is revealed. But this is one of the other ten percent. She was murdered."

"I'd like to look at the body. I want to know what was done to her."

"It's a mess, Danny. The rocks are unforgiving. I have pictures. That should do."

"OK. I'll follow your advice. Any pictures in the knapsack?"

"A few. You'll sort that out."

"Thanks, Hugh. When did she die?"

"Last night. Roughly between nine and one."

Danny turned to Nadiri. "Any further questions?"

"Not now. I have some thoughts, but let's look at what we have before I make any suggestions."

The knapsack and a winter coat were in another room. The coat was typically Canadian, lined, with down inside and a hood. The pockets contained a toque, a library slip from the Robarts Library at the University of Toronto, some tissues, and two paper clips. The knapsack had a wallet, a hijab, a brush, a comb, lipstick, a pen, a yellow marker and a purse with change. It also contained a Presto card, more tissues and a book from the library, *A History of Islam* by Phyllis Nadri.

The wallet contained forty-five dollars, a driver's licence, several identification cards for the university, a debit card, two bandages and pictures of Halima. The pictures were of people who might be her family—a man, a woman in a niqab, a young man and Halima in a hijab—and one with six young women of a variety of ethnicities, including Halima, in jeans and tops, laughing. Danny was glad about the pictures, not only for what they might reveal. He wanted to have an image of Halima Nizamani in his mind. Now, it was up to him to deal with the person who murdered her. He could not bring her back, but he could bring some justice to the end of her life. He felt a responsibility to the young woman.

Danny called McIntyre and told her what he had found out from Hugh O'Brien and Halima's possessions. "Has the family been informed?" he asked.

"Not yet. I wanted you to get a look first. Perhaps it would be useful if you and Nadiri informed them?"

"Yes. I don't like doing it, but there are too many open questions. We have their address from her wallet. We'll go directly to their place in Scarborough."

IV

By the time Danny and Nadiri arrived at the apartment complex where Halima's family lived, it was six in the evening and dark.

In the car, Danny asked Nadiri what she thought. "I don't want to get ahead of myself here. Let's just say this is one of those cases where we might need to fully understand what my best professor called the sociology of the event. On the other hand, it could just be a random murder by a terrible human being."

"I like the term 'the sociology of the event.' How come I didn't take a course with your professor?"

"You were too busy learning about politics. Every sociology major will tell you society is more important than politics."

"So will Edmund Burke and John Stuart Mill. Even the dreaded Machiavelli. We're not as blind as you guys think."

"I agree. But as a cop in Toronto, sociology is more important in understanding the context of a killing than politics is."

"I've been sold on that for a long time. One of my professors would say the first rule of good teaching is to know who is in front of you. Applied to being a cop, you realize the first rule is to know who you are investigating. People are similar. They have greed, pride, kindness, empathy and foolishness. But their worlds differ, and you need to understand those worlds."

"Well, sir, we might make a sociologist out of you yet."

They got into the building easily. They followed someone entering with a key, and took the elevator to the fourth floor of the six-story building. They knocked on the door of the apartment where the Nizamani family lived. The elevator and corridors had an odour of cumin, coriander and nutmeg, Pakistani spices.

The door was answered by a young man, about twenty-five-years old, who was the same person in what Danny thought was the family picture in Halima's wallet.

Danny and Nadiri identified themselves and asked if the parents were home.

The young man responded in a hostile manner. "We haven't done anything wrong. Why are you bothering us?"

"We have news about a young woman who we believe lives here. We would like to speak with Mr. and Mrs. Nizamani."

They were admitted reluctantly to the foyer and were asked to wait while Mr. and Mrs. Nizamani were summoned.

Mr. Nizamani came. Nadiri thought she saw a shadow of a woman in a niqab in the background. The man did not invite them into the apartment. The son hovered behind his father.

"Are you Farid Nizamani?"

"I am. Why are you here?"

"I have news about your daughter Halima."

Nizamani's voice raised as he said, "I have no daughter."

"Mr. Nizamani, perhaps I am making a mistake." Danny took one of the pictures he had brought with him, the one of the family. "This is certainly you and the young man is your son. The young woman in the photo is Halima. Is she not your daughter?"

"I had a daughter named Halima. She disobeyed Allah, me and the family. She is no longer my daughter. Whatever she has done, she now looks after herself."

Nadiri touched Danny on the arm. He nodded and she then spoke in her first language, Farsi. The only things Danny understood were references to Allah and the Qur'an.

Farid Nizamani looked surprised, but Nadiri's technique worked. He said, "I'm not fulfilling my responsibility to guests. Please come in."

They entered a living room with furniture and pottery in the style of their homeland. They were asked to sit. "May I get you some tea?" Nizamani asked.

Danny looked to Nadiri to respond. She again spoke, this time in Urdu, saying what Danny thought was thank you.

Farid sat across from them. The son went to the kitchen to bring the tea when it was ready.

"I am telling you again, I have no daughter. She shamed our family and would not mend her ways. I tried to persuade her. She didn't obey. I told her she was now an orphan. Whatever she has done is not my responsibility."

"I have bad news, Farid," Danny said. "Your daughter is dead. She was killed yesterday. Her body is at the morgue."

Farid recoiled and a horrifying sound came from the kitchen. It was a wailing that pierced both Danny's and Nadiri's hearts, clearly the sound of a mother beginning to mourn her child. It was a sound no one should have to make.

Farid paid no attention the cry. He said, "This is what happens when a child disobeys the tradition and shames the family. Allah has sent a message. Let Allah's will be done."

The son brought the tea, though the three of them ignored it. He again hovered behind his father.

"What is your name, son?" asked Danny.

"Jameel."

"Jameel, can you help us learn how your sister died? This is, I'm sorry to say, a murder investigation."

The young man glanced at his father. In fear, Danny thought. "I tried to protect her. I tried to get her to behave properly. I watched over her. She wouldn't listen to me or to our father."

There was very little to be gotten in that room. Danny ended it. "Farid, Jameel, I will need one of you to come to the morgue to identify the body. I will send a car tomorrow morning at nine to take one or both of you to do so. Constable Rahimi and I will be there." Danny got up.

"I have no daughter," Farid repeated.

"You have no living daughter, that is true. You'll find it's not so easy to efface a child."

V

Danny and Nadiri were silent as they left the building and walked to the car. Both were emotionally torn by what they had experienced. Silence was their first response. In the car, as they got onto Finch to make their way west before going south to the police station, Danny broke the quiet.

"What did you say that got us into the living room?"

"I spoke in Farsi, though I'm pretty certain that Urdu is the Nizamanis' language. I hoped he would at least surmise my background was Islamic. He did. I referred to the Qur'an and the importance of treating guests in a welcome manner. When he offered the tea, I used one of the few Urdu expressions I know—the words for thank you very much, bahut bahut shukriya."

"That was useful. It helped to make the exchange somewhat civil. Thanks."

"Did you ever have a case where your Hebrew was useful?"

"Oh, yes. About five years ago. There was a case involving some people in the Orthodox Jewish community, including some Israelis.

Hebrew was useful in telling them I knew where they came from. There were some older people involved, a generation ahead of me, and with them I used my Yiddish, which is not at all as fluent as my Hebrew."

"What do you think of the case so far, sir?"

"I think we need to interview all three of the Nizamanis separately at the police station. We need to find out what's been going on. The idea that Halima was killed because her family abandoned her might be true. I don't want to go as far as to say she was killed by her family yet. I also think we need to interview Halima's friends—the other five women in the photo and anyone else who pops up. We need to get a sense of what her life has been like in the last year or so."

"Sir, I wonder if it would be more useful if I were to first interview Mrs. Nizamani alone."

"Tell me why. I think I know, but I want your perspective."

"I'm a woman. And I'm from a culture that has Islam as part of its daily life, even if my family and I are Persian rather than Arabic. She might remove her niqab in front of me if we are alone, which she almost certainly wouldn't do if you're in the room. Also, I can ask her certain questions that she won't answer if a man other than a member of her family is present. I think we'll learn more this way."

"You make a good case for your proposal. Let me think about it. If we do it that way, we should rehearse what we want to ask."

"Absolutely."

"I'm pleased you took the initiative and asked. I'm glad you decided to just be yourself and not clam up after the earlier goof."

"Bahut bahut shukriya, sir."

VI

Danny skipped his squash game that Sunday morning to meet with Nadiri and Sydney McIntyre at eight o'clock, before going to meet the Nizamanis at the morgue.

"Let's decide how to proceed," McIntyre said. "I imagine you've already spoken about this between yourselves."

"Of course," Danny replied. He first briefed McIntyre about what had happened on the visit to the Nizamani home the previous evening.

Then, he said, "I want to interview the three immediate family members as soon as possible. Here at the station, and all separately. Both of us will be present for the men and Nadiri will see Mrs. Nizamani alone. Then I want to find out about Halima's life. See her friends, maybe talk to her teachers. I'd also like to go to The Bluffs to look at the location where the body was found. Not that I think I'll find anything that was missed, just to get a feel for what occurred."

"Do you think we need to consider that this may be an honour killing? The murder of a young woman gets media attention. I'll need to have a press conference soon. Danny, I'd like you there when that happens."

"Yes, ma'am, it may be an honour killing. Every word out of her father's mouth was angry, even hateful. But we don't know that it is. Yet. Let's not jump to the stereotypical conclusion. Of course, Nadiri and I will probe in that direction. As for the press, let me know when the conference occurs."

"OK. And before the conference we'll take ten minutes to discuss how to handle it. Do you need more support?"

"I doubt it. Maybe to find out who her friends were. But not to do the interviews. Only Nadiri and I should do them. Let me have Taegan or Connor or both of them and I'll get them to do some probing into Halima's circle."

"I'll see who can be spared. Let's get going."

Danny and Nadiri took the short drive to the morgue. They got there before the car arrived from Scarborough with Farid Nizamani. When the car arrived, Farid Nizamani and one other person exited. They both entered the building. Farid introduced him as his brother Maher, Halima's uncle.

The identification was brief. O'Brien and his assistants had cleaned up the face as best they could. Instead of entering the morgue and seeing the body on a table, the procedure now was to go to a room with a television monitor and project the face on the screen. Both men nodded and said it was Halima.

Danny and Nadiri tried to be as quiet and respectful as possible through this procedure. Danny then asked if either man wanted some tea or coffee. They were surprised, but this was a way for Danny to let them know he needed to talk to them. Danny ordered tea and Nadiri kept an eye out for its arrival.

Finally, Danny said, "I'm very sorry for your loss, gentlemen. It's a terrible thing when a young person leaves the world."

"Inspector," the uncle said, elevating Danny's rank knowingly, "when might we leave? This is a hard matter."

"It's Sergeant," Danny replied. "This is a bad business, I agree. But it's also a murder investigation. I need to interview the immediate family, Mr. Nizamani, in addition to yourself and several others."

Tea arrived and there was a pause. "Those interviews have to be conducted soon. The sooner the better. So, I'm going to give the two of you a choice. We can do the interviews now or you can go home, take care of whatever needs to be done for a few hours, and we will send a car to take you back to the station at four this afternoon."

"Must it be so?"

"Yes, it must. We need to catch a killer. And we need to get going as quickly as possible. You may know things that will help."

The brothers exchanged some talk in Urdu. Then, Maher turned to Danny and said, "We will go home now. We'll return this afternoon."

"That's fine," Danny said. "Not only will the two of you return. Your sister-in-law and nephew will need to be interviewed. They must come along this afternoon as well. It will take some time. If you let me know your preferences, we can provide food and drink."

After the brothers left, Nadiri asked, "Why did you let them go? Now they can build a story among the four of them."

"Several reasons. If they have a story, they've already discussed it. I also want them to think we're open, that we're not accusing them of murder. And I don't want defence attorneys claiming we're abusing our authority. Let them do some thinking. That won't hurt."

"Sounds right. In the meantime, what should I do?"

"Start finding out what you can about her friends. If Halima left home, she had to sleep somewhere. Sunday may not be a good day for doing this, but get organized so we can work efficiently tomorrow. And get some lunch along the way. It'll be a long day. I'll see you at the station at three-thirty."

VII

They decided Danny would interview Farid Nizamani in a regular interview room, one with a two-way mirror so McIntyre could watch. Another male member of the force would also be present, though he would be instructed to act as a silent observer. At the same time, Nadiri would interview Mahshid Nizamani in an office with an observing female officer present. The office would have no mirror, no window and a door that looked secure. They thought the two parents would likely take longer than the uncle and the brother.

Farid Nizamani was escorted to his interview room by an officer. Danny waited ten minutes and then he and the observer entered.

"Farid, this is an official interview. I am putting on the tape recorder. The time is four-fifteen. How are you feeling, Farid?"

"I don't want to discuss my feelings, Sergeant Miller, unless you tell me my feelings are part of the interview."

"No, they're not. Tell me, Farid, how did you get along with your daughter?"

"She was raised properly. She was taught about our traditions and the respect she is to give to her father and the other men in the family. We instructed her in prayer, about Allah, and about Islam."

"Did you and your daughter get along well?"

"She was a good child until she was sixteen. She knew her place in the family and her duties. She followed the rules of our people. Then, something happened. She began to ask if she could go out without an escort from the family. I found things like lipstick in her room. She read books that were not correct for a woman to read. She persuaded me to let her exchange her niqab for a hijab."

"Did she like the high school she attended, Cedarbrae Collegiate in Scarborough?"

"She tried to stay late at school. Clubs, she called them. They were profane, dirty. I had her brother keep an eye on her. He would report to me that she removed her hijab, that she had Western clothes in her locker and changed into them sometimes. She had friends who were not of our community."

"What did you do?"

"I tried to direct her properly. I thought she was moving back to a proper life until I refused to give her permission to go to university. I wanted her to meet a man from Pakistan, to marry and live a normal life."

"What happened?"

"She went crazy. She screamed and refused to do any work in the house. She became more disobedient, staying out late at night."

"How did she get to go to university?"

"We made an agreement. She could go to university if she conformed to our ways and rules. She fooled me. She was a perfect woman at home, but her brother followed her and reported on her behaviour outside the house. She changed clothes, ate foods that are forbidden, and started having boys as friends, not from our community, as well as girls."

"When did you learn this?"

"About a year ago. I did what a father is supposed to do. I took advice from our imam and from other members of the family, especially my older brother, who leads the family."

"What did you tell her?"

"I told her she was going too far. I told her she would cease to be my daughter if she continued in these ways. She was choosing an evil path, one that shamed our family."

"Did you use force? Did you hit her?"

Farid thought for a bit. "I did everything a man who believes in Allah and the Qur'an is supposed to do."

"Did you use force?"

"Sometimes it is necessary to protect the family."

"When did she leave home permanently?"

"Three months ago, when school began in September. I told her she was forbidden to return to school, that we would not pay her fees. She was to stay home and behave like a proper Islamic woman. I suggested we could arrange a good marriage for her."

"She left?"

"She left and did not return. I told our imam and the family that she was no longer our daughter."

"Did you hear from her after she left?"

"No."

"Did you look for her?"

"No."

Danny asked if Farid wanted a break or something to drink. He requested some water and Danny turned off the tape machine while the observing officer went to get bottles for the three of them. Danny told Farid he would step out for five minutes to take a break. "Please stretch and take a break yourself," he added.

In the corridor, he saw McIntyre. "You're being nice, Danny," she said. "Do you think you should push more?"

"I'll push. This is a first interview. I don't want to totally alienate him at this moment. We've learned a lot. If what you're partly talking about is to get him to admit that he hit Halima, that will happen. He won't get to avoid it."

"OK. Keep going."

Danny returned, opened his water bottle, took a swallow, turned on the tape, and continued.

"Farid, where were you on Friday night between nine and two?"

"I was home. My wife was home, and she will tell you I was home. My son came home at about eleven, and he will tell you I was home."

"Did anyone else see you at home?"

"No."

"Did you talk with anyone on the phone?"

"I spoke with my brother earlier. At about eight. No one else. I don't like where this is going. Do you think I killed Halima? For me, she no longer existed."

"I need to have the facts, Farid. That's all I'm doing."

"My daughter died, for me, months ago, maybe years ago. You do not understand."

"I think I do understand. Is there anything else you want to say now?"

"She brought it on to herself. I told you. Allah has spoken. Allah has given his judgment."

Danny concluded for the time being. He thanked Farid, turned off the tape, and told him he was free to go. "My colleague is speaking with your wife. We will also need to talk with your son and your brother. There is a place you can wait while they're being interviewed. Thank you again for your time."

VIII

While Farid Nizamani entered the interview room, Nadiri was escorting his wife Mahshid to the office where they would talk. Trailing behind them was Constable Rose Fielder, who would also be present.

There was tea in the room, and Nadiri had brought some biscuits from a halal bakery, which she put on a plate in the middle of the desk, along with serviettes.

Mahshid Nizamani was dressed in a black niqab. She was shorter than Nadiri, about five feet three inches. However, her body language as she sat down made her seem smaller than that. She was bent and did not look directly at Nadiri. She was someone who knew how to disappear.

Nadiri had met with Danny beforehand to discuss how she should approach the interview. He advised her to go slowly. "The most important thing is for you to build some trust," he had said. "After that, perhaps we'll learn something useful."

"Mrs. Nizamani, I am very, very sorry for your loss. I can't imagine how terrible this must be for you," Nadiri began. "Can I ask you for your full name?"

The woman looked up, still focusing to the side of Nadiri. "My name is Mahshid Nizamani."

"Thank you," Nadiri said. "I need to tell you that your daughter was murdered. We are looking into this to find the murderer and to bring them to justice."

Mahshid nodded and said, "You cannot bring back my daughter. She is gone forever."

"You're correct. We cannot bring her back. But there is something we can do for her. We can find who murdered her and bring that person to justice. That's my job and the job of my superior, Sergeant Miller."

Mahshid did not respond with words. She looked around her, taking in the office and the space.

"This office has no windows, as you can see. It is also locked. It has no mirrors. We are recording this interview, but there are no cameras. The only people who can see you are me and Officer Fielder. If I can be open with you, this is because we have some understanding of your customs and traditions. I was born in Iran."

"Are you one of the people of Islam?"

"I am Persian. We have some of our own customs and some Islamic customs. I spent my first years in an Islamic country."

"I don't know anything. I don't know why you are questioning me."

"You do know many things. You spend a lot of your time pretending not to know. There is not much you can do for your daughter now. This is one of the things you can do."

She looked up and was silent for a time. Nadiri let the silence do whatever it would. Finally, Mahshid Nizamani loosened the headdress part of the niqab to show most of her face. She sat up a bit straighter.

Nadiri worked hard to not look surprised. This was not because the face was revealed. What shocked her, even though she had thought it might be so, were the bruises on her very sad face that had been hidden by the garment.

"How can I help my daughter? How do I know you will not tell what I say to my husband?"

"No one will tell your husband. The information will be limited to those who are investigating. They are Officer Fielder, me, Sergeant Miller, his superior, Inspector McIntyre, and possibly a few others who are experts. This isn't a public matter. It's not a family matter."

"I don't know if I should believe you. Tell me how I can help my daughter." She paused and held up a hand. "Tell me what will happen to my daughter's body."

"Of course." Nadiri had never done this before. She was close to tears for this woman, knowing it may be unprofessional, but also knowing she had to go on. "Your daughter's body will be released to the family for burial. The family will do what is proper in your tradition."

"What if the family refuses to take the body?"

Danny had anticipated this when he was discussing how to proceed with Sydney McIntyre and Nadiri. Sydney had provided an answer Nadiri now repeated.

"We have a solution, which I would like to ask you about. We have had this happen a few times before your loss. There is a respected imam—he is the imam at a mosque on Danforth Avenue—who would then conduct a service in the tradition of Islam. Halima will be buried in an Islamic cemetery according to the proper ritual."

Mahshid nodded. "How can I help my daughter?"

"You can help by answering my questions. Before that, may I get you some tea?" She nodded again. "Then let's take a five-minute pause."

Fielder was already out the door to fetch the tea.

When they settled again a few minutes later, Nadiri asked, "When did you last see your daughter?"

"Two weeks ago."

"Where?"

"In the apartment. I am not permitted to go out alone."

"How did that happen?"

"I gave her money—what little I saved—when she left a few months ago. She was smart. She bought me a phone before the last time she left. She never called. I would call her when it was safe to come. She only came for a short time."

"How did she look?"

"Thin. Frightened."

"Did she talk about her life?"

"Yes. She lived with a kind friend near the university. She took loans. She wished to make a different life from mine."

"Did you approve?"

"She is my daughter. I love her. I support her. I do not wish to discuss my life."

"Did your husband ever mention her after she left?"

"It was forbidden. For him, she was no longer his daughter. He believed she had shamed us and the large family. He wanted her to be like the traditional women in Islam."

"Did your son help?"

"He sided with his father ... My son is afraid of his father."

"Why?"

"Because his father will punish him if he does not behave properly."

"Would your husband hit him?"

"Yes."

"Did your husband hit Halima?"

"Yes."

"Who do you think might have killed your daughter?"

"I don't know."

"Do you think that a member of the family might have killed your daughter?"

"I don't know."

"Was your husband at home with you on Friday night?"

She pointed to her face. "Yes."

"Mrs. Nizamani, it is very courageous for you tell us these things. We will not fail you."

Mahshid nodded, realizing the interview was ending. She began to adjust her niqab.

Nadiri leaned closer to Mahshid. "I want you to know that this is not the last time we will be speaking. For now, you have been very helpful. I also want you to know that you can call me anytime. Here is my card. You have my number as a police officer and on the back, I've written my home number."

Mahshid Nazimani took the card and it disappeared into her clothes. She was adjusting, making herself again almost invisible. Her posture changed. Her eyes became glazed and neutral.

Nadiri escorted her to a place where she could wait while the interviews continued. She asked Rose Fielder to wait with her.

IX

When Nadiri returned to the main office, she asked about Danny's whereabouts. She was told he was in the interview room with the uncle. Nadiri went to her desk and made some notes. Then her shoulders dropped, and she took a very deep breath. Ten minutes later, after Danny had finished with Maher Nizamani, the two went together to interview Jameel.

Maher Nizamani had been openly hostile. He supported his brother entirely and told Danny that Farid had done the right thing. "You don't understand," he had repeated several times, because Danny kept saying that the murder must be investigated. He took seriously his recently-inherited role as head of the larger family, the father having died a year earlier. He contrasted his own daughters' proper behaviour with that of Halima. His alibi was no more secure than Farid's. He said he was at home on Friday night, along with his wife and two daughters who would testify to that.

Jameel was by turns fearful and loudly hostile. He wouldn't tell them anything about the family. He was proud his father had given him the responsibility of looking after his sister, even if that meant spying on her and being verbally abusive. He clearly feared what would happen to him in the family if he said the wrong thing. He said he came home at eleven after being with friends. His mother and father were there when he arrived and he never left. He gave the names of two friends who would vouch for him.

It was seven in the evening when they met with McIntyre and Taegan, who McIntyre had arranged to be assigned to the case.

"What have we learned and where do we go from here?" McIntyre asked.

Danny summed up his interviews. Nadiri then gave a running account of her interview with Mahshid Nizamani. At the end, she said, "I'm very sympathetic. This woman is not even permitted to mourn properly. She took a big risk in going as far as she did."

"Yes, you're right," Danny added. "For her, this is an act of resistance, if not rebellion."

"You did well to get her to open up even as far as she did," McIntyre said. "Let's not let her down."

"I'm really very sympathetic with her," Nadiri said. "I've seen what some religions can do to women."

"I agree," replied McIntyre. "But let's remember we're not fighting a feminist cause here. We're investigating a murder. Keep some distance."

"I will. Though I must tell you her concern for the body of her daughter got to me."

"When it fails to get to you, leave the force" said McIntyre. "Still, keep the distance."

She turned to Danny and asked, "Where do we go now?"

"We widen the net. We need to get to her friends. We need to find out where and with whom she was living and probably talk to boyfriends. Nadiri did some preliminary probes via the picture, but she didn't get far. I have an idea. She was attending classes at U of T. It's reasonable to assume she had friends attending some of them with her. I suggest that Nadiri and Taegan go to the registrar's office at the university tomorrow morning, find out what classes she was taking, and make a plea to her friends and others in those classes throughout the week. As you know, not every class meets on Monday. But in a few days, we should have some contacts and they will yield more contacts. We'll get informed." He looked at Nadiri and Taegan. "I'll call the registrar tomorrow morning to let him know you're coming."

They looked at McIntyre. "Yes," she said. "Many in the class will have read about the murder. Let's move as quickly as we can."

"We'll be at the Registrar's office at nine," Nadiri said.

"And what will you be doing tomorrow, after your call?" McIntyre asked Danny.

"I will be devoting the morning to reviewing and thinking about the Frawley case. Maybe a few days away will help me to see something new."

McIntyre shook her head, though she was smiling. "You don't give up, do you?"

"No, ma'am. It's part of my charm."

Danny returned to his office and called Avi, since he had not seen him on the weekend. They had a good chat and agreed to meet for lunch on Tuesday. Danny would drive up to Avi's school, pick him up, and they would go to the local kosher deli, a treat for the two of them. On Thursday, Avi would sleep over at Danny's. That evening they would make potato latkes for Danny's annual Chanukah party, with forty or so guests, which was on Saturday night.

When he arrived home, Danny knew he had four things to do: unwind, get some food, think some more about the case, and think about organizing his Chanukah party.

Life still happened, even in the face of murder and death. That's a good thing, he thought.

X

Nadiri and Taegan's visit to U of T on Monday morning was a success. The registrar's office cooperated quickly, and they learned that Halima had been enrolled in four courses, two of which met that day, at eleven and two.

They contacted both professors, who were happy to give them time in the classroom to help find the murderer of their student.

There were fifty students enrolled in Halima's eleven o'clock psychology class. The professor introduced Nadiri and she made her plea for help. While watching the students enter, she and Taegan thought they spotted one of the women in the photograph. They were correct. She was Maureen O'Connell and she raised her hand to identify herself even before Nadiri finished speaking.

They got some important information from Maureen O'Connell. She identified all the other women in the photograph. Most importantly, she identified herself as the person who gave Halima a place to stay.

"I have an apartment on St. George Street, five blocks north," she said. "Halima and I have been friends since we were in a course together two years ago. The apartment is owned by my parents. We live in Barrie. My parents bought it when I came to university—as an investment as well as a place for me to stay. Halima crashed with me when she could no longer go home." By this time Maureen was in tears as she recounted what she knew.

"Did she seem any different in the last week or so?" Taegan asked.

"No. She had a lot of troubles, including financial problems, but she was determined to graduate and move on. I don't think she was different in the ten days or so before she was killed. She was in touch with her mother—I don't know if you know that—that meant a lot to her. She talked about the sadness of her mother's life. She even talked about wanting to rescue her sometime in the future. Things at home were very, very bad."

"Did she have a boyfriend?"

"No, not a steady boyfriend. She dated."

"Did she date men of any particular ethnic group?"

"Anyone. She wanted to put her old life behind her. She didn't date a lot lately. She was very tense about her situation."

"Do you know if she was sexually active?"

Maureen hesitated. Taegan continued, "This may help us. It doesn't matter now."

"I feel I'm violating our friendship, but you're right. If it can help catch the murderer, that's what matters." She took a deep breath. "She was sexually active. I think she only discovered her sexual side in the last year or so."

"Did she sleep around?"

"No. But once a week or so, she would go to a bar on Queen Street looking to socialize. Usually, she found a partner for the night. She told me she couldn't handle a serious relationship at this crazy time."

"What bar?"

"It's on the strip between Bathurst and Spadina. That's all I know."

Nadiri asked, "Was she sleeping with men, women, or both?"

"Men. She said she was wildly heterosexual. She laughed and said at least her father would approve of that."

Maureen gave them contact information for Halima's other friends. Then, Nadiri and Taegan asked if they could come to the apartment to see where Halima had lived and look through her things. "Let's go," Maureen replied. The three of them, Nadiri in a pantsuit, a modest blouse, and an open overcoat, Maureen in jeans, running shoes, a T-shirt with an image of a rock group on the front and an anorak, and Taegan in uniform, walked up St. George Street. They passed the Christian Science Church on their way to the apartment.

The one-bedroom apartment was in a condominium that had been converted from a large old private home, a mansion really, and added to at the back. Maureen's apartment was at the rear, overlooking the schoolyard of the local elementary school on Huron Street.

Halima slept on a bedroll at night in the living room and Maureen had made room for her things in closets and the tiny bathroom. "She studied in the library a lot," Maureen said. "I think she was trying to tell me she respected my space. That was how she was. But we would often have supper together."

Nadiri and Taegan learned Halima had few possessions, not many clothes and but for Maureen would have been living very rough.

Through more tears, Maureen asked, "What do I do with her things? Should I contact her family?"

"No," said Nadiri. "I'll help you pack them up, if you want me to. I'll take them to the divisional offices as evidence."

"Thanks, but I think Patty and Andrea, and other friends, will want to help with the packing. We can say goodbye together."

Nadiri and Taegan left, telling Maureen she had been very helpful. Taegan added, "You were a real friend. You did as much for your friend as you could." Nadiri had never seen Taegan this active in an interview. She thought his own youth helped him relate deeply to what was happening. She now understood why Danny liked him so much.

XI

Danny spent the morning at his desk, reviewing the Frawley file, thinking, making notes, circling relationships and putting lots of question marks on the paper. He thought of the case like a castle with many doors, maybe like the city of Venice, which he had once visited, where, if you took one bridge, you are in a new labyrinth. He wondered how to take the right bridge to solve the riddle.

After some time, Danny was convinced the answer lay in the past. There seemed to be nothing in Frawley's life in the last several years that would result in someone killing him. He would now try to find the right bridge in some past action or event. He had already considered Frawley's history, but he would now do so again, this time going deeper.

Sydney McIntyre popped into his office at noon and he told her his conclusions. She agreed, but added, "If it was simply some crazy person who killed someone at random, we're at a loss, Danny."

"Yes. But I'd like to pursue his past."

"By all means. I dropped in to ask that you, Nadiri, and Taegan meet me in my office at three. I've arranged for an expert on honour killings to come and talk to us. I think we'd benefit from a discussion."

"Sure."

"I'd just like to discuss the dynamics. I'll see you at three."

Nadiri and Taegan finished with Maureen O'Connell at one-thirty and drove back to the divisional headquarters. Nadiri complimented Taegan on his questioning as the two of them became more comfortable with one another.

"I'm beginning to see how Sergeant Miller works, ma'am," Taegan replied. "This case really hits home. There are lots of honour killings in Jamaica, not only about religion."

"Taegan. I am not 'ma'am.' Inspector McIntyre is 'ma'am.' If I were meeting your mother, she would be 'ma'am.' Like you, I am a constable. I am Nadiri."

"Yes, ma'am," he said. They both laughed.

When they arrived at the station, they briefed Danny. "We're making progress," Danny said. "Now let's talk to the other friends and anyone else who comes forward. I'd like to find some of Halima's sexual partners. Let's try to find the name of the bar on Queen Street."

They worked until three and then went to Sydney McIntyre's office.

Nadiri was surprised to see who else was waiting for them.

He was about fifty, with greying hair and something of a belly, the kind that develops when young men who are in shape get lax as they grow older. His eyes were brown, his nose a bit bent—probably it had been broken, perhaps more than once, a long time ago—and he had a very strong mouth and chin. He stood as they entered.

McIntyre introduced him. "Detective Sergeant Miller, Detective Constable Rahimi, Constable Green, this is Professor Howard Mandelbaum of the Sociology Department of the University of Toronto. He has helped us on occasion in the past."

Mandelbaum said, "Good to meet you two men. Constable Rahimi and I know each other. How are you Nadiri?"

"I'm fine, sir. It's very good to see you again, even under these circumstances."

"Likewise. I gather you didn't take my advice and go on to graduate school for your doctorate."

Nadiri blushed. "No, sir. Things happened. And then I joined the force."

"If you are who I think you are, Professor," Danny said, "then I can assure you that Nadiri is putting your teaching to good use. Only a few days ago, she taught me the concept of the sociology of the event."

Mandelbaum smiled. "She was a fine student, passionate about her subject, always trying to do her best. And she had a good sense of humour. I'm really pleased to see you, Nadiri."

Nadiri didn't know what to do or say. McIntyre rescued her, saying, "Let's get down to business. Professor Mandelbaum is one of Canada's experts on honour and honour killings in society. I thought a discussion with him might help us."

Mandelbaum took over. Danny and the others felt his great energy as he began to speak. He was simultaneously powerful and warm.

He began, "I don't want to subject you to a fifty-minute introductory lecture on honour killings. I'll say a few things and then you tell me what you want to know. I've been briefed on the case by Inspector McIntyre.

"First, honour killings are as old as our species, probably older. Some argue that certain animals commit honour killings as well. They are part of social customs and taboos. Many societies accepted honour killings as legitimate. Some still do. It's one of those things where social customs either override legality or become part of legality.

"Second, if you look up honour killings online, most sites will only speak about honour killings as part of the religious side of a society. They're wrong. The concept of honour is all over the place. In certain places you can be killed for looking at someone in the wrong way or stealing something that has value to a family or another group.

"And third, in Pakistan, honour killings have a name. They are called karo-kari. This is a compound of two words. Karo means black male, Kari means black female. The terms began as references to adulterers, but have come to mean any kind of behaviour that's seen to be improper or immoral, mostly related to the understanding of the rules of Islam. I will add that there is nothing, nothing at all, in the Qur'an that refers to or encourages honour killing. Period.

"Why kill? This restores honour to a group, usually for the family, and for the extended family, this is the main unit of identity and social organization. Not having honour means a kind of shaming of the family, even ostracism of a sort.

"Enough. Now you ask me what you want to know, and I'll try to help."

McIntyre began. "This family, or at least the male members of the family, the people who lead it, abandoned Halima Nizamani. Isn't that enough to restore honour? Why would they kill her too?"

"They may have tossed her out of the family, but to others in the community, she's still part of their unit. She would still be viewed as doing shameful acts."

"So, there are two units here," Nadiri said. "The family is the basic unit. Islam, or at least how they understand the codes of Islam, is another unit. What if I'm a member of a family and I engage in forbidden acts, I become Western, and this is only known to the family?"

"Good point," Mandelbaum said. "I still think you should go to graduate school."

He continued, "The family loses honour when other families know that the acts of one of the family members are violating the codes. If they keep it within the family, then there's no honour lost. But that's very difficult because the families in any given community interact regularly, not only at the mosque. They go to the same markets, the same shops. It's very difficult to keep it inside the family."

"But, if they fix it inside the family, all is well?" Danny asked.

"They don't lose honour. So Nizamani tried to fix it inside the family. He made an arrangement with his daughter. Remember, there's nothing wrong with a woman going to university as long as she follows the rules. She is expected to wear proper clothing, to keep company with her own people, not to be involved with males."

"Help me further," Danny said. "Define the family."

"Another good question. This is not the family as it has evolved in traditional Western culture. This isn't mom and dad, two kids and a dog. This family means the whole of the extended group. It can be hundreds of people in some places. Halima's actions affect her second cousins, her aunts and uncles, great aunts and uncles, and a whole bunch of others. Since they have so many restrictions, who you can marry is very limited. Many are related to one another in one way or another. An analogy would be Mennonite communities here, or shtetels in Eastern Europe before the Holocaust. For example, my mother and father, both immigrants to Montreal from Eastern Europe, are distant cousins, and the family tree has many branches. I have cousins I don't even know exist."

"So, if Halima had kept the bargain with her father she might still be alive," McIntyre said.

"From what you told me, I would guess that she never meant to keep the bargain," Mandelbaum said. "You will have to decide whether that is so and whether it matters."

"Then, Maher Nizamani, who is the uncle and leader of the family, could have killed her or arranged to have her killed?" Taegan asked.

"From what you have told me, yes. Did they? That's your job to find out."

"Sir," Taegan followed up, "I don't want to get off topic. I come from Jamaica, where there is a lot of violence that goes unpunished. Is it about honour?"

"Yes, a lot of it is about honour. Not about religion, but about losing face. You are shamed if you don't do the right thing socially. This is where social codes are far more important than legal ones. Let me take this back to our killing. The social code demands that the male Nizamanis do something about Halima. In places in Latin-America, a bride is supposed to be a virgin. If she isn't, she's returned to her family. The male members of her family are expected to punish—usually that means to kill—the male in the community who slept with her. Failure to do so would dishonour the family and they would seriously lose standing in the community. Courts often accept honour killing as a defence."

"So," Danny said, "we have two codes fighting one another. There is the civil code, Canadian law, which we uphold, and there is the law of the community, often tied to religion. If that is so …"

"It is," Mandelbaum interjected.

"… then this occurs in other ways with many groups. For example, you mentioned the Mennonites, and there are very Orthodox Jews, Catholics who belong to Opus Dei and organizations of that sort, and neighbourhood gangs with their own rules."

"You got it," Mandelbaum said. He looked around. "Anything else?"

There was silence, the kind in which everyone is thinking.

"You've given us a lot to chew on, Howard," McIntyre said. "Thanks."

"Anytime. Get in touch if you want to talk about anything else as the case moves on. We could also meet in my office one-on-one. I'm informing you that there will be an examination on the subject on Monday morning at nine. No multiple choice. All complicated essay questions."

It broke the heavy weight of the conversation and they all laughed. Mandelbaum shook hands with everyone, very warmly with Nadiri, and took his leave. "Now I'll go back to my day job and subject my students to that fifty-minute lecture."

XII

The next day, Danny got up at six to practice his violin. He had done so for an hour when he came home on Monday, but realized he needed some rest, and went to bed early. Now he could get in a couple more hours before going to work. He mainly worked on his technique, on his tone, and on the Vivaldi piece they were rehearsing. A part of him realized he was doing this because he feared embarrassing himself in front of Gabriella.

This morning, Nadiri and Taegan were assigned to find more friends, to interview them, and to get as much information as possible. They were also going to check with the two friends Jameel Nizamani said would support his alibi. Danny and Sydney McIntyre were to meet with the press at ten o'clock.

The press conference went well. Even experienced and hardened news people were very sympathetic regarding the murder of a young woman and they wanted to help. McIntyre and Danny told them what had occurred and what they were doing. Both appealed for help in statements that would be in the newspapers and on the local television.

When the question of an honour killing arose, they dodged it. "We still don't know what this is," McIntyre said, "and we're not going to make that assumption until we have hard facts."

Danny added, "In the meanwhile, the family is helping us with our inquiries."

They did not tell the press what they had found out from the people at the morgue that morning. Farid Nizamani refused to accept the body. They would contact the imam on the Danforth. Danny made a mental note to make certain that he and Nadiri attended the funeral.

Danny then drove north and picked up Avi for lunch. They went to Bathurst Street, to the kosher deli near the Baycrest Centre. They both ordered soup and smoked meat sandwiches, Danny's without mustard.

"What have you been up to?" asked Danny.

"Not much, Dad. School takes a lot of time. And the basketball team is doing OK. There's not much room for anything else. I have good friends at school and I hang out with Leo and Deborah."

"Not many people appreciate that you're doing two schools in one. You have the usual stuff—English, History, Science, Math—and then the Hebrew curriculum. How many Hebrew courses do you do in the high school?

"Four—language, history, Torah and Talmud."

"Is it too much? I worry about that."

"I don't know it any other way. I've been in Hebrew Day School since kindergarten. They tell us we've developed fabulous time management skills, which may be true. I don't know. I like the school and I like to study."

After a pause, Avi continued, "Dad, do you believe in God?"

Danny was stunned and paused before answering. "You expect me to answer that question before I finish my sandwich? Or maybe I should try doing it standing on one foot while eating my sandwich? OK, son, I'll do the Jewish thing and answer a question with a question. Why do you ask?"

"I wonder sometimes. I daven and praise a just and merciful God in the prayers. My teachers accept that God is good and righteous while teaching the Shoah. I just wonder."

"Doubt isn't a bad thing, Avi. Doubt means you are thinking, you're not adopting a fixed position and claiming the truth because you assert it. Frankly, I trust rabbis who admit doubt over those who claim they have the whole truth and I must follow their version of reality to live a proper life according to their understanding of God."

"Mom and I saw you on the news last night. Halima's murder is all over the news. Do you think it was done by people who believe they're following their version of what God wants them to do?"

"I don't yet have the answer to your question, Avi. I wish I did. I really want to catch her killer. I can say, to you, that her father and others in the family have very firm ideas about how they think their God wants them to live. And I think, however the case turns out, this almost certainly contributed to her fate. They don't have doubt, and that permits them to do things you, I and many others would regard as immoral."

Danny grinned. "Well, I've finished my sandwich and I haven't given you a proper answer. You have to get back to school and I need to get back to chasing Halima's killer. Let's continue this discussion on Thursday evening."

"OK, Dad. It's been bothering me."

"I see that. Don't let it bother you. It is a question we all ask many times during our lives. I'm still grappling with it at my age."

In the car, Avi said, "You have doubt?"

"Yes, I have doubt. I don't know for certain that God exists, Avi. I do know that, even if he doesn't, it's important to have an occasional conversation with him. That sounds paradoxical, but that's where I am."

"I think I get it. Some of my teachers wouldn't accept that."

"None of my teachers did, as you can imagine. But you're of a different generation. I'd like to think that some of your teachers, even some of our friends and relatives who might disagree, would be willing to discuss it."

XIII

Nadiri and Taegan returned to the office at four in the afternoon to report to Danny. They all settled in the office and Nadiri asked, "Anything new on this end, sir?"

"No. Nothing has come in. We've had a few calls from people who were around the Bluffs that night, but nothing important has turned up. What do you have?"

"Not much. I'll start with Jameel. His two friends, Mohammad Jarwar and Hassan Gurmani, both said they were with him all evening, hanging around a park nearby. Taegan and I don't know whether to believe them. Given what Professor Mandelbaum said, they might be lying on his behalf in the name of the family. They weren't convincing."

"We interviewed three of Halima's friends. They are Pamela Smith, Cassandra Pereira, and Heba Teynori. All students and all are devastated. But we don't have more than Maureen O'Connell provided, with one exception. They all adored Halima and they all sympathized with her plight. Two provided lunches for her by making extra sandwiches and taking stuff from their homes. They said Halima was determined to make her own life. They admired her courage. We did learn one important thing."

Taegan said, "We know the name of the bar on Queen Street that she often went to. It's the Queen's Arms. It's known among young people as one of several bars where people go to find a partner for the night. We don't know the name of the person she picked up."

"That's good. We need to follow up," Danny said. "We need to take a picture of Halima to the bar and ask the employees what they might know. Maybe even ask the patrons, though I wonder if that might scare someone off."

Nadiri said, "Cassandra Pereira, who told us the name of the bar, also said that there was little action early in the week. Thursday begins the weekend, even if folks work on Friday. I know from my work as a constable that Thursday is pub night at the three Toronto universities."

"I'll go there tonight," Danny said, "just to get a feel of the place and ask the employees the relevant questions. Let's see what comes up. Then, if it makes sense, the two of you could go on Thursday to see if we can identify Halima's recent sexual partners. Check with Cassandra Pereira to see if she went with Halima, if you haven't done so. It may be worth taking her along with you. If you go, Taegan, no uniform."

"Hurray! It will be my first time in plainclothes."

"Don't worry, Taegan. Unless you screw up in a manner I can't imagine, it won't be your last."

"Thanks, sir. That means a lot."

"You've earned it." Nadiri nodded. She admired Danny's willingness to give praise when it was deserved. In her experience not many superiors did that. Some criticized you when you messed up and took you for granted when you did well.

Danny went home, ate supper, did another hour of violin practice and laughed at himself for doing it. At nine o'clock, he drove across the Danforth to Bloor, turned left on Spadina to get to Queen, then turned right and found a parking spot. He walked to the Queen's Arms.

It masqueraded as a British pub, with a dart board and ales and bitters on tap along with the usual drinks. Though it served food, it seemed to Danny mainly a place where people gathered to drink. Musical groups Danny had not heard of—not that he knew much about the young music scene—were advertised for Wednesday, Thursday, Friday and Saturday nights.

It was Tuesday and the pub was sparsely populated, perhaps a fifth of capacity at the long bar and the tables. Some people were drinking alone.

Danny went to the bar and introduced himself to the server. Then he took out a picture of Halima and asked, "This is the woman who was murdered last Friday. We know she frequented this pub. Do you recognize her? Can you tell me anything about her?"

The young woman, Mary by her nametag, recoiled. "My God. I didn't make the connection. Is this the woman who was in the news?"

"Yes. Do you know her?"

"I didn't even know her name. I recognize her. She's been here about six or seven times, with a girlfriend. Let me call the other bartender over."

The other bartender was a young male named Jim who came over to hear what was happening. He too recognized Halima.

"Did either of you talk to her?"

Jim said, "We exchanged a few words. She ordered a drink … I think a vodka Martini was her drink, usually. She was very polite, the kind of customer who says please when she places an order, and thank you when she receives it. She tipped normally, not cheap and not showy. I got the impression she didn't have a lot of money."

"Mary, did you speak with her?"

"Once. It was early, and I had time. I said there weren't a lot of interesting men in the bar that early and she agreed."

"Can we go to a table? Can someone take over for you?"

"I'll get the manager," Mary said, and she went into the rear.

Danny introduced himself to the manager, a man of about forty who identified himself as John Raveson, and explained the situation. Raveson agreed to look after the bar while Danny interviewed the others. "I'll want to talk with you afterwards," said Danny to Raveson, who nodded.

They settled into a table in a private corner. Danny continued, "Please think carefully. This bar has a reputation as a place young, single people hang out. I'm certain that Halima Nizamani came here with the hopes of meeting someone."

"Does this mean we're in trouble?" Mary asked.

"Not that I know of," Danny replied. "Sex between consenting adults is not our business unless there is foul play. That they meet here is something that we know about, but it's not illegal. Let's go on about Halima. Do you know who any of her partners might be? Specifically, do you know who she might have gone with last Thursday or Friday?"

"There is one regular who she went with a while ago," Jim said. "I remember because she was really nervous when she came in and seemed at a loss on how to pick up a guy. He's not here now. I know his first name is Mark. Seems like a nice guy. I also know that he works in some financial house on Bay Street. A lot of our male regulars are from there, some young lawyers, some financial guys, whatever they do to make money. There are some women from there, but not many. I don't think they like to mix work and bed. Generally, the women are students, a lot of graduate students, from U of T, York, or Ryerson."

Danny looked at Mary. "I think I know the guy Jim is talking about," she said. "One of us can identify him when he comes in. Probably not tonight. Tuesday is dead. The game begins a bit on Wednesday, and on Thursdays, Fridays and Saturdays it is standing room only, very busy."

"Do you know anyone else she might have gone with?"

"There is a guy," Mary said. "Not a regular but he was here once or twice last week. I remember because he ordered a double scotch, single malt, as he was sweet-talking Halima and she ordered the same. She gagged on the drink as she tried to knock it down. They laughed."

"Could you recognize him if he comes in again?"

"I don't know. It was busy. It becomes a blur. A lot of the men dress alike. They even stand and talk alike. They think they're cool. But I could try."

"Good. Thanks. I appreciate your help. Some members of my team will be here on Thursday night to see if we can find the last guy or two she went with."

"Officer Miller," Mary said, "Do you think she was killed by one of those guys? On the news they were saying it might be a family thing—an honour killing?"

"Honestly, I don't know. We need to talk to a lot of people. We'll get the murderer, but we need to have the facts."

"Good," Jim said, "I really hope you get the son-of-a-bitch soon."

"Thanks. Please let Mr. Raveson know I'd like to talk to him."

When Raveson came over, he asked Danny if he could bring him something to drink.

"Ice water would be fine," Danny said. "We're going to need your cooperation. Halima Nizamani picked up someone or perhaps two people in this bar last week. We need to talk with those people."

Raveson said, "We'll cooperate. We don't want any difficulty with the police. Besides, if this helps catch the murderer, that's fine. It wouldn't be good publicity if they met here and she got murdered by that person, but that's life."

"This is a miserable business and we want results. It's clear this city wants results. A lot of people have adopted Halima in the last few days."

"Absolutely."

"What I will be doing is sending two of my team members here on Thursday night to liaise with you and your service people. I need to have Jim and Mary here because they have some memories that will be useful. I assume there will be more staff on Thursday."

"Yes. It gets really busy."

"So, they will talk with you and your staff and see if we can identify others who might help us. The goal is to find the one or two men Halima slept with last week. There will be a third person with them, one of Halima's friends who came here as well."

"No problem."

"They may have to make a plea to the whole house. It depends. But they may have to take the microphone."

"No problem. We want to help. Big time."

Danny then told him the two from homicide would be Nadiri and Taegan. He asked, "Does the owner have to know?"

"I'm one of four partners. I'll let the others know."

"Good. Let's get going on Thursday night."

"I did overhear," said Raveson. "Jim and I agree. Let's find the son-of-a-bitch, whoever he is."

Danny took a drink from his water glass and stood up. He shook hands with Raveson, waved to Mary and Jim, and left. He felt he had come far in a few days. Now, on the way home, and later while listening to a Bach prelude at home, he pondered where to go from here.

XIV

They had a team meeting on Wednesday at nine, prior to the press conference at ten.

At the meeting, Danny reported on what he had learned at the Queen's Arms and indicated that Nadiri and Taegan were to follow up on Thursday evening.

"Anything else?" McIntyre asked.

"Yes. I want us to see the young woman … what is her name? Cassandra something …"

"Pereira," Taegan said.

"Yes, Cassandra Pereira. I have a sense she might be useful to bring along if she also frequented the Queen's Arms. Could you look after this, Nadiri?"

"Will do, sir."

"We should check Jameel's alibi again. I'd like to see him here on Friday morning. Also, on Friday morning, after the report on what happened Thursday night at the bar, I want to see the two young men who vouched for him. Separately. Here."

"What are you thinking, Danny?" McIntyre asked.

"I wonder whether their stories will agree with one another if I meet with them separately. Maher's alibi is secure because his family will back him up. He was at home. Not that I totally buy it. Farid's alibi was confirmed by Mashid Nizamani. Of course, I don't think for a moment Mrs. Nizamani had anything to do with the murder of her daughter. But Jameel's alibi can be confirmed or broken with proper questioning."

"Do you think he killed his sister?" McIntyre asked.

"You know me. I don't go that far. I'll decide what I think about that after I confirm or break the alibi."

McIntyre asked, "Is there any way we can move faster? I'm getting heat from upstairs. This is something the city cares about."

"I don't want to blow it by pushing it too fast, ma'am. I expect to know a lot more by Friday night. Then we can, I hope, go very fast. This isn't the Frawley case. It'll break soon, I think."

"OK. I'll take care of upstairs. I'll let them know a breakthrough should come soon."

McIntyre and Danny met with the press and reported that progress had been made, especially in knowing the whereabouts of Halima before she was murdered. They also reported that Halima's friends were very cooperative. Again, they made a plea for information.

"So, Inspector, when do you and Sergeant Miller think you will solve this?" asked Rosalie Daniel, the reporter from the CBC.

"Soon, Rosalie. It's moving along well. I hope that we'll have a lot more to say by the end of the weekend," Danny answered.

"People are concerned, Sergeant."

"So are we. Every effort is being made. Again, we'll know a lot more by Sunday."

"I'll hold you to that," Rosalie said.

"You can."

"Thanks, everyone," McIntyre intervened. She didn't like the tone the conference was taking. "We'll report to you and the city regularly." She and Danny turned and walked out slowly.

"They're getting restless," Sydney said to Danny once they were alone.

"I get it. But the last thing we need is to trample on someone's rights or to decide who did it with so little hard evidence that the prosecutor can't make a case."

McIntyre sighed. "You're right, but I feel like I'm sandwiched between your carefulness and the desire of everyone to have this solved."

"As they say, ma'am, that's why you get the big bucks."

Nadiri reported later in the day that she had contacted Cassandra Pereira. Danny was correct. She also went to the Queen's Arms, sometimes with Halima, and she readily agreed to accompany Nadiri and Taegan the next evening.

Danny met with Nadiri and Taegan beforehand. "I don't want to go faster than we should. That can be a mistake. I have a feeling we'll be far ahead by Friday evening. I think all of us should take a little break. We've been working day and night. Go to the gym, get some sleep, watch a movie, whatever. This can't move forward until tomorrow night when you both go to the bar."

"I'm not certain I get it, sir," said Nadiri. "We can do something now, can't we?"

"What?"

"I don't know. Something."

"Don't push it. Timing is important."

"I don't know if Jameel's alibi will stand up. I'm going to interview the three of them. They say they spent the night together. Now they think we believe them. Maybe they did spend the night together. If they didn't, that opens a wide avenue. Who knows, you may also find an important avenue tomorrow night. I believe one of the two, or both, will lead us far."

"What will you ask them on Friday?"

"It's not complicated. I'll ask them to tell me what happened at the park that evening."

"Eureka, sir!"

Danny laughed. "Yes, Archimedes?"

"I got it. It's so simple. Professor Mandelbaum told us a story. He tells stories in class all the time. It's as if he explains things by telling about behaviour."

"Tell us the story, Nadiri."

"There were two friends who were poor students. Not that they were stupid. They just didn't come to class regularly. They handed in assignments late. They made excuses for everything. They missed an important exam, a mid-term I think. They went to Professor Mandelbaum in his office and asked for a make-up. He asked them why they had missed the exam. Oh, they said, we would have been here, but we were driving to school and the car got a flat tire. So, Professor Mandelbaum said he would give them the make-up. He made up a new exam, same format, same material, and he put the two guys in separate rooms. However, he added one more question, which he put at the end of the exam. The question had two words, 'Which tire?'"

Both men were delighted with the story.

"You got it, Nadiri. I'm going to ask them the equivalent of 'which tire?' I'm liking your professor more and more. Now, both of you, get some rest. We have a busy few days ahead of us."

XV

Soon. The chase was no longer enough. It was time to act again. It was fun knowing that his new quarry was to be hurt, but now it was becoming more important that he do it. He wanted all these men to know why they would die.

The first time he was unclear about what he would do, beyond telling Frawley what he had done and what pain he had caused. Frawley begged forgiveness, he said he lived a godly, righteous life. Frawley infuriated him. Frawley said that if he hurt him he would be in sin. Finally, he grabbed the nearest available weapon and struck Frawley. And struck him again. And again.

Now he was clearer. He would carry a weapon with him in case one was not available. He would wear gloves. He would be careful. Next week there would be two who would be the recipient of his revenge. And they would know why.

XVI

Danny spent the rest of Wednesday and Thursday morning catching up on paperwork. He took time for himself, in addition to the usual Wednesday night meeting of the Bloor Street Chamber Group. He went to the community centre on Thursday morning to make up for not having played squash on Sunday. He managed to get a game with another player whose partner was ill. He was creamed, but he enjoyed the workout. Afterward, he took a walk along Bloor, going to the west, stopping into a bookstore to browse and getting a snack at a coffee shop. It helped. He felt better. After giving it more thought, he did not change his mind about how to proceed.

Then he drove to the Islamic cemetery in Richmond Hill for the burial service for Halima Nizamani, conducted by the Danforth mosque. He asked Nadiri to join him, but she told him that in the Islamic religious community women did not attend these ceremonies. Nadiri had a hard time explaining this to Maureen O'Connell and the other women friends who wanted to attend. They finally accepted the restriction as part of Halima's tradition and held a separate memorial service for her on the weekend. The imam had brought several male members of the mosque with him to serve as mourners. Two elders lowered the corpse, which was in a white linen shroud, into the ground, laying it on its right side, so it faced toward Mecca. Those present then participated by putting several handfuls of earth onto the corpse, saying a prayer. Then there were other prayers before the grave was filled. A further prayer was said after the gravediggers had finished their work. Later, the imam later told Danny this was the final plea for forgiveness for the dead person.

Danny watched this dignified ritual with admiration for the imam and his friends. While they were saying the final prayer, Danny whispered the Kaddish, the prayer for the dead in the Jewish tradition. He didn't think Halima would mind at all.

Halima would be mourned. By her mother, by her good friends, and by many in the city. It might not be traditional, but she would be in people's thoughts.

XVII

When Danny got home after the funeral at five-thirty, Avi was already there. This was the night when they would together make about one hundred and fifty latkes for the party on Saturday.

Danny 'kept kosher' at home, meaning he followed the rules about food that were in the Torah and had developed as custom over the centuries. All the food in his home was kosher. Meat and dairy were not eaten together. There were separate sets of dishes and silverware for meat and dairy, and even separate dish towels. Among other practices, some foods, such as pork and shellfish, were forbidden.

While it seemed strange to others, to Danny it was normal. He had lived this way at home all of his life. And though he might occasionally break the rules outside by eating at certain places, he never broke them at home.

There was another reason he followed the rules. Avi was kosher, as were Ruth and her family, and several of his Jewish friends. This meant they could eat in his home with no worries about violating *kashrut*, dietary laws central to Jewish life.

Avi and Danny had a modest supper and then got ready to make the latkes, which would be frozen and reheated in the oven before the guests arrived on Saturday. Since it was early December—Chanukah came early this year, or, as Danny preferred to think about it, Christmas came late—the Sabbath ended at about five o'clock, at sundown, so there would be no problem for a party that began at seven.

For such a simple peasant dish there are more recipes and variations than are imaginable. Every Jewish cook has their own favourite way of doing it. In this case Avi had the hard job of grating the potatoes and a bit of onion. Danny got rid of the excess water, and put in salt, pepper, egg and a bit of flour. Then he shaped the pancakes and fried them in peanut oil. They were made in batches.

Both father and son cheated. Each would occasionally eat one of the latkes that just came out of the pan. Avi thought it a terrific treat.

They continued their discussion from two days earlier. Avi introduced the subject as they were working in the kitchen.

"I thought about what you said about doubt. I wonder whether some of my Hebrew teachers ever have doubt. They don't seem to show it much."

Danny said, "I think that teachers who are most open to discussion about religious matters, tradition and interpretation might have doubt on occasion. Doubt requires an open mind, a willingness to test your beliefs."

"So, doubt isn't a sign of weak thinking?"

"Not at all, in my view. Doubt is a sign of being willing to reflect.

Weak thinking is to always have certainty. Those kinds of people, including some I am dealing with now as a detective, aren't open to reflection."

"Does your childhood friend at the Kollel, Rav Goldstein, have doubt?"

"I think he does, though he is a man of the Torah. He certainly tolerates people like me far more than most of the hardhat types. For someone like him, I think doubt is just a piece of the way you confirm your beliefs. It goes with an active mind. And Aaron certainly has an active mind."

"OK. I want to think more about it."

"Good. Be flexible. Let your beliefs evolve. Don't be rigid. Especially at your age, you should be testing your ideas and developing your own mode of life. I'm not certain I'll always agree with you, but I'll always respect that you're a thinking and sensitive person. Very important."

They were almost done with frying but they needed to wait for the latkes to cool before putting them away.

"Any homework?" asked the parent in Danny.

"Nothing I can't do tomorrow morning. I always get to school early. Let's watch the Leafs game."

"Sure. They're no longer a lost cause. We may even get a Stanley Cup in my lifetime, something I'd given up on only a few years ago."

They sat on the couch together with ice cream for dessert and turned on the game. It was the middle of the second period, and the Leafs were beating the Devils two to one. Avi cuddled up next to Danny, who put his arm around his son and tucked him into his shoulder. 'Heaven,' Danny thought.

XVIII

Nadiri, Taegan and Cassandra Pereira drove down to Queen Street together on Thursday night. Cassandra was very vibrant. Her family had emigrated from Portugal. She had no difficulty discussing the bar and what occurred there with the two young detectives, though she did say her parents would go berserk if they knew what was going on.

"Do you think someone Halima went home with might have killed her?" Cassandra asked.

"We don't know," Nadiri replied. "They could have. Someone there might have information that could help even if he is not the killer."

"I read she was choked."

"Yes, she was."

"Maybe she was choked by a Karim," Cassandra suggested.

"A Karim?" Taegan asked. "What's a Karim?"

"Oh," Cassandra answered, "That's what we call someone who likes rough sex. Once somebody has the reputation of being a Karim, people who don't like that kind of sex avoid them."

"Named after Karim Bogasha?" Nadiri asked.

"I guess so."

Karim Bogasha was an infamous Torontonian. He was a public figure, formerly a star performer for the radio station CLUB, a bon vivant, someone regularly asked to act as emcee for award ceremonies in the arts, a tastemaker, fawned upon by many. Six months ago, four women pressed charges against him. He was accused of engaging in rough sex, hitting, beating, choking, and other matters, without the consent of his partners. He admitted to the acts, but claimed they were all consensual. But once these four women went public, the gates opened and by now at least a dozen such complaints were filed with the courts.

He was a public figure and the media had a fine time taking down one of their own. The same journalists and pundits who for years had gushed about Bogasha's simple charm, his cleverness as an interviewer, his boyish good looks and his interest in the arts, now revealed they had secretly always thought of him as narcissistic, egocentric and rude. He had a bad temper and treated those who helped him in his work with contempt; he was feared rather than loved. He was immediately fired from his main job, was disinvited from events held by several groups with whom he had made engagements and became a pariah in a matter of a few days. He continued to protest his innocence, but the vast number of women who came forward belied his claim. Still, his trial had not yet begun. For the moment, his lawyer told him to stay quiet and lay low; he was in a self-imposed house arrest.

"So, the famous Karim Bogasha is now infamous as a rogue," Nadiri said. "Not quite what he anticipated."

"Thanks, Cassandra," Taegan said. "We'll be on the lookout for a Karim."

"By the way," Nadiri added, "if we do interview some people you'll need to disappear, Cassandra. Is that OK?"

"No problem."

They got to the club at nine o'clock. Both Danny and Nadiri had spoken on the phone earlier in the day to John Raveson, who again confirmed his cooperation.

Nadiri, Taegan and Cassandra settled in a corner and looked around.

"It's early," Nadiri said to Cassandra. "Do you see anyone we should be thinking about?"

"I see some regulars, but no one I saw with Halima. I'll keep looking."

They hung around for an hour, not making any further progress. Nadiri then went to the bar and asked one of the bartenders to get Raveson, who came immediately.

She introduced herself, showed identification, and told him, "As we discussed, I want to go to the microphone and make a plea. I thought I'd let you know so you can be present."

"Thanks, Officer. I'll go tell the band to stop playing whenever you need to talk."

"Let's do it now."

Nadiri followed Raveson, stayed behind while he talked to the band's leader, and then went up on the stage. She nodded to the band, which stopped abruptly. People looked to the stage.

Nadiri took the microphone and started her well-rehearsed speech, one which she had passed by Danny, who helped her with some revisions of the original.

"People, my name is Detective Constable Nadiri Rahimi. I am part of the team investigating the murder of Halima Nizamani." She unfolded a large reproduction of a picture of Halima. "This is the woman who was murdered last Friday. You will likely know of her because the media has followed the case very closely."

She looked around. The Queen's Arms was nearly full, standing room only. People nodded. "Halima, as some of you probably know, frequented this establishment. We have good reason to believe she sometimes made a friend for the evening. It's important for our investigation we speak to anyone who drank with her or spent an evening with her, especially recently."

Again, she paused, which Danny advised. "Let it sink in," he had said. "Go slowly."

"We suspect no one here. But in any murder investigation it's necessary to know how the victim spent her last few days. I'm certain you will understand this. Halima was one of your own and she was brutally murdered. For her sake and for the sake of the decency of our city, we must catch the murderer. So, I ask you, my partner and I will be at a table in the back. Please, folks, make yourself known to us if you have anything to relate. This is very important. You can help us catch the murderer of someone who has friends here."

There was a buzz, and several people began to move to the back.

Nadiri and Taegan talked to two women and two men. All had seen Halima. The two men had had a drink with her the week before she was murdered. The two women remembered Halima but couldn't identify any men she might have accompanied out of the bar.

The fifth person was the one they were seeking. He identified himself as Keith McLaughlin, a broker for one of the major firms on Bay Street. He was forthcoming in telling them that he and Halima had left the bar together at about ten-thirty last week, the evening before Halima was killed. They went to his condo nearby and had sex.

Nadiri and Taegan wanted more privacy at this moment and so they asked Raveson if they could use his office.

"Is this necessary?" McLaughlin asked.

"I don't like the line because it's used too much on television and in bad novels, but I'll use it," Nadiri said. "We can talk here or at the police station. Your choice."

McLaughlin was about thirty years old. He was well-groomed and dressed in expensive casual clothes. He seemed willing to cooperate.

He told them that he and Halima had met each other last Thursday, when he offered to buy her a drink. She agreed and they ordered vodka Martinis. They chatted, had another drink, and then left for his place. They had a third drink when they arrived at his apartment and then had sex.

"Did she sleep at your place?" asked Taegan.

"No, we had sex, some pillow talk, then she got dressed. She told me she didn't have a lot of money and could use taxi fare. I called for a taxi at about one o'clock and gave her some money—forty dollars I think. We said goodnight and she went downstairs to wait for the taxi at the desk with the concierge. That's it."

"Keith, are you a Karim?" followed up Taegan.

He squirmed a bit. "You guys already know the lingo. Very fast." He took a big breath. "Let me tell you what happened. I do like rough sex. You can find that out from several of my partners and, if you want, I'll supply names. I am not Karim Bogasha. Every one of those women will let you know it was consensual. I'm very careful about that."

"We will check if necessary. What happened with Halima?"

"She didn't know I liked being rough. I started and she withdrew. I backed off and asked her what was OK. She said she'd had enough of men hitting her, that if this was what I needed she would leave. She was angry. I told her I respected her wishes. I would be happy with good consensual sex. She thought about it and said she didn't want to find me hitting her midway into our involvement. I said I could be trusted. But I also said she should leave now if she was uncomfortable. We talked for a while. She then came and gave me a kiss. And we had pleasant sex. That's it."

"What did you talk about?"

"Our lives. What she did at school and what I did at work. Some stuff about our backgrounds. I sensed she had family troubles, but she didn't want to talk about that."

"Did she indicate she thought she might be in danger?"

"No. She was … how do I describe it? … restless. But that's all. We parted on good terms. I would have liked her to stay for the night. She wanted to go home."

Nadiri came back into the discussion. "Where were you last Friday night?"

McLaughlin looked at her. "Officer, you don't think—"

"I don't think anything, Mr. McLaughlin. "This is a question we ask everyone."

"Fine. I was at a family event—my parents' fortieth wedding anniversary, a party for forty people at the Granite Club. It began at about seven. We had drinks, then dinner, then speeches, then dessert and coffee. My older brother and I spoke, congratulating our parents."

"When did it end?"

"About ten. Afterwards I drove my aunt and uncle, who are elderly, to their home near Bayview and Don Mills. That must have been until at least ten thirty. My uncle doesn't walk well—he uses a cane—and I escorted him to the door. Then I turned around and went home, to my condo three blocks from here. I parked in the underground garage, went up, had a nightcap, listened to some music and went to bed. That's it."

"It sounds like a foolproof alibi, Mr. McLaughlin. We'll check. Please give Officer Green the names of people at the party, especially the names of your aunt and uncle."

"I understand. No problem."

"Thanks for your candour. I think you saved yourself a lot of grief, and us a lot of time, by being forthcoming."

"Frankly, Officer, I was really troubled when I saw on TV what had happened to Halima. Do you think it might have been someone from here?"

"We don't know yet. We'll work it through."

"Please catch the guy. Now that I've talked to you I feel better, but I'm even angrier about her death. She was a nice person."

"That's what everyone tells us, Mr. McLaughlin. I don't believe the good always die young but, in this case, that is so. We'll get him. Please don't leave town. We may need to talk again."

XIX

Danny met with Nadiri and Taegan the next morning at eight-thirty. They briefed him on what happened at the Queen's Arms. Jameel Nizamani and his two friends were being brought in for questioning at ten.

When they finished, Danny said, "It looks like you got that rarity last night—a quick resolution of an issue. I doubt Keith McLaughlin is our man, though of course we'll check out his alibi. The information from the others simply supplements what we learned from Cassandra and Halima's other friends. Taegan, start checking out McLaughlin. No need to talk to everyone on his list. Use your judgment. Nadiri and I will be busy with Jameel and the others for quite a while."

They first interviewed Jameel Nizamani. He was nervous and it was hard to interpret him clearly. People are nervous when they are in a police station answering questions. It could be as simple as that. Danny thought it might be more complicated, that he was nervous out of fear of his father, his uncle and the family. He needed to do the right thing and he was in an encounter he didn't fully understand.

Danny began, "Jameel, we're here because we need to confirm some facts. We need to be certain what happened. Just be straight and you will be fine."

"Yes, sir."

"First, you told us you were out with friends and returned home at about eleven in the evening. Your mother and father were at home when you returned. Is that correct?"

"Yes, sir. My father was watching something on television. My mother was in the bedroom."

"Good. You also told us you spent the evening with your two friends, Mohammad Jarwar, and Hassan Gurmani."

"Yes."

"You stated you hung around at the local little park, called Joseph D. Lesage Park, a small green space in your neighbourhood."

"Yes, sir."

"And what time would you and your friends have arrived at the park?"

"About eight o'clock. I don't know the exact time."

"That's fine. Not a problem. Did you arrive at the park together?"

Jameel's eyes begin moving around, looking one way and another. There was a pause. "I met them there."

"They were there when you arrived?"

"I think so."

Danny let it pass. "Did anyone else see you?"

"I don't know. Nobody was in the park. Only young people hang around it at night." After a moment, he added, "Maybe some people walked by. I don't know."

"So, you were in the park until about eleven. Is that correct?"

"Yes, sir."

"What did you do?"

"What do you mean?"

"Well, you didn't just sit around for three hours. Did you talk? Did you smoke? Did you play games on a tablet or something? Did you play cards?"

"I don't remember."

"Did you leave the park?"

"No. We hung around there."

"What did you do?"

Jameel was becoming very uncomfortable. Danny and Nadiri let the quiet continue. Finally, he said, "I have a smartphone. We played some games."

"What games?"

"War games. Things like that."

"Do they have names?"

More shifting around by Jameel. More silence.

"I don't remember."

"Who won?"

"What do you mean?"

"Games have winners and losers. Who won?"

"I did most of the time."

"Who was second? Mohammad or Hassan?"

"They were about equal."

"Thanks, Jameel. Did you do anything else?"

"We just talked."

"What did you talk about?"

"You know. Things guys talk about."

"What do guys talk about?"

"Soccer. We talked about soccer."

"Which team do you root for?"

"Manchester United."

"Do your friends root for the same team?"

"Yeah. I think so."

"Thanks. Jameel, do you have a car?"

"No. My father has a car. Sometimes I get to use it."

"Do your friends have cars?"

"Hassan has a car. He works for a delivery service."

Danny let some time go by. Then he said, "Jameel, do you have anything else you want to tell us?"

"No."

"Do you have any idea why your father said Halima was no longer his child?"

"She behaved in a bad way. She didn't follow the rules of Allah. Women are supposed to obey their father and the family. She became filthy."

"Did you try to help her?"

"I followed her sometimes. My father and uncle told me it was my duty to try to get her to do the right thing. I told her many times she should change."

"Did you report her movements and friends to your father?"

"Yes. That was my job as an older brother."

"OK, Jameel. That's all for now. We may need to speak with you again later." Danny rose, turned off the machine and followed Jameel out of the interview room. He told the officer outside to put Jameel in a room alone. He was to have no contact with his friends. Danny also made some calls to impound the two cars and to have the forensic people look at them.

He took a break to get some water, accompanied by Nadiri.

Nadiri asked, "What do you think, sir?"

"I think we might have a big piece of the puzzle. We'll find out shortly."

The second interview was with Hassan Gurmani. He was short, about five and a half feet, and dressed in jeans and a shirt that may not have been washed for a while. His body posture was aggressive.

"Hassan. Thank you for being here. We need to ask some questions."

"Are you accusing me of anything?"

"No. You're friends with Jameel. You know the family. We just need to find the facts so we can know what happened. I'd like to think this is a friendly interview. Are you related to Jameel and the Nizamani family?"

"I'm a third cousin. I am part of the larger family."

"I'd like to ask what you, Jameel and Mohammad did last Friday night."

"Sure. We hung around the little park. From about eight to eleven."

"Did you leave the park at all?"

"What do you mean?"

"Did you take a ride? Did you go somewhere to get a bottle of pop or water? Did you get something to eat?"

"I don't think so?"

"You don't remember?"

"I don't remember."

"Did you arrive at the park together?"

"No. I met them there."

"Were they there when you arrived?"

"I think so."

"You think so?"

He fidgeted. "I'm pretty sure."

"What did you do in the park?"

"We hung around."

"Did you kick a soccer ball? Did you play games on a tablet or something like that? Did you talk? Did you perhaps smoke? What did you do?"

"We talked."

"About what?"

"You know. Things guys talk about. Girls, sports, work."

"What sport?"

"Hockey. I'm a big Canadiens fan."

"Did you talk about the Blue Jays?"

"No."

"Did you talk about soccer?"

"No."

"Did you play any games? Did one of you have a device on which you could play games?"

"We had a tablet. We played some games."

"Which ones?"

"Some war games. I don't remember the names."

"Who was the best player? Who won?"

"I won."

"Who was the second best?"

"Mohammad. Jameel is lousy."

"Do you have a car?"

"Yeah. A five-year-old Nissan Sentra. I use it for my work with a delivery service."

"Do you work part-time?"

"Full-time."

"Do you go to school?"

"No."

"Did you use your car on Friday?"

"For work. Yeah."

"Did you use it Friday night?"

"No."

Danny let some time go by and then said, "Hassan, how do you feel about Halima's death?"

"She asked for it. Everybody knew that she was cheating when she went to school. She dressed in Western clothes, stopped wearing even a hijab, went out with men, read books she should not be reading. She shamed her family."

"So you're not sad about her death?"

"She was no longer a member of the family. She brought great shame on all of us. Her father and Jameel tried to make her see what's right. She wouldn't listen or obey."

"Thank you, Hassan. I need to talk with Mohammad now. I may need to talk with you later today."

They took another five-minute break. Nadiri said, simply, "Which tire?"

"Yes, Nadiri, which tire?"

The interview with Mohammad went in a similar direction. He had them arriving together, kicking around a soccer ball, leaving the park for a short time to get some shawarma take-out at a local restaurant, interested in the Barcelona soccer team.

When Danny asked him if they had used a car that evening, Mohammad said they didn't. When he asked him about his feelings about what happened to Halima he echoed Hassan, even more firmly. "She deserved it," he said.

After finishing with Mohammed, Danny made certain that the cars were being taken for examination. This was a priority and McIntyre had arranged it quickly. They were on their way to the garage for examination.

Lunch was brought to the three young men sitting separately. They were assured that all the food was halal. Danny and Nadiri also took some time to review what they had learned and to have a sandwich. Danny had coffee and Nadiri had some juice. They agreed on what to do.

Jameel was called in for a second interview.

"Jameel," Danny said, "We need to ask some further questions."

"Why? I told you what you wanted to know," replied Jameel, though he looked still very nervous.

"You didn't tell us the truth. Your story and your friends' stories don't match. Here's what I think. I think you and Hassan and Mohammad agreed that 'you would say you were hanging around Lesage Park. I don't think you thought about what you would say if someone asked what you did. Again, your stories don't match. You didn't tell the truth."

Jameel stayed quiet, and he looked like a trapped animal.

"Jameel, I want you to know, on the basis of what we have, I could arrest you for obstructing justice."

More silence.

"What happened, Jameel? I also want you to know that the police have taken your father's car and Hassan's car to a place where they will examine them for evidence. If there is a single hair of evidence that your sister was in one of those cars we will find it. And we will identify it via DNA. Do you know what DNA is?"

"Yes."

"So, Jameel, tell me where you and your friends were on Friday night until eleven."

Jameel was silent. So were Danny and Nadiri.

Finally, he spoke. "We went for a ride in Hassan's car."

"Where? Be prepared to know that I will ask this question to your two friends."

Silence.

"Was your sister in the car, Jameel?"

Silence. Then Jameel collapsed. "I didn't do it."

"What didn't you do?"

"I didn't kill Halima."

"Who did kill Halima?"

"Hassan. He put on gloves and choked her. I think he was trying to scare her, to force her to obey. But he killed her."

"And then what happened?"

"You know what happened. We went to The Bluffs and threw her body down the rocks."

"Who threw her body down the rocks?"

"Hassan and me. Hassan brought three pairs of gloves. She deserved it."

"Jameel, did your father and your uncle encourage you to do this?"

"I followed her a lot for the last year. I tried to tell her what was right. I reported what she was doing to my father and uncle. They said the family needed to cleanse itself from filth and our shame must end."

Danny sighed, very sadly. "Jameel Nizamani, I am arresting you for obstruction of justice and for accessory to murder and for desecration of a corpse. I think you should acquire a lawyer."

"You're arresting me? I told you I didn't do it."

"You did it, Jameel. You conspired in the death of your sister."

They took Jameel out to be booked and placed in a cell.

Then, they interviewed Hassan and Mohammad a second time. Hassan claimed that Jameel did the murder and that he only was there. Mohammad confirmed Jameel's story.

After the paperwork was finished and all three men were in cells, Danny and Nadiri met with Sydney McIntyre and Taegan.

"When did you know?" McIntyre asked.

"I didn't know until this morning, when Nadiri reported on the interview with Keith McLaughlin. I had a sense it could go either way. It could have been a result of Halima's sexual escapades or that Jameel was involved in some way. Or both. Once we ruled out McLaughlin … Taegan?"

Taegan said, "McLaughlin's alibi works, so far. I talked to the Granite Club, the aunt and uncle, and several guests."

"So, once we ruled out McLaughlin, I went hard for Jameel. If I'd been wrong we would have been nowhere. But 'which tire?' was the question they could not agree on."

Taegan and Nadiri laughed. McIntyre looked puzzled. "I'll tell you a story told by Howard Mandelbaum later, ma'am. That's where the phrase comes from."

McIntyre said, "Alright, you're a good team. You're entitled to a private joke. Here's what I'm going to do. I've put every available forensic person onto Hassan's car. If we find something, then I think we're foolproof. If we don't, I still think we have a good case. I'm going to release a press bulletin indicating we have arrested some people for the murder of Halima Nizamani. No names yet. I'd like to call a press conference for tomorrow morning to give the names and some information. If we have evidence from the car, even better."

"Let's go over what we'll say beforehand," Danny said.

"Of course. I'll call it for ten tomorrow and we can meet at nine in my office. In the meanwhile, everyone take a deep breath and relax. You've earned it mightily."

"Let's not forget that James Frawley's killer is still out there," Danny said.

"You are relentless," McIntyre replied.

"Yes ma'am."

Later that evening, the forensics team reported they had found several female hairs in Hassan's car as well as a ring that could not fit any of the fingers of a grown man. The hairs would be sent to be matched with Halima's DNA, which they had gotten from her hairbrush in Maureen's apartment. The ring would be shown to her friends.

The next morning, the press conference was packed. The journalists and the media knew the arrests meant a breakthrough had been made.

McIntyre did the briefing, giving the basic facts. Three men, including Halima's brother, were being charged with murder or accessory to murder, among other charges.

The questions were incisive but friendly, and Danny handled most of them. A press officer was present, though Danny wondered what she would do if he goofed. Was there a trap door beneath him?

"What led you to the brother?" *The Globe and Mail* reporter asked.

"We didn't rule out anyone until the facts ruled them out. It got narrower as we went along."

"Did you always think it might be a family member?" asked Rosalie Daniel of the CBC.

"Not at all. I want to emphasize this. We had a wide, intensive search. We included lots of people. Many who we questioned were very helpful. And they were not offended when we asked where they were on that Friday night. I don't have to tell you that crimes of violence are often committed by those close to the victim, but not always. We kept a very open mind and narrowed it down as we went along."

"Have you informed the parents of the three men?" *The Toronto Star* reporter asked.

"Yes," said McIntyre.

They were patient, knowing that this was a story that the city needed. Halima had been adopted by lots of people, and they needed a clear resolution.

Finally, McIntyre ended it. "Thank you, everybody. And I want to thank all those people who helped us, especially Halima's close friends. We may yet have further information, which I'll release as we get it."

Rosalie Daniel intercepted Danny on the way out. "Danny," she said, "I owe you an apology. I was little too aggressive, even for me, the other day."

"Thanks. I understand. I was as anxious as you were to get this solved. I just had to do it the right way. So, it holds. Now go and do what you do. Tell the story to the city."

In McIntyre's office, she praised the team. "Take off until Monday morning, when I hope to have news about the ring, at least. Maybe the DNA. I'm pushing, but the lab can't go faster than it takes. Let's meet at nine on Monday. One more thing. The chief of police and the mayor called and wanted me to send their appreciation. At least we sometimes get thanks from above."

"I'm off," Danny said. "I have a holiday to celebrate tonight." Danny realized he was very tired and was going along on adrenaline. Still, he looked forward to the evening.

XX

There were about forty guests, probably more than his house should hold, but it worked. Avi invited eight friends. Ruth and her family came and brought two couples Danny knew. From the Sunday squash group there were several regulars and their spouses. Five members of the chamber group came. One of them was his violin partner Olga Nevsky, another was a wind player, Benjamin Grynbaum, who brought his clarinet and was not offended when his friends called him Benny Goodman. Two new invitees were Nadiri and Gabriella.

Ruth, Irwin, Deborah and Leo arrived a half hour early to help Danny and Avi set up the food. When she arrived, Ruth hugged Danny, wished him a *chag sameach* and then said, "I saw you on the news. I'm glad you got the people who harmed that fine girl. I'm proud of you."

They organized the food. In addition to the ton of latkes, there were bagels, cream cheese and lox and several salads—Egg, Tuna, Israeli, Greek and Caesar. Wine, juice and a punch would be served throughout the meal. And for dessert, there were *sufganiyot*—jelly donuts, also a tradition on the holiday for which oil was an important symbol.

When most people had arrived, they gathered for the service. Because it was Saturday evening, this meant that first there would be Havdalah, the ritual by which Jews conclude the Sabbath. Danny asked Avi to conduct the short service, which included wine, a spice box and candles. Avi did so beautifully, and the group, which included mainly Jews, responded in Hebrew.

After that, Danny asked Irwin to give the blessings for the Chanukah lights. Ruth gave Danny a nod, which he cherished. Irwin did the blessings and then read an addendum in Hebrew, reminding those present of the sacred quality of the lights. Danny translated the traditional statement into English as Irwin paused half-way through and at the finish. There was a song afterwards, in Hebrew, which was sung by most of those present, offering thanksgiving for the victory over the oppressor and the rededication of the Second Temple.

Then Danny said, "It's an old saying among us, and I'll say it again—they tried to destroy us, we fought them, they failed, we survived; let's eat."

People mingled happily. Several congratulated Danny on solving the case and he did his best to shrug it off. He spent some time with Nadiri and Gabriella and introduced them to Avi and to his family. The noise in the room was the right kind. Danny liked Chanukah because it celebrated freedom and the need to fight oppression. It wasn't one of those times when you were supposed to reflect on how sinful we all are.

After people had finished eating, Danny took out his violin. Nadiri, in a corner chatting with some of Avi's friends, was stunned. The rest of the group smiled. It was time for singing.

Danny began his playing with some mournful Jewish melodies, fiddler in his living room. Then he moved to playing a bunch of Hebrew and Yiddish folk songs, starting with *Mi Y'malel*. People started singing and soon there was a chorus. There were a lot of repetitions in the songs, as well as, in some, a chorus that was often repeated. Gabriella listened carefully and joined in when she could.

Danny moved from one song to another. There was the dreidle song, special on Chanukah, and Hava Nagila , which was traditional. Then came *Tumbalalaika*, which had a terrific chorus, and *Rozhonkes mit Mandlen*, which was as sweet as its title. Danny was happy. There was joy in his house.

He finished the singing by playing *Ma'oz Tzur*, whose English version is *Rock of Ages*. As the group was singing this last song, Benny opened his case and took out his clarinet. He and Danny then played klezmer music, often improvising together as they moved along. By this time, Avi and his friends were moving furniture and tables to the edge of the room.

After klezmer, the two musicians started a slow hora. Avi, his best friend Jordan, and several others, including Ruth, Deborah and Leo, moved to the center of the room. They formed a circle and danced, holding hands. Those watching clapped to the rhythm of the music. A few others joined the dancing. Danny was amused to see that Nadiri was one of them. Then Danny and Benny started playing faster. And then faster. And faster. Those dancing managed to keep up for a time; then a few dropped out from exhaustion. Finally, the two musicians resolved the tune and it ended. Everybody in the room applauded. *Mazel Tov*, they shouted. *Chag sameach*.

This year something new was added, which Danny hadn't planned. As the dancers were on the couch or the floor catching their breath, and as the larger group watched, Olga went to Danny with her hands outstretched. She was asking for the violin. For her, Danny made a very rare exception. He handed it to her, his most precious and intimate possession.

She started a Russian song, a lament, very slowly, capturing the mood of the group. Then, she played soulfully, sweetly, one of the most famous Russian folk tunes, *Oy, da ne vecher*. It was beautiful and reminded many of them how closely Russian folk culture and Ashkenazi Jewish culture were intertwined. Three of the people present knew the Russian lyrics and they whispered the words together. It was a perfect coda to the evening.

People began leaving, on their way out telling Danny how much they enjoyed this annual tradition. Danny thanked Benny for his playing and gave Olga a big hug and kiss, which embarrassed her.

By eleven, Danny and Avi were almost alone. Gabriella had stayed and was helping with the clean-up. "You don't need to do this," Danny said.

"I don't mind at all. It also gives me a chance to invite you and Avi to the annual St. Mike's Choir Christmas concert at Koerner Hall a week from tomorrow. It's at two o'clock. I'll be conducting, and we could go out for some supper afterwards. Here are two tickets."

"I'm sorry, Ms. Agostini," Avi said. "My mom already has something planned for that day."

"Another time, perhaps. Where did you learn to dance like that?"

"I don't know. I've been doing it since I was a kid. Like language, we learn it without knowing it."

"Good comparison," Gabriella replied. "I never thought of it that way. It is a language."

Danny picked up one of the tickets. "Thanks. I'd like to go. I'll be there. Now, I feel guilty putting you to work here."

"I'll just help get everything out of the living and dining areas."

"OK. Then I'll take you home."

"No you won't. My car is parked a block away. We've had this discussion," Gabriella said, smiling.

"You win. Let's clean up and I'll walk you to your car. That I insist."

The three did their chores companionably, Avi explaining more about Chanukah in response to Gabriella's questions.

Danny and Gabriella then walked to her car, Gabriella putting her hand into Danny's arm. "What a terrific boy you have. I teach kids the same age. He's a delight."

"I think so. It's a wonder to think that I helped bring him into the world."

"I enjoyed tonight a lot, Danny. A nice bunch of people and I learned a lot. Wonderful vibes. You are a very unusual man, Daniel Miller."

They reached the car. This time they were not awkward. They embraced and held it for longer than necessary.

XXI

After all the events of the last week and the energy of the evening, Danny was worn out, and had trouble getting to sleep. He lay in bed thinking about Halima, about the Nizamani family, and about Gabriella. Avi, with the innocence of a fourteen-year-old, fell asleep as soon as his head hit the pillow.

In bed, Danny skipped his squash game to try to sleep in. He was awakened at nine by the phone. It was Sydney McIntyre. "I hope it's not too early, Danny, but I know you want to be informed. Good news. The ring has been identified by both Maureen O'Connell and Cassandra Pereira as belonging to Halima. They would be ready to swear to it in court."

"Thanks, ma'am. I'm pleased. I think that wraps it up, though if we get the DNA evidence, too, that would seal it."

"Absolutely. Let's hope for it. In the meantime, have a restful Sunday."

Danny knew he would never get back to sleep. He also knew Avi would probably sleep until noon. He decided to go to the community centre after all, not for squash but for the shvitz, then a schmooze with his friends over coffee and a bagel.

When he appeared in the sauna, several of the group congratulated him, having seen the news on TV. He nodded, wished those who were Jewish a *chag sameach*, went into a corner and closed his eyes.

In the cafeteria, Joe Solomon congratulated him again, and said, "Did you see today's Star? They're singing your praises. You're a hero, Danny."

Danny laughed as Joe passed the newspaper across the table, and said, "Lots of others deserve credit, especially my partner, Nadiri Rahimi, who some of you saw last night at my Chanukah celebration."

Those who were at the Chanukah party thanked Danny again. Mike Ryan, who was a friend from his boyhood neighbourhood, added, "Hey, Danny, is this party only for members of the tribe? When we were kids we used to share celebrations. What happened?"

"You're right, Mike. Next year you and Louise will get an invitation. It will do your Catholic soul good to hear Hebrew and Yiddish again."

"Definitely. Having grown up in our neighbourhood, I wouldn't know how to speak if I didn't have words like schmuck, meshugah and heimish in my vocabulary. Yiddish is a very good language for a lawyer."

"For anyone," chimed in Joe. "A bissel Yiddish ist sehr schoen ."

While the affectionate banter continued among the men, Danny read the piece in *The Star*. He thought it was overdone in terms of the praise of the police, not that they couldn't use decent publicity. The article recounted the case, more or less got how it was solved, and dealt with the tragedy of the circumstances. Halima was properly lamented. They had somehow gotten the story of the family not accepting the body, and the fact that Danny had attended the funeral. He was also given credit for arranging the funeral, which was untrue.

Danny looked up. Eddie Siegal kidded him. "So, Danny, how does it feel to be a celebrity?"

"Come off it, Eddie. I'm just a nice Jewish boy who grew up near Bathurst Street. What's in The Star is about fifty percent of the truth. This is my fifteen minutes of fame."

They went on to other subjects. Danny left shortly thereafter, saying, "I have to wake up Avi so he can get his homework done, and then take him over to Rachel's place. See you next week."

Driving the short distance home, Danny reflected on what was happening. He didn't like the publicity, in part because it was both overdone and ignored others who deserved credit. More than that, he had chosen a private life and he liked it that way. In the age of cyberspace, Danny knew people could lose their privacy very quickly. He took pains to retain his agency and be the one who shaped his own way of life and his own identity. You could look him up online, but you would not find anything about him apart from professional matters. He was determined to not be a public person. As he once said to Sydney McIntyre, in trying to get out of appearing at a press conference, "Anonymity suits me."

He reflected that his heroes were not celebrities. They were people like Ruth and his friend at the community centre, Jacob Schmuelovitz. People who lived their lives quietly, who were kind, who treated others with dignity, who did their jobs without fanfare. These people, he thought, were the glue who held together society, who helped make for a decent civilization.

It was, he thought, a very Canadian way of looking at the world. He remembered, in his very first political science course, reading an American scholar who defined politics as, "deciding who gets what, when, where and how." The class discussed this and one of his fellow students quoted William Lyon Mackenzie, the first mayor of Toronto, who said that, "politics is the science which teaches the people of a country to care for each other." The people he admired were those who daily did the ordinary things that helped us take care of one another.

He arrived home, put the orange juice on the kitchen table and woke up Avi.

Two minutes later, the phone rang. He looked at the display and saw it was Nadiri.

"Hi, Nadiri."

"Sir, bad news. I got a call five minutes ago from Mahshid Nizamani. She told me she stabbed her husband and he's on the floor bleeding."

"Call an ambulance."

"I did."

"Call Fifty-Two Division to send people over to the apartment. I'll meet you there."

"Yes, sir. See you soon."

Danny raced. He told Avi, gave him money for a cab to get to his mother's place, got into his car, and sped as fast as he dared to the apartment in Scarborough.

When he arrived, there were already two police cruisers in front of the building and several officers at the entrance. An ambulance was at the door. He watched as a stretcher came out and was put into the ambulance, which then put on its siren and left.

Danny identified himself to the officer at the door who seemed to be the senior person.

"Is there a detective upstairs?"

"Yes, sir. She went up ten minutes ago."

"Good. Officer, I see two female officers. Which one has more experience?"

"Officer McClellen, sir. The other officer, Officer Hart, is fairly new to the force."

Danny walked over to McClellen, introduced himself and said, "Officer, I need you to come upstairs with me. I will want you to be present when Detective Constable Rahimi, who is upstairs, interviews Mahshid Nizamani. She admitted she stabbed her husband."

"Yes, sir," McClellan said. Let me know what to do."

"I don't want you to do or say anything unless Detective Rahimi or I ask something of you. I want you to be there. Mahshid Nizamani is a devout Muslim and she will be more comfortable with a female officer than a male. I want you to be there to witness what's happening in case this goes to court. One more thing. If Mahshid Nizamani at any time loosens her niqab, I want you to register what her face looks like. If, at any time, she is willing to show her arms or other body parts, I want you to note what they look like. After this is finished make notes about her appearance. Don't discuss her appearance with Officer Rahimi until after you make your notes. Got it?"

"Got it."

They went upstairs. A shocked Mahshid Nizamani was in the living room on a couch. Nadiri was sitting next to her, holding her hand, not saying anything. When Danny and Nora McClellen entered, Mahshid Nizamani adjusted her niqab.

Danny sat across from Mahshid Nizamani and said, "Mrs. Nizamani, I need to ask a few questions. Do you understand me?"

She nodded.

"What happened? I know you told Officer Rahimi you stabbed your husband."

"I took a knife from the kitchen and I stabbed my husband."

"Did anything special happen, which caused you to do this?"

She hesitated and seemed to be trying to gather enough strength to answer. Finally, she said, "My daughter is dead. My son killed her and is in prison. My husband did this and now he hits me every day. I took a knife and stabbed him."

"Mrs. Nizamani, I have to discuss some things with Officer Rahimi. Officer McClellen will wait here with you."

The two of them left the apartment and went into the hallway. Nadiri said, "Sir, I'm pretty sure she is not fully together. What she did was wrong, but I understand it."

"Nadiri, we're not going to deal with right and wrong in this conversation. I would like you and McClellan to with her. I'll wait outside. I'd like you to ask her if she will remove her niqab so both of you can see her face. Take in what it looks like. If you can get her to show you her arms and legs, that would also help. I've asked McClellen to take notes about what she sees without discussing it with you. You make notes as well. Inform her we'll be taking her to the station. I'll arrange for a psychiatrist to speak with her there."

While Nadiri was in the apartment with Mahshid Nizamani, Danny called the station and told them to get hold of Sydney McIntyre and inform her what was happening. He went downstairs and asked the officer which hospital Farid Nizamani was taken to. He learned it was Scarborough and Rouge. He called and, after some forceful words and an exercise of his authority, got through to the emergency room. He was told Farid was pronounced dead on arrival."

After twenty minutes, Nadiri and McClellen escorted Mahshid Nizamani to a police car. It was chaotic when everyone involved in the case arrived at 52 Division, but Mahshid Nizamani was treated gently. She was first interviewed by Dr. James Smythe, the forensic psychiatrist. Smythe reported that she was in shock, could not be questioned at this time and that she needed food and some sedation. Mahshid Nizamani seemed to Danny to be in a kind of walking coma, hardly in this world at all. Afterwards, McIntyre, Danny and Nadiri met in McIntyre's office. "I thought it was over," McIntyre said.

"So did I," Danny said. "But, strangely, I'm not surprised. She showed that she had her own inner life when we saw her last week. She lost her daughter and her son will soon be on trial for murder. And then her husband still abuses her."

"I know I'm supposed to keep a distance, ma'am," Nadiri said. "Even at a distance, I'm very sympathetic. Both as a person, and as a woman who grew up knowing her culture."

"I am too, Nadiri. Who wouldn't feel sympathetic? We'll leave it to the justice system to sort it out. I think the right thing will be done."

They talked some more, needing the conversation to help deal with all they had seen in the last ten days. After half an hour, which was therapeutic for the three of them, McIntyre looked at Danny. "I hate to tell you this, Danny. We're going to have to have another press conference. Tomorrow morning, I think. I'm going to recommend to the communications people that we draw up a bare bones press release for now. Tomorrow we can give whatever details we decide are relevant."

"I can't tell you it shouldn't happen, ma'am." Danny took a deep breath. "What time tomorrow?"

"Ten o'clock. I'll see you here at eight-thirty."

When they left Danny and Nadiri continued the conversation. Finally, he said, "I'm going home, Nadiri. I need to find some quiet space and listen to some music."

"Sir, I want to thank you again for inviting me to your celebration last night. I had a wonderful time, especially talking with Avi and his friends. I can't remember any time in my life when I was more surprised than when you took out your violin. Wow. Amazing. Is there anything else I should know about you, like the time you climbed Mount Everest?"

"Hardly, Nadiri. My sister played the piano and I was started on the piano also. As usual, I rebelled. I wanted my own instrument, not Ruth's. I'm told I was hopelessly determined and very annoying and rude, so I got my way. I started the violin at five and it's always been a part of me. I noticed you joined the hora. I didn't know Persian women danced."

"We have a long tradition of dance. The name for dances is Raqs. We have what's called in English a line dance, not a hora, though it's similar. It's called Baba Karam. Your sister took my hand and started to teach me the hora. We also have dances for women, for the times when the sexes are separated, as your very religious people do. It's called Khaliji."

"Interesting. I think it's time I go home Nadiri. I need some quiet time."

The press conference the next morning was as crowded as the one on Saturday. McIntyre handled most of it, giving the facts, noting that Mahshid Nizamani confessed and that she was under medical care at this time.

As it was winding down, *The Globe and Mail* reporter asked, "Detective Miller, do you think that Mahshid Nizamani will go to trial?"

"I can't comment on that. The justice system will handle the case from here and this issue will be in the hands of the Crown Attorney. If it goes to trial, the courts will do their job."

"Sergeant," Rosalie Daniel asked, "What's your opinion?"

"Rosalie, Mahshid Nizamani has undergone a kind of suffering none of us in this room can possibly imagine. In the last ten days she has lost her daughter, seen her son indicted for the murder, and become a widow. Those are facts, as is the fact she stabbed her husband, who died from the wounds. My opinion is we need William Shakespeare to help us understand what's happened. We are in a Shakespearean tragedy and all of us need to reflect on it."

The press conference ended on that note as McIntyre shut it down. She knew Danny had given the press their lead.

XXII

Danny slept. He slept at night and took naps during the day. He needed to deal with the last ten days both consciously and unconsciously. He finished the paperwork on Monday and then took Tuesday and Wednesday off to catch up and assimilate all that had happened.

On Wednesday afternoon, he took a long walk to Spadina Avenue, across the street from the community centre, to the offices of the University of Toronto sociology department, to meet with Howard Mandelbaum. Danny had called Mandelbaum on Monday to make the appointment.

He found Mandelbaum's office and knocked on the half-open door.
"Come in, Sergeant. Sholom aleichem."
"Aleichem sholom, Professor. Thanks for seeing me on such short notice.
"No problem at all. By the way, I'm Howard."
"Danny."
"How can I help you?"
"I wanted to talk with someone who knew the Nizamani case but had a different perspective from those of us who were involved in it so intimately."
"I'm not certain my opinion is all that different from yours or Sydney's," Mandelbaum replied. "I have enormous empathy for Mahshid Nizamani. I'm ashamed to tell you, I don't feel sorry for her husband. I don't want anyone killed, but I get what happened."

Danny replied, "I keep thinking that if anyone is responsible for the death of Halima it is Farid Nizamani. His brother, Maher, also bears some of that. Yet we had Jameel in jail and Farid just keeps being violent."

"Do you think you could have made a case against Farid?"
"Maybe. We could have arrested him for assault. I think the Crown could have made a criminal charge of counselling or abetting murder. Whether that would stick would have depended on how good a lawyer he might have had and on the Crown Attorney. Could we have charged him with murder? No."

"And you're troubled?"
"I'm troubled that our justice system is imperfect in this way."
Mandelbaum spoke with his body, his eyebrows raised, his two hands spread out.

"Howard," Danny continued, "I'm not a kid. We live in an imperfect world. We do the best we can."

"Danny, we try. That's what we do. We try. Do we always succeed? No. But we keep trying."

"Fair enough. I thought you'd understand. I have a bigger question."
"Shoot."

"You understand society."

Mandelbaum gave Danny a quizzical look and said, "You're setting me up."

"Maybe. I want to know what you think we can do to end this craziness that permits—even encourages—acts like honour killings. How do we get these people to accept the civic code?"

"Most do," said Mandelbaum. "We still have people who accept a belief system that arises from their professed religion. I think it's really a social code, not a theological one. They take comfort in it—in its certainty. And many males get an ego feed because they are given power and status. Of course, it's not only Muslims who do this. Some Christians do, too. And in our tribe, there are Chassidim of several varieties who will do their best to follow the rules of their group rather than the law of the land. For example, in Israel there is a guy with a hard-hat and a beard who goes around stabbing gay people because—he claims—they are filthy. What we can do is to try to educate people in tolerance and in accepting differences. Enough. I'm lecturing again."

"Do you think we'll always have the Jameels, Farids and the hard-hat guys who justify violence?"

"I think we make progress, at least here. Try it this way. In Toronto, slightly more than half of us were born outside of Canada. Slightly more than half identify themselves as visible minorities. There are many languages spoken by young people attending our schools. Yet, I'm not fully certain why or how, we get along, at least as much as we do. The glass is more than half full. For every Jameel there are hundreds of Nadiris."

"You're probably correct. This last week has gotten to me. Let's keep doing our jobs."

"Danny, do you know what will happen to Mahshid Nizamani?"

"No. At the moment she's unfit for anything. She's getting help. My guess is she'll be charged with second degree murder, because the death was not planned or deliberate. I expect her lawyers will have her plead what we call NCRMD, not criminally responsible due to a mental disorder, brought on by the abuse she sustained from her husband. She could also plead self-defence based on battered woman's syndrome. I doubt she'll spend time in jail."

"I wonder what will happen to her," Mandelbaum said. Her story is not over. What will be her story?"

"I don't know. I admire her in some ways, but it'll be hard."

"She made a decision, Danny. She decided not to continue the life she was in, without her son and daughter. Maybe her children gave her some consolation. Now there is none."

Howard continued, "Danny, you talk about what is just in these circumstances. Do you think Mahshid Nizamani decided that she would do what is just?"

Danny pondered this for a time. "I wonder if that wasn't going on in her mind, even in her unconscious. We'll never know."

"Do you play chess?" asked Howard.

"No. I was taught the game as a kid but never really played. I know how the pieces move, that's all."

"You should play, Danny. It's a terrific game. It requires some of the skills you use as a detective. Making choices, strategy, seeing the whole board, understanding your opponent."

Danny replied, "At the moment, squash is my game. When my knees give out, maybe I'll take up chess."

Howard took the tangent. "My game is hockey." He pointed to his nose. "That's how I got this bent schnoz. Playing hockey on outdoor rinks in Montreal, without helmets. So this is the result of my opponents' elbows on the ice. Their Gordie Howe moments."

Danny smiled. He was pleased the conversation had become lighter. "Do you still play?"

"Rarely. Old man games. But I referee now. At George Bell Arena in the Junction for a low-level minor league. I am, as you can see, becoming corpulent. I'd be fat without it."

"I bet you root for the Canadiens."

"Of course. That's my equivalent of being a fanatic. They can do no wrong. Next to my family, they are my oldest loyalty."

"You were talking about chess."

Do you play?"

"Yes. Not as well as I would like, but I'm acceptable. Here's where I was going about Mahshid Nizamani. In chess there's a concept called zugzwang. It's one of those German words combining two things into an idea. Zug means move and zwang means compelled. It can only occur well into a game. The concept is that your opponent has you in a bad position. But even worse. It's your move and, even though you are in a bad position, every move that you can possibly make will put you in even a worse position. In chess you can't pass, you must make a move. Usually, if you are in a zugzwang you resign. Mahshid Nizamani was in a zugzwang. What could she do? She changed the rules of the game. She took agency. Her future doesn't look wonderful, but it's better than her life would have been with Farid."

"Not a bad concept. I hope we Jews never find ourselves again in a zugzwang again."

"Yes. That would be real progress," Howard said.

Danny gathered himself to leave. "Thanks, Howard. I'll reflect on this."

"Truly, Danny, anytime. Let's have the occasional coffee or lunch."

"Sounds good." Danny rose and started to put on his coat.

"By the way," Howard said, "you were wrong when you spoke to the press."

"In what way?"

"It was worse than anything Shakespeare wrote about, not that he didn't understand the nature of tragedy. This tragedy wasn't Shakespearean. It was much more like a Greek tragedy. One of those stories where people go blind, they marry their mother, they serve the remains of their children to the horrible father; far worse things."

"I never thought of that. You may be right."

"Do you know the story of Procne and Philomela? It's a Greek myth.

"Never heard of it."

"Look it up. The Nizamani tale is as tragic as that one. With an exception. Procne and Philomela, who are sisters, get transformed into birds to escape their tormenter, Procne's husband. If I remember correctly, one became a swallow and the other a nightingale."

"Would that Mahshid Nizamani could become a swallow or a nightingale," Danny said. "Then she would know freedom. See you, Howard."

PART III

I

The next day, Sydney McIntyre asked to speak with Danny. "I just have a lot on my mind, and I need to speak with a colleague," she said. "Sometimes you feel a little lonely in this job."

She also wanted to talk about the Nizamani case, and raised matters similar to the conversation Danny had with Howard Mandelbaum. Danny told her what he had said to Mandelbaum and Mandelbaum's responses. "I feel the same way," McIntyre said. "There's an unhappiness around the whole affair. Danny, I'll assign you a case when something appropriate comes up. In the meanwhile, catch up on the overdue paperwork, take a break from murder, and perhaps I'll ask you and Nadiri to work on some cases of violence that come across my desk."

"That's fine, ma'am. The Nizamani case took something out of me. I could use a short pause."

"Danny, I think it's time you abandoned the 'ma'am.' Please call me Sydney."

"I'm old-fashioned. I like some of the formal courtesies. I don't belong to the generation that thinks they can call anyone by their first name and that means they're friends. Can we compromise? It will be Sydney when we're alone and ma'am when we're with others in a professional situation."

McIntyre smiled. "Sometimes, Danny, you're so traditional you make it radical. I accept the compromise."

"Good," Danny replied. "I see from the board a new case has come up."

"Yes. It's the murder of a man who works for Stevenson and Marks LLP. He's not a lawyer, but an expert on compliance who works for the firm. I've assigned it to Ed Morgan."

Danny winced. Of all his colleagues, Ed Morgan was the only one he disliked, something well-known to McIntyre. Morgan was about sixty and close to retirement, and he liked to pose as what he called "a real old-fashioned cop." To Danny, that meant that he treated women with veiled contempt, when speaking to Danny he sometimes said "you people" when he was angry, which was often, and he argued that criminals were now treated like they were royalty. Danny thought he would have probably put handcuffs on Mahshid Nizamani and dragged her down the stairs.

The homicide squad tried to reassign Morgan five years ago. The union grieved and the judgement of the arbitrator was that he was "competent," since he did get convictions some of the time. So, Morgan would be with them until he got his pension in a year and a half.

Danny's face asked two questions as McIntyre read it. She responded, "Let's not get into Ed Morgan. He's here, we're understaffed and he has a decent partner to help. As for what I think you're also asking, as far as I can tell this has nothing to do with the Frawley case. This person, Edward Michaelson, was gay and married. His husband didn't do it and they had what seems to be a fine and loving relationship. He was active in his Unitarian church, the one on St. Clair, and he volunteered in the food bank. He was very social. Also, he was stabbed, a totally different MO from Frawley's killer."

"OK. I still have Frawley on my mind."

"Of course. There's something else. I want to let you know, informally—you haven't heard this—that your name has come up in discussions about promotions. There will be at least two inspector positions vacant in the next year or so and people start looking early. I've been asked about you. I don't have to tell you what I said. You're on what might be called a long short list. You'll probably also be on the short short list. What happens from there is out of my hands."

"I like what I'm doing, Sydney. Your job requires more desk work than I care for. I don't know. Thanks for letting me know. I'll put it way back in my mind for the moment. My father, who himself rose up to a high position in a large firm, had many maxims. One of them was that you should never accept a job that hasn't been offered to you."

"Good advice. I'll remember that," McIntyre laughed.

"It may also come to nothing. Thanks for letting me know. And thanks for the good words you put in for me."

II

On Sunday, after his ritual squash and socializing at the community centre, Danny went to the annual St. Michael's Choir School Christmas concert. Gabriella was one of two conductors, and he enjoyed watching her do it from the audience. The music ranged from sacred choral singing to popular songs. There was even a moment when the audience, composed in part of families of the boys in the school, was asked to join in. It was joyful, different from Chanukah in every way, but very pleasurable in its own fashion. Danny was especially impressed by some of the singing of the senior choir, putting it in the same league as the best boys' choirs in the world.

He met Gabriella at the stage door a half hour after the end of the performance. He mused that here he was, in the cold of December, a stage-door Johnny. They went to supper at a Thai restaurant nearby and settled into a booth in the back.

"Lean back, Gabriella," Danny said. "I know how much tension there is in both the preparation and the performance."

"What did you think?" she asked.

"They were terrific, especially the senior boys. You must get a lot of pleasure teaching them."

"I do. Though I wonder if the school could expand its musical culture. Its mission is to teach and support sacred music. These boys sing every Sunday in the Cathedral, at mass."

They looked at the menu. "I eat here regularly," Gabriella said. "It's all good." Then, "Oh, Danny, I'm sorry. I should have thought. Can you eat here?"

"Yes, no problem. They have lots of things that I eat. I eat out. I can always find something I like on the menu. I'm a sucker for Chinese food. Thai is close enough. Eat what you like. I'm having the chicken in green sauce with rice."

Gabriella reflected, as the waiter came around and looked at her. "You go first," she said to Danny, who ordered.

She looked at Danny and said, "A famous line." Then she turned to the waiter, saying, "I'll have what he's having."

Danny laughed. "When Harry met Sally becomes when Danny met Gabriella," he said. "You don't have to do that."

"I like the chicken dish. I'll have to give this matter some thought."

They discussed some of the performances and the school. Danny then asked, "You said the kids in the choir performed at the mass in the Cathedral. Do you go to mass?"

"Maybe once a month. I need to go to the Cathedral occasionally to see how the boys are doing. I've never sorted out whether I'm going to see the boys or going to mass. It's complicated."

"These things always are. Especially if it was part of our childhood and associated with certain memories. These days I only go to shul for the annual yahrzeit, a tradition to honour the memory of my parents. But when I do go, all sorts of thoughts cloud my mind. Even the smell of the place affects me."

"You're right. I admit I take comfort in the ritual, in the appeal to more than just belief. I find it very warm. But if I do it too often it loses that. I don't think that for me it's about belief. I think it's about identity."

"Same here. Those Yiddish songs I played move me more than the prayers."

Their food arrived and they began eating. They were quiet. Gabriella liked that the quiet was companionable, that neither of them felt forced to fill the silence.

As they were awaiting dessert, she said, "I think I owe you a story."

"No, you don't. You'll tell me when you feel it's right. No need."

"I think it's the right time."

Danny nodded and she continued, "You asked, charmingly, why I'm single. Well, I'm single but I'm not single. I was married when I was twenty. It was one of those things that came about because it was supposed to come about. He was … is … a nice person. We had a boring, even difficult time because we had little in common besides being Catholic. He wanted to make money, which he has done in the trucking business, and I wanted to make music, which I have done. Our intimate life was, to be nice—and I've thought about the right word for a long time—dutiful. We were supposed to make babies. But we were also very awkward and, slowly, over the course of three years, we didn't make a baby, and we had stopped talking to each other about anything meaningful. Maybe we had never talked about anything meaningful. We had lived together for three years and never had a real conversation. It grew painful—for both of us."

"I can imagine," Danny said. "Rachel and I were another story, but it has some similarities."

"Maybe it's the story of more people than we think. Anyway, I asked for a divorce. Not out of malice, I just wanted a life."

"So being a Catholic makes this complicated matter even more complicated."

"You get it." Gabriella managed an ironic laugh. "But then, you are the only person I know who has ever asked me about Opus Dei."

"So, what happened?"

"A very long and difficult episode in my life. I'll fill you in on the details another time. What happened is we separated, and then got a civil divorce. We tried to get an annulment from the Church but it wasn't agreed to. So, I'm married according to the Church and I'm divorced according to the laws of Ontario, Canada and the rest of the world."

"A very Talmudic problem in my background. What happened to your former husband?"

"He started making his money, he found a nice Catholic woman who loved him, he married her and they have two kids and seem to be living happily ever after."

"How does the Church handle his remarriage? He is, if I get it, committing adultery theologically, not civilly speaking."

"There are a number of parishes where the priest will just turn a blind eye. A lot of Catholics in North America divorce and remarry. Opus Dei people, and others, would regard him as a heretic, even deserving excommunication. Certainly, they would refuse him communion. But there are other churches where people like him can just get on with their lives. Pope Francis has helped."

"It sounds like you Catholics have as many rooms in your house as we Jews do. I'm not alone at all. In fact, I am in the majority, in believing there are very many ways of being Jewish."

"It's the same with us."

"But how does this affect your work at the school?"

"I knew you were clever, Danny. There is a 'but.' What happens is it's finessed. I've not re-married, so I am married. I use the name I was born with, but so do others. And, of course, they're intelligent and good people. They would never in a million years think my life outside the school is anyone's business."

They had finished their dessert. "Thanks, Gabriella. I'll need to tell you more of my story, though not now. One story is enough for now."

The bill came and Gabriella grabbed it first. "I'll get it," Danny said. "It's to celebrate the great work you did today."

"Good try, Danny. No. You'll have to get used to my independence, even though you are a gentleman—even an old-fashioned gentleman sometimes, which I adore. I invited you. My turn."

"I know when I'm defeated. I give up. Uncle."

Danny had brought his car, thinking correctly that on a Sunday he might be able to park reasonably near the concert hall. He assumed Gabriella would have taken the subway.

When they were in the car, parked on a side street, Gabriella said, "Face me, Danny." He did so. She then gave him a kiss, which turned into a lengthy one by both of them.

When they ended their embrace, she said, "I'm not used to this, Danny. I want it. However, I may need to go slow and steady."

"I'm not used to it either. Let's take comfort in one another and move at whatever pace seems right for both of us. This is about us. We choose."

He drove her home. They again kissed and embraced in the car. Danny knew something big was changing in his life, as he took the short drive to the Danforth and his house.

III

The call from Sydney McIntyre came on Wednesday morning. "It's earlier than I hoped, Danny. We have a new murder. We'll talk later.

In the meantime, get over to 219 St. Clair West. The doctor's office on the ground floor."

By the time Danny and Nadiri got there the place was cordoned off by the local police. Danny looked around but didn't see any other cars.

They identified themselves to the officer at the entrance. The name on the door of the doctor's office was Dr. William Gentrey, MD, FRCPC, RSC, which sounded familiar to Danny.

"Anybody in there?" Danny asked the officer.

"No, sir. The body was found by his nine o'clock appointment. She's very upset. One of the officers is speaking to her in the car. We confirmed he's dead and then left the scene for you and forensics. The forensics people are on their way."

Danny looked at the officer's name tag. "Thanks, Honeker. Keep everybody out except forensics."

He and Nadiri went into the office. It was one of several on the ground floor of the apartment building, and had its own entrance from the street. They walked into a reception room, which had a desk and a place to leave boots and hang coats. To the rear there was another room, which patients entered to wait for their appointment and a washroom. Gentrey's office was in the front with two doors, one which led to the waiting room and another which patients used to leave the office, which led to the reception room.

'A psychiatrist's office,' Danny said to himself. The waiting patient and the leaving patient were not supposed to see one another. If they have cancer, Danny thought, they can have an ordinary waiting room, but if they have mental issues there is, at least according to Dr. Gentrey, a need for privacy because of the stigma associated with it.

The body was in the office, on the floor in front of a bookcase containing medical books and journals. His head was bashed in.

In the few minutes before forensics arrived, Danny and Nadiri looked around carefully, not touching anything, not wanting to contaminate the scene. It was a doctor's office, though the doctor being a psychiatrist there were no medical tables or instruments. In Gentrey's office there was the bookcase, a desk with a picture of a family of four, lots of papers, including handwritten notes, and two comfortable chairs facing one another across the room, undoubtedly one for Gentrey and one for his patient.

The Forensics team arrived along with the pathologist. This time the pathologist was a woman in her early thirties, with whom Danny had not worked before.

"I'm Emily Chow," she said as she entered. "I'm new, on probation, and I was called." Danny introduced himself and Nadiri and they shook hands as Danny related what he knew. They waited outside while the forensics team did their job. After fifteen minutes, Chow came outside and they went to a private place to talk.

"Sergeant, Constable, it's pretty clear. Dr. Gentrey died from wounds to his head. They were made by a stone or a large rock or something of that sort. Whatever the instrument, it was about twelve centimetres in width or length. I estimate—this will need to be confirmed—that Dr. Gentrey was about five feet eight inches tall. His killer was a bit taller, given the position of the wounds. His killer used his right hand. Obviously, Gentrey was killed from behind."

She paused. Danny asked, "You said 'wounds.' How many?"

"Two or three. Again, I'll probably know better after doing the autopsy."

"The usual question, Doctor Chow. When was he killed?"

"The usual answer, Sergeant. I can't know for sure. But I take it that you would like a preliminary estimate." Danny nodded. "Don't hold me to it until I do the autopsy. My guess is he was killed yesterday in the late afternoon or early evening, certainly not this morning."

"That helps."

"Good. Do you want to attend the autopsy?"

"Possibly. Let me know."

They shook hands and the efficient Dr. Emily Chow left. When the forensics people finished, Danny and Nadiri did a further investigation of the office. All professional. Lots of patients' files in a locked cabinet.

When they returned to the station, they met with McIntyre and briefed her. Then, Danny asked, "Why is the name familiar to me?"

"He's a very prominent man," McIntyre said. "He used to appear on radio and TV as an expert on mental illness. He also was the kind of person who bridged fields. For example, when Stratford did Hamlet several years ago he was one of the lecturers on the play in a series they had. And something else. He was involved three years ago in an incident with a cyclist."

"That's it," Danny said. "That's where my memory tried to give me a push."

"It got a lot of publicity," said Sydney. "What I remember is he was driving along Bloor Street, near Bay, one evening, going home. His wife was with him. They had just had a dinner to celebrate her birthday. Then, a young female cyclist came alongside, on the driver's side, as he began to turn left. He nearly hit her. She started banging on his window and yelling. He tried to get away, but she jumped onto his car and blocked his view. The car hit a pole, with the young woman between the pole and the car. She died."

"Wasn't he arrested?" Nadiri asked.

"Yes. And there were witnesses. I'm a little vague about this part. The cycling community was very angry and used this incident to raise issues about safety and respect. Gentrey was seen to be a pompous establishment type by some of the cycling community and the media. He was arrested and then released on bail while waiting to see if there would be a trial. A few months later, the Crown Attorney said there was not enough evidence to warrant a trial. Again, lots of publicity. Gentrey, as far as I know, tried to just go back to his normal routine. But it undoubtedly affected his life."

"So," Danny said, "on top of everything else, we will need to investigate what might have arisen from this incident. Three years is a long time."

"It may or may not matter," McIntyre said. "However, it needs attention."

Danny turned to Nadiri. "Could you assemble a file about the bike incident? The names of witnesses and those protesting would help."

"Yes, sir."

"Now, let's get back to the net," Danny continued. "We will have to deal with both his personal life and his professional life. Could it be a relative? Yes. Could it be an unhappy patient? Yes. Lots of research."

"We need to be comprehensive," said Sydney. "I'll get you some help."

"Taegan and Connor, please. And anyone else you can spare. This might be one of those cases that get solved by just digging."

"I'll try. Also, I found Gentrey has a connection to CAMH. He worked there in addition to having his own practice on St. Clair. We have a connection there who we consult occasionally, just as we sometimes use Professor Mandelbaum. I'll see if he can help."

"Sounds good." Danny looked at Nadiri. "Let's go to work."

IV

The next morning, Danny attended the autopsy, mainly to see the head wounds and get a sense of what happened. Dr. Chow confirmed there were certainly two blows to the head, possibly three. She also confirmed time of death, between five and eight on Tuesday evening.

Nadiri was putting together matters related to the bike incident and Taegan and Connor were interviewing relatives. Danny went to see the family at their home in Forest Hill, not far from Gentrey's office.

Louise Eamons was Gentrey's wife and they had a daughter, Moira, and a son, Liam, both teenagers. They were in a kind of horrific shock. Still, when Danny asked, they said they were willing to talk. He learned little. Louise Eamons was a psychologist who had her own part-time counselling practice. The children were at Forest Hill Collegiate.

"Our lives changed three years ago, with the bike incident," said Eamons, with just a trace of bitterness in her voice. "Bill was no longer asked to do public appearances, although he was found not culpable. Some people avoided him. He himself felt responsible for the girl's death. He even wrote a piece about it for The Walrus, dealing with how life can change in a few random seconds."

"Did he have any enemies?"

"None. He was a kind person. A fine man. Now, in a few seconds, my life and those of my children have been forever changed. Diminished, really."

"But surely there was some anger from the cycling community and others?"

"Yes, but that was three years ago. It didn't go away, but Bill was determined to get on with his work and his life. It got far less important after about a year."

"What about family or work?"

"He was a model father and uncle. When his parents were alive he helped look after them."

"And professionally?"

"What are you thinking, Sergeant?" Louise Eamons asked. "Do you think psychiatric patients want to kill their therapist?"

"Of course not. Psychiatric patients are patients, Ms. Eamons, just as patients with pneumonia are patients. What I mean is that it's highly likely that your husband was killed by someone in his life. This was almost certainly not a random killing. Like everyone, he had a complicated life. Family, friends, acquaintances, professional associations, patients. And maybe others. I just want to know if there is someone out there who was angry enough—or even disturbed enough—to want to do this."

Eamons calmed down. "I've thought about it. No one comes to mind. Bill was a gentle soul. I'll think some more."

"Good. I've troubled you enough for now, Ms. Eamons. I am truly sorry for your loss. We'll do everything we can to catch the murderer."

"I don't mean to insult you, Sergeant, or your work. Sure, catch the murderer. The only thing that can truly console me is to have my husband back."

Danny nodded and ended the interview. She's right, he thought, but all I can do for her husband is to find out who destroyed what seemed to be a nice family.

V

The second deed was done. Michaelson did not beg, though he too asked for forgiveness. He offered support, counselling help, even money if it would be costly. He told Michaelson that he needed to offer him a life. "You robbed me of twenty years," he had said. "Now, I'll take some years from you in return."

Life is getting much better, he thought. His psychiatrist actually said that perhaps soon they might only need to meet once a week rather than twice.

Most significantly, he rented a new apartment, one near enough to the beach to walk to the boardwalk. It was in an attic, but it was an improvement from the dingy place he would be leaving. He thought of it as a symbol of his new self. He had a self now.

Work was getting better. He was getting some praise from his boss. And he had enrolled into an on-line computer course. He sometimes did not do the lessons as carefully as he should, but he said to himself that he was learning something.

For the first time in many years, he thought regularly about the future.

VI

The Gentrey killing required a lot of digging. Sydney and Danny organized a bunch of police officers, led by Nadiri, who would look into Gentrey's life, including finding out about his patients. Alibis would be asked of many people.

The psychiatric equivalent to Howard Mandelbaum was the head of psychiatric services at CAMH, Dr. John Everson. Danny made an appointment immediately, Everson fitting him in to a very busy day.

Danny went to CAMH at Queen and Ossington at ten o'clock the next morning. He found his way to Everson's office and sat in a waiting area, dedicated to several offices on the same floor. Everson was a bit late, and Danny looked around to survey those waiting alongside him.

There were five others. One, a young woman of about twenty was dressed in what would have passed in the 1960s as hippie style, and she had her nose and eyebrow pierced. She was reading a magazine. Another was a man of about forty, dressed in frayed clothing though there was an attempt at grooming and cleanliness. His right foot went up and down in a persistent tic. He looked at Danny while Danny looked at him. A third was in a white medical coat, seemingly impatient. Another was a grey-haired man in his seventies, reading *The Globe and Mail*. The last was a woman of about forty, well-groomed in a suit, sitting as far away from the others in the area as possible.

Danny mused on the stereotype of madness. Are these people mad? Of course not, though some of them, perhaps all, were in need of counselling. Are they functional? Of course. And Danny realized seeing these people on the street would belie the notion that 'mad' people look mad. He wondered what these people might think about him, sitting here.

The people in the room changed in a short time as those present met with their doctor. By the time Everson appeared to ask Danny to join him, four of the five were gone, replaced by others who had their own individuality.

Everson was a man of about fifty, with full-white hair and a strong chin. His blue eyes seemed reflective, and his manner was, like many in his profession, that of a listener. Danny asked him about Gentrey.

"He was an unusual man, Sergeant. Not only was he a fine analyst, he had a breadth of learning that very few of us in the profession attain.

He bridged fields. For example, he could use his psychological knowledge to gain insight into art and literature. He was extremely well read. I have no idea where he found the time for it, but this was a person who could talk with philosophers about Descartes and with literary people about George Eliot."

"What kind of person was he?"

"Bill was a decent man. He was very engaged professionally. There were people who were a little afraid of him because of his vast knowledge, if that's where you're going. But generally, he was kind and warm. He was something of an enthusiast simply because he had such an active mind."

"What happened to him after the bike incident?"

"Are you asking about his professional life? We were colleagues, not close friends. I don't know a lot about his personal or family life."

"Tell me what you can."

"Bill was clearly very disturbed about the incident. He felt he was responsible, though he didn't say much about it. As you probably know, he was dropped from the public airways for a time because of the notoriety, and that bothered him. But he continued his professional life in a manner that meant that the incident receded after a time."

"Tell me about his professional life."

"He saw patients three days a week—Monday, Wednesday and Friday—at his office on St. Clair West. His practice was varied. He had patients who were psychotic, some who were depressed. His patients came from a wide range of backgrounds and wealth. A general practice. Here, he saw some patients and did research. In the last several years he was very interested in refugees who had undergone trauma in their homeland and how they handled their new lives. Lately, he was also working with children of refugees. He published some interesting and insightful studies. Given his range of publications, Bill could have been a professor at the university, but he preferred the clinical life."

"Let's move on to the violence. Please tell me about violence in your profession. It's not something I've thought about."

"Here I can talk with confidence. I've done some research in this area. Let me note that there is violence between patients and professionals in the health profession as a whole. Not a lot, and not regularly, though enough that every provider is aware that it's around. Nurses, doctors, therapists, and others.

"In the psychiatric profession, many have experienced verbal abuse and some have had to deal with physical assault. As well, there are a number of instances of patients wounding or killing their analyst, usually patients who are psychotic. It goes with the nature of the work. We often work with people who are in serious difficulties."

"Talk about the relationship between the psychiatrist and the patient."

"Sergeant, I could talk about this until morning. From the beginnings of psychiatry this has been an important matter. What do you want to know?"

"I want to know if a patient could have killed William Gentrey."

"Yes, it could have been a patient. The term we bandy about when talking about the doctor-patient relationship is transference. It refers to the patient seeing the analyst as a stand-in for an authority figure. It could be a parent, a teacher, anyone. The patient then transfers the emotions about that figure to the analyst. Hence, the analyst becomes someone who might be hated."

"What about the analyst to the patient?"

"It only gets more complicated. Patients can have erotic feelings about an analyst. And the reverse can occur. There are many instances of analysts relating in erotic and other ways to patients. It becomes very intimate. It's not just about fixing the brakes on your car. There are even instances where the analyst will envy the patient or admire them. Some analysts don't like to cure their patients, if the word 'cure' means making them ordinary and taking away their distinctive personality."

"Let's get to the case. You say it's possible the murderer was a patient. What kind of patient?"

"Psychotics. Not your ordinary neurotic living in a big house in Forest Hill and wondering about the meaning of life. Someone whose grasp on life is tenuous, who is given to violent mood swings."

"Can you help us? We're going through Dr. Gentrey's files in his office. Yes, I know they're confidential, but we have a warrant. Can we show you some of them? We also have a warrant to look into his files here."

"Of course. Anything I can do is fine."

"Good. Could I ask you to look at the files here? I have a feeling this case is one that goes deep into someone's psyche. We'll need to be very sensitive to find a motive."

"I'll get one of our younger people to look at our files with an eye on the issue of violence. Then I'll get back to you."

Everson continued with a reflection. "The human mind is a puzzling thing, Sergeant. We humans are a lot more complicated than they thought we were prior to the twentieth century."

"Frankly, Dr. Everson, I think life in general is more complicated these days. We police uphold the law, but there are times when the law seems inadequate to the human elements of a case. I recently had one like that."

"You're referring to the honour killing, of course. I watched you on the news. A very difficult matter. I won't tell you I condone killing, but I am, like most people I know, very sympathetic to Mahshid Nizamani. Bill was interested in the case. He talked about it as something that required more than just following the rules, something that occurs in clinical matters from time to time."

"I'll get on with my job, Doctor. I'll be getting back to you for some help with the files and for some further explanations. Transference is interesting. There's the famous Patty Hearst case where the person abducted sympathizes with her captors, and there are many instances of transference in relationships between police and gangsters. I'll have to think about it."

"Good point. This is the kind of thing that made Bill special. He would come up with an angle and a way into a problem that opened it up far wider than the rest of us."

"I'll get out of your hair now. I appreciate your seeing me on a busy day."

"My regards to your inspector."

VII

Nadiri was ready to report to Danny when he returned to the station.

"First, let's discuss the patients," Danny said. "I learned from Everson there is violence in psychiatric medicine. We're still working through the files, but we've looked at a majority of them. There are four that seem to fit. The patients have some violence in their background. They seem, to us, unstable. A lot of the patients are just ordinary people like the rest of us, with a need for some counselling to sort out whatever is troubling them. As we know, ordinary people commit murder on occasion."

"Yes, sir. But you asked us to look for files that fit some pattern of violence."

"Fair enough. Could you separate those files and let me see them? I may need to show them to Dr. Everson. He's arranging to look at Gentrey's patients at CAMH."

"The bicycle story is a complicated one," Nadiri said. "It was a big deal because of Gentrey's high profile in the city. Inspector McIntyre had the basic facts correct. I'll add a few. Gentrey claimed he hadn't had a drink at the birthday dinner because he was driving. That was confirmed by a breathalyser test. Witnesses to the incident were all over the place. Some claimed that the young woman, Elise Edwards, had beaten on the front driver's side window, as Dr. Gentrey and Ms. Eamons had stated. Others weren't certain. All agreed she had screamed, some said she used vulgar language, two said the language was threatening."

"Makes sense there are several versions," Danny said. "It was a very short and very confusing half minute or so."

"Thirty-seven seconds, said the Crown Attorney. That Elise Edwards wound up on the front of the car, on the driver's side, blocking his view, is agreed upon by all but one witness. The one who disagreed said Gentrey might have had a view. Then the car swerved and hit a pole and she was crushed. Ms. Eamons called 911 near the end of the incident. She asked for an ambulance and told the operator there was an injury and a bad accident. The cycling community exploded. Many accused Gentrey of manslaughter, even murder. Many said the legal system was covering up for a prominent person. Many people made threats. Gentrey's lawyers asked the police to look into some of the more open threats. We have a file of the people who openly threatened violence to Gentrey, even Eamons and their children. The incident became a … what is it called?"

"A cause célèbre."

"That's it. What should we do?"

"I'd like you to get a file of the major figures from the cycling group. Who leads them? Who spoke to the public for them? Who are the people the news stations would interview? And then I want a list of those who made open threats, with what was said. I agree three years is a long time, but we need to deal with this properly. Once we have all the information I'll assign tasks."

"Do you want to talk to the family of Elise Edwards? There are parents, Robert Edwards, a banker, and Marilyn Everson, who owns an interior decorating shop. And two siblings, Belinda and Sebastian."

"I don't think so. Not yet at least. Did any of them send threatening messages to Gentrey?"

"No. They hired their own lawyer and they tried to stay private. A few interviews just after the event and then they refused to speak again in public."

"They've had enough. I'll only speak with them if it seems necessary along the way. Again, what is the name of Elise Edwards' mother?"

"Marilyn Everson. Coincidence?"

VIII

It was Friday and, after reporting to Sydney McIntyre, Danny went to Ruth's to join her family and Avi in the Sabbath meal. As usual, he stopped at the kosher bakery to get some sweets for his hosts as well as some for himself for the weekend. It was December, so the Sabbath came early. Luckily, he got to the bakery just before it closed.

Danny let himself into the Feldman home, announced his presence and went to the kitchen to find Ruth. They tried to get a bit of time each week to themselves, to have some sister-brother moments together. He gave Ruth a hug and a kiss and then asked, "Where are the kids?"

"Leo and Avi are playing some game in the basement. Deborah should be here at any moment."

Ruth put a piece of homemade gefilte fish on a plate with a piece of bread and set it down before Danny. "Your Chanukah party was terrific, as usual. We enjoyed it. Irwin was pleased that you asked him to give the blessing."

"It wasn't diplomatic, Ruth dear, you're my closet kin. It was just right."

"Doing the right thing sometimes works. I'm comforted by that."

"Anyway, I had fun. I will never forget the sweet Olga asking for my violin."

"I wondered. I know it's the only possession you value. I remember when Momma and Papa gave it to you. You were sixteen, just about fully grown, and they were told by your teachers to get you a better instrument. You had talent, they said, and you needed a proper instrument to develop. So, they got me a grand piano three years earlier and then got you your wonderful violin. I know for a fact it cost a lot more than my grand piano. But it was worth it. It's meant a lot to you."

"Frankly, Ruth, I don't know how I would survive without it. I'm not that talented. I'm pretty good. Maybe very good. But some of the people I play with are excellent. They put up with me."

"Nonsense, they wouldn't let you join them if you didn't have the stuff."

"That's what Gabriella says. Sometimes I wonder."

"Modesty is a fine trait, Danny. But undervaluing yourself is not smart, and you are smart. Speaking of smart, tell me about Gabriella. She seemed a very fine person. And I really liked your new young partner. She has spunk. I like her energy."

"Nadiri is doing well. About Gabriella, speaking of talent, she is a fine musician. A terrific flautist. An excellent conductor. She also plays the violin very well and a few other instruments."

"Don't avoid the question. Tell me about Gabriella."

"It could turn into a relationship. I think I hope it will do so, though I admit it's a little scary after all this time. I find her intelligent, sensitive, warm, and kind. She has all the right values. We seem very comfortable with one another. To get to your question, her relationship to her Catholic background is very similar to my relationship to Judaism. She is who she is. She's not religious, though she will not abandon her tradition or family, both of which give some meaning to her life."

"How about finding a nice Jewish girl who's as odd as you are?"

"You certainly tried, and I gave it a shot. I'm in my forties and I've found Gabriella. As you say, she's a splendid person. I have no problem making a commitment to a good person. Remember Ruth, we're not talking about a traditional life here. If we get together, we will do so on our own terms, terms which will not hurt anybody else. But for both of us, there is no possibility of a marriage, kids, and all that goes with that."

"I understand and I want you to be happy. I'll start talking with

Irwin. My guess is the three kids will handle it better than he will."

"I need to have a heart-to-heart with Avi. That's what matters most to me."

"As it should."

When dinner was served there were ten places set at the table. In addition to Danny's family, there was another family of four who Danny had not met. They were introduced as Sam and Linda Parkel and their two daughters, Leah and Naomi. They were members of the Feldman's synagogue, and Leah was in Avi's class at the Maimonides College School.

They all settled in comfortably, enjoying the singing and the ritual, having a warm time at the table.

Midway through the meal, Irwin asked Danny about the Gentrey case. "Are you involved?"

"Yes, but you know I can't talk about it until it's over."

"Well, you did a terrific job on the Nizamani killing. I'm certain that this will be solved as well, in due course."

Sam Parkel entered the conversation. "Gentrey was a fine man, a credit to our profession. A renaissance man."

"What's your role in the profession, Sam?" Danny asked.

"I chair the psychology department at York University. Several years ago, I tried to recruit Gentrey for one of the new Canada Research Chairs, but he said he was happier doing clinical work and research at CAMH. He seemed to be the perfect fit for a faculty that stresses interdisciplinary studies."

Deborah asked, "I know you can't talk about Dr. Gentrey, Uncle Danny, but can you speculate about what might happen to Mahshid Nizamani?"

"You're not the first to ask me that, Debby. Of course, it's out of the hands of the police now and the justice system will work it through. I'm not certain she's even fit to stand trial. People like Dr. Parkel will make that decision."

"We talked about it in my law and society seminar," said Deborah. "It's really a moral dilemma, what my professor calls a quandary. Objectively, she is a murderer. But actually, several of my fellow students defended her."

Ruth dove into the discussion. "It's a good example of how the law has to be seen as a guide, not as something rigid. Not only as a woman, but as a citizen, I hope she finds a decent life."

"The law will make the decision," said Irwin.

Leo broke in. "The law might not be the right place to make the judgment. Maybe we need a Solomon for this one."

"I think we do, Leo," Danny said.

Naomi said, "Mr. Miller, I remember you referred to Shakespeare in speaking about the case. What was it Shakespeare wrote? 'First, kill the lawyers.'"

"Where is that from?" Linda Parkel asked.

Avi said, "Henry VI. I think the exact quote is, 'the first thing we do, let's kill all the lawyers.'"

"Why the first thing?" Ruth asked.

"Because," Avi answered, "they're talking about a utopia. In the utopia there is no need for laws. As in Gan Eden, all are happy."

"In Gan Eden there's no need for most of us," said Danny. "No lawyers, no police, no psychologists." He looked at Leo, adding, "And no need for soldiers for defence."

"Well," Ruth said, "we've been expelled from the garden. We're imperfect. So, I guess, children, we need laws. Still, the law sometimes doesn't work as humanely as we would like."

"I won't argue with you," Irwin said. "I can only say laws help make us civilized. The rule of law is sometimes the only thing standing between decency and chaos."

"I agree, Irwin," Danny said. "We do need laws. If we're civilized we sometimes don't realize how fragile civilization can be. I think both cases, Nizamani and Gentrey, reflect that."

The conversation continued until the end of the meal, after which grace was said.

As they were leaving, Danny went to speak with Sam Parkel. "Could I meet with you for a coffee, Sam? I have a few questions I want to ask. All this is informal, though it's confidential."

"I'd be delighted. It's been a great pleasure meeting you and Avi." Sam took out a card from his wallet and wrote his home phone number on the back. "Call anytime."

"Good. Shabbat Shalom to you and the family." Danny hung around a bit and helped with the cleanup. He found it comforting being around Ruth and the children.

He met Nadiri the next morning to get up-to-date and move the investigation along.

"What about the cyclist incident?"

"There were lots of aggressive communications, some threatening. It's hard to decide which were serious and which were just outbursts. So, I decided someone who spoke out once wouldn't be on my list. Here's a list of eight names, those who wrote emails or tweets more than once, in some cases four or five times. They did stop after a while. No one kept it up for more than a few months."

"Who did the media speak to about the cycling issue?"

"There's a group called the Union of Cyclists that advocates on behalf of the cycling community. There are a few others, but this one seems to be the major organization. It's headed by a woman named Deirdre Upton. I have the address and phone number."

"Alright. I'd like you to get in touch with those patients you identified. Go easy. If they have a plausible alibi, just let it go. If not, don't push too hard. Get some impressions. We can get back to them. Also, get in touch with the cyclists who wrote the threatening notes and do the same. If you need help because of the numbers involved, get it from Taegan and Connor. I'll get in touch with Upton. And there is then the group from CAMH. Dr. Everson should be ready with that list shortly. We'll get to them then."

"What you're saying is there's no breakthrough."

"Nothing at all. I feel that we just have to slog away at this one, and the breakthrough will come.

"I'll get on it right away, sir. By the way, could I ask for Tuesday afternoon off? There's a personal matter I need to look after."

"Certainly. Unless there's an emergency, it's yours. You've been doing six- and seven-day weeks. You're entitled to an afternoon off."

"I don't mind the work, sir. I'm finding it very meaningful."

"Good. But work should be a part of a life, not the whole of it. We do better at work if we have a fuller life. Don't neglect those things that matter to you, like your family."

"I know you don't sir. I'll be careful."

"Sounds good. Let's get to work. You should know I intend to take off tomorrow. A Sunday will do me good. My rationale, and it is really a rationale for my own benefit, is sometimes you have to let things percolate for them to get solved. Tomorrow they percolate."

IX

It was the period of holiday between Christmas and New Years for most of the city, though not for the police. They made certain members of the force had their holidays—non-Christians like Danny and Nadiri always worked on Christmas Eve, Christmas Day and Boxing Day—but their services never paused.

Still, the city had a slightly different feel. Schools were out and shoppers were legion searching for Boxing Week bargains. Lights lit up the main shopping areas and many houses. It was a pause before winter—a long winter usually, often going into early April—took hold. This week there was holiday in the air. Next week the routine would resume and people would be walking with shoulders hunched against the cold. The holiday lights would dim.

Danny did his usual squash, shvitz and bagel in the morning and then went home. He had a date later in the day. Gabriella had invited him to her place for dinner. "It's time you saw where I live," she had said. She had checked with him on food because she said she wanted to make an old-fashioned Italian meal. Danny told her that if he ate in a Thai restaurant, he could eat in anyone's home, so not to worry. Gabriella said that any meat would be kosher—she had had the adventure of going to Bathurst Street to a kosher butcher for the first time a week ago to scope it out—and that she would not mix meat and dairy. "Anything else?" she had asked with a smile and concern.

Danny squeezed her hand, saying, "You've covered it for me."

At five o'clock Danny entered Gabriella's condo carrying two bottles of Italian wine, one white and one red. He took the elevator up to the fourth floor and found her apartment.

Gabriella welcomed him with a hug, told him to hang up his coat and took the wine into the kitchen. She showed him around a very charming apartment, full of colour and light. The living room walls were a rich red, and there were posters and a few small original pieces of art on the walls. The furniture was cozy and comfortable.

"I was lucky," she said as she showed him around. "This place has two bedrooms. It gives me a place to do some work and to have a guest. It was only slightly more expensive than a one bedroom on sale at the same time and I decided that, if I was going to take on a mortgage for life, it didn't matter if it was a bit bigger than I thought it should be.

But the real bonus is there's only one wall next to a neighbour, in my bedroom. I can practice here and not bother anyone, and I can listen to music as loud as I like. My neighbour hears me sometimes, but she says she doesn't mind."

"It's terrific. People like us need our own place. You probably like coming home here."

"I do. After the divorce having this place was one of the things that kept me sane, and even happy."

The kitchen was a galley, but Gabriella made room for a stool for Danny to sit on while she cooked. He thought this was as good as being in Ruth's kitchen. It smelled very different, a pungent tomato sauce smell, with hints of pesto and oregano. Not chicken soup and brisket, the regular Friday night fare of his sister. Nonetheless, he recognized Gabriella's smell as soul food, as much as was Ruth's.

"Open the wine, Danny. The white first."

They talked about the chamber group and what was happening. They had moved from Vivaldi to Bach. They were practicing two of the Brandenburg Concertos, numbers 1 and 3, and there were some issues regarding the harmony. Gabriella tested some ideas on Danny and he responded.

After a while, Gabriella said, "Go sit at the table, Danny. I'm ready."

She first served an antipasto plate. It had tomatoes marinated in olive oil and herbs, artichoke hearts, olives, pickles, almonds, walnuts, pine nuts, yellow peppers and some sausage, all accompanied by homemade garlic bread.

"There is a first here, Danny. Can you guess what it is?"

Danny surveyed the food. "A first for you or a first for the world?"

She smiled. "Both. I'll give you a clue. Taste the sausage."

Danny took a sliver and then took a bite. "You're kidding. It tastes like kosher salami."

"That's because it is kosher salami."

"It actually works, Gabriella. Amazing. This whole plate is delicious."

"At least I think it's a first. As you probably know, Jews have been in Italy since before the time of Christ. I wonder if some of them didn't do a version of this in Rome or Venice."

"Could be. I'll bet Avi and his cousins would go wild for it. They eat various versions of kosher pizza as if it were candy. And pizza bagels are in every home in the community."

The main course was veal piccata accompanied by a small side of penne with a rich tomato sauce.

"Open the red," she suggested. "We can save the rest of the white for cooking."

Danny ate and felt as warm as he had on Friday night. "This is terrific. Where did you learn to cook?"

"My parents were immigrants and they came here with my grandmother, my mother's mother. My Nonna took me under her wing early. I would go into the kitchen and she always had a treat for me and my sister. She died when I was eighteen, but her food remains in the world. As a teacher, you always hope your students will help you to be in the world beyond your given years. For my Nonna, when I make her recipes, she remains in the world."

"A fine idea. Family and culture have tastes and smells. And food is so central to our being, not only our physical being, but our spiritual one as well. For me, Chanukah has important tastes and smells. For you, Christmas must feel the same."

"Certainly. There are reasons why the kitchen is so central in our two cultures."

Danny had finished his food. "Now," he said, "I owe you a story."

"As you said, Danny, not necessary."

"Necessary for me, my lovely cook."

They each took a sip of wine and Gabriella topped up their glasses. "I'll try to keep it brief," Danny said.

"Like you, I married early. To Rachel Stern, a lovely Jewish girl who I had known since we had attended the same Hebrew high school, the one Avi is in now. She was bright and she was inquisitive, though she was always a person who didn't take a lot of risks. We married and had Avi a few years later. But what happened is that she grew more observant, like many of her friends, in her twenties and early thirties, and I grew less so."

He took a sip of wine. "So, we began to argue, quietly, no raised voices, about how to behave and how our home should be as the years went on. She disliked that I worked on Saturdays. No, even more, she disliked that I didn't mind having to work on Saturdays. She began to dress very traditionally—long skirts, elbows covered, hair covered.

"I understood what she needed and didn't feel she was doing the wrong thing. But I couldn't see living the rest of my life that way. And, to be fair, she didn't like thinking about living the rest of her life with this kind of Jew.

"By the time Avi was five, we were living two separate lives. Again, to be fair, we both tried to adjust as much as we could, but it didn't work out. So, we separated for a time. The separation ended in divorce."

"But you didn't have the problem Scott and I had with the Church?"

"No. There's a religious side to divorce for Orthodox and some Conservative Jews, and Rachel, by the time of the separation, was very Orthodox. It's called a *get*, and, in the masculine culture of the Orthodox, it is given by the male to the female. In our case there was no issue. I did what was ritually appropriate and we are divorced in both the civil and religious worlds. Rachel met what seems to be a nice man through the Orthodox network and she's remarried. They have two daughters. Mutual friends tell me she's happy. From what I can tell from Avi, she seems content. I'm glad of that. The complication was I would have liked for Avi to live with me. Not that Rachel is a poor mother, it's just that I love him so much. It was not to be. We made an arrangement and we abide by it. We're civil when we're in the same room. One day I'd like to have a good conversation with her."

"Well, Danny, your story is not all that different from mine. I think there are a lot of stories like that out there. Some people stay. You and I could not. We have, in our own ways, made a life."

"Ruth has been wonderful. She's on my side at all times, though she often disagrees with me."

"My parents died in an accident six years ago. My sister, a younger sister, Beatrice—she pronounces it the Italian way, Bee-ah-tree-chey, and won't answer to the North American 'Bee-tryce'—is my link to my past. There are aunts and uncles—we're not close, but we spend Christmas and other occasions with them and they are good to us. Time for dessert, Danny. Very simple after this meal. Some peaches and ice cream. Don't worry, it's … what do you call it? … neutral ice cream. From a store next to the butcher, who told me about it."

"Pareve, it's called. Do you think of everything?"

Gabriella brought out new wine glasses and the corked white bottle. "We can have some more white with dessert. No, I don't think of everything Danny. I haven't figured out what to do after dessert."

"The dishes of course."

"No, Danny. I think I'm going to leave the dishes. That's not like me at all. I'm not obsessive, but close to it, when it comes to being neat. I think I'd like to go to the living room and cuddle."

"I'd like that as well."

They sat on the couch together, Gabriella leaning on Danny's shoulder, kissing from time to time. After some time she looked up and said, "Come, Danny." She stood, took Danny's hand and led him to the bedroom.

X

Danny woke at six o'clock, with Gabriella at his side. He looked at her for a few minutes, in a kind of trance, thinking her so very beautiful and reflecting on how fortunate he was. This was new to him. However, he also knew he had to get to work today, though Gabriella had the day off for the school holiday. He got out of bed as quietly as he could, pulled together his clothes and closed the bedroom door as he left the room. He went to the bathroom and neatened up. Then he dressed and went into the kitchen and did the dishes. He left the warmest possible note for Gabriella, telling her he would call later in the day. He went home, showered, shaved and went to work.

The day was an organizing one. He first got in touch with Deirdre Upton and made an appointment for the early afternoon. Then he called John Everson.

"Good morning, Sergeant," Everson said when he picked up. "I hope you had a good weekend."

"Good morning to you, Doctor. I'm following up. Have you had someone go through Dr. Gentrey's files at CAMH?"

"Yes. I can report to you now."

"If you don't mind, I'd like to meet about this later today. Have you any free time? I don't think it'll take long."

There was a pause. "As usual, I'm booked. Can you come at five?"

"Absolutely. See you then."

He then met with McIntyre to report what was happening.

"Danny," she said, "you seem to have covered the bases. Do you think we should have a professional look at the files in Gentrey's office?"

"I thought about that. Not yet. Let me get the report on the people

Nadiri and the team have identified. If I think we need to go further I'll consider it. I want to clarify a few other things first."

"This might be a tough one. Still, none of us think it was random. We just have to slog through the process and something will open up."

"That's what I think, Sydney. Have we missed anything?"

"It depends on how big you want the net to be. Right now, we're looking at his personal life, which seems to yield nothing, his outstanding patients, and something from the bicycle incident. If that doesn't work, we'll get a bigger net. Keep in touch."

"By the way, how is the great detective doing with his corpse? Perhaps Morgan thinks the victim deserved it because of his sexual orientation?"

"This isn't like you Danny. Though I understand where the anger comes from." She paused and then said, "We're not getting far on that one. We'll see."

"Well, to be nice, I remember you said he had a good partner. I agree. Ted Sloan is a good guy. If he hasn't made progress, then it must be a difficult problem. Ted should get a medal when Morgan retires."

"No comment, Danny. If you become an inspector, you can't talk like that."

"I disagree, Sydney. If I become an inspector I can only talk like that to other inspectors." He smiled, "Not to lowly sergeants."

She laughed. "OK, Danny. I get it. Now let's both get on with the day."

Deirdre Upton, the president of the Union of Cyclists, operated a large bicycle shop that did both sales and repairs in Bloor West Village. Danny drove to the area a bit early, found a place to park, and walked around the main shopping district. He liked to get a feel for those parts of the city that were not well-known to him. He was impressed with the shops and the energy of the area running from Jane Street to Runnymede on Bloor. It still had a United Church feel about it, though there were now Thai restaurants and eastern European delis scattered about.

Danny found the large bicycle shop in the middle of the area, went in and asked for Upton. She was a woman of about forty-five, slim, blonde and energetic. She took him into her office in the rear of the store and offered him coffee as they settled.

"How can I help you, Detective?"

"Frankly, I'm not certain. As you know, I assume, Dr. William Gentrey was murdered several days ago."

Upton said, "And you think a cyclist, or someone in our organization, did it?"

Danny answered, "No, I don't think that. The incident was three years ago. I think a direct line of cause and effect running from a member of the cycling community to the killing is unlikely."

"So why are you here?"

"Because in my business you have to cover all the possibilities. I said it was unlikely, probably highly unlikely, but I still have to ask."

Upton started to interrupt, but Danny held up his hand and continued speaking. "You know, Ms. Upton, that there were a lot of hostile communications sent to Dr. Gentrey, some threatening, some openly suggesting violence. Those cannot be ignored. So, let's talk quietly and let me get the information I need to help solve a murder."

"When you put it like that, I understand. Sorry. We're used to being told that our projects are in the way of progress, or that we are in the way of the car."

"That's not what I'm asking. I'll add that that's not what I think. What I get is that the death of Elise Edwards was in part the result of a kind of anger. I also get that, in anger, some people threatened Dr. Gentrey, some several times. Help me to understand it."

"There is an anger. We feel we're not respected or listened to. It has gotten better in the last few years. All you have to do is check the streets and see the bicycle lanes introduced. On Harbord Street, on Sherbourne, even on places like Wellesley Street and Bloor. Cyclists have rage, just like drivers have rage. Some drivers just ignore us or feel we're in their way. They have a powerful machine and we are on a little two-wheeler. Many cyclists can't afford a car, and need the bike to get to work and to shop. Many cyclists feel they're contributing by biking. They don't pollute and they take up a hell of a lot less room than a car, especially a big car with only a driver in it."

"Would a cyclist harm a car or a driver?"

"Detective, there are over one hundred thousand regular cyclists in Toronto. Some are a little crazy. There are over a million drivers in Toronto. Some of them are also crazy."

"Fair enough. I agree. Why the threats to Gentrey?"

"I'm not saying I agree with the threats, though I understand them.

Cyclists feel threatened by cars. I want to add that the Gentrey incident did a lot of good. It made our advocacy easier. It helped push forward our agenda."

"Do you know of any cyclists who are especially violent, or, in your own words, a little crazy?"

"Sure. Do you know of any drivers who shouldn't have a licence?"

"Do you know of anyone who might have had a grudge for three years and who might have committed an act of violence against Dr. Gentrey?"

"If you'd asked me this question two years ago, I would have given you several names. I think the matter has passed. But I can think of two or three people who continually get into trouble with the police because they're violent and who we have helped. I don't know them well. I've not heard any of them say anything about Dr. Gentrey for the last two years."

"Can you give me their names, in confidence?"

"I don't like it, but we'll cooperate. I think you're looking in the wrong place."

"You may be right. But this is murder. We have to look even in places that aren't likely to fit."

They parted after Upton wrote down three names and gave the piece of paper to Danny. Danny ended the exchange by saying, whatever happened as a result of their conversation, he would report the outcome to Upton.

It was cold, but the sun was out and the sky was blue. Danny had some time to put in before going to see Everson, so he walked into Swansea, another area he knew little about. He walked south on Windermere and, after a few quiet residential streets, bumped into Rennie Park. The park, in addition to being a fine open space, had both an outdoor hockey rink and a skating oval.

He wandered over to the rink and saw the ice being prepared for a hockey game. The game was clearly between two bantam teams, kids he estimated to be nine or ten years old, waiting at the gate impatiently for the machine to finish its job resurfacing the ice. The oval was next to the rink and there were a bunch of people on skates circling it, a skating oval with some trees in its middle. The skaters ranged from retired elders to three-year-olds. It was, he felt, a very serene space, a real neighbourhood gathering place, with families enjoying themselves with their neighbours. What a nice city Toronto was to have this, and other public spaces like it, as part of its daily life, Danny thought. Danny walked to an isolated bench, sat down and called Gabriella.

"Hi, Danny," she answered. "I feel like a bum. I'm still in my pyjamas while you've been working all day."

"Still? I didn't see any pyjamas last night."

Gabriella giggled. "OK. When I woke up I put on my pyjamas and haven't gotten dressed all day."

"Very luxurious."

"It's a fine feeling, Danny. I hope you're feeling the same."

"Glorious, Gabriella. Terrific."

"Good. I want this, Danny."

"I want it, too. Let's just keep going at our own pace."

"Sounds right. When I walked into the kitchen I knew I had the right guy. There is a saying among women that the perfect man is one who can make passionate love until four in the morning and then turn into a pizza. My perfect man is someone who can make passionate love until four in the morning and then does the dishes."

They talked for a while, at random, wanting to hold on to the magic. Finally, Danny said he had to go to CAMH. They agreed to meet for dinner the next night. "Come to my place at seven," Danny said. "We can walk to the Danforth and find a quiet meal."

Danny walked back to Bloor, found his car and drove deeper into the city to meet John Everson in his office at CAMH. This time there was only one person in the waiting room. The clinical day was nearly over. Danny went directly to Everson's office. He knocked and Everson invited him in.

"Hello, Doctor. It looks like I extended your workday."

"This is important. Your days are, I would guess, often longer than mine, Daniel. Can I call you Daniel? I'm John."

"Everybody but my late father calls me Danny. To him I was Daniel."

"Good. My resident pulled three files. I think they're marginal in terms of possibly revealing the killer, though you can never know. These are copies. Please destroy them when you're finished."

"I can't destroy them. They'll go into a file that is confidential."

"Good enough."

"Why do you say they're marginal?"

"There isn't a regular pattern of violence. Some of it's verbal. In each case there are outbursts, but I don't see any of them as leading to a killing."

"We'll look at them and see what we do. We do have some files from Dr. Gentrey's private practice. We can compare. If they're not like them, we may just back off on these for now."

"Use your judgment. You and Sydney will be sensitive to the matter."

"Have you helped us in other cases?" Danny asked.

"Several. In part, trying to get profiles. I'm one of several psychiatrists on your list of advisors."

"I sometimes wonder if we shouldn't have a full-time profiler or psychiatrist. I do like the idea of consulting outside experts. In the Nizamani case a sociologist was very helpful."

"I'm happy to help. Like you, my colleagues and I are civil servants of a sort. Medicine's not a business here."

"Good point. I'll get back to you on how we do. I'll let you go home now. By the way, I ran into a coincidence. The young woman who died in the Gentrey bike incident was named Elise Edwards. Her parents are Robert Edwards and Marilyn Everson. There are probably a bunch of Eversons in Toronto …"

Everson put out his hand to interrupt. "I'll answer your question. She was my niece. Marilyn is my sister."

Danny sat still and just looked at Everson. He knew that the psychiatrist, who used this technique regularly with patients, would understand that he wanted him to continue.

"Elise was my goddaughter. She had a history of erratic behaviour from childhood. In fact, she was diagnosed early as bipolar. She was very bright, very inquisitive, and very opinionated. But she had mood swings that seemed uncontrollable. Six months before her death she attempted suicide. The family did everything we could."

"I'm sorry for your loss. It must have hurt."

"It did hurt. I come from a culture that says you take these things with a stiff upper lip, you don't show your emotions. But yes, Danny, it hurt. And I needed to support my sister and brother-in-law in a hard time."

"You were still able to work with Gentrey?"

"As I told you in our earlier conversation, he was a colleague, not a friend. And neither the family nor I held him responsible for the death once the facts were revealed. Bill came here, sat in the seat you are occupying, and we talked. He was genuinely remorseful."

"I have a child. I don't know how I would go on if I lost him."

"Marilyn is tough, but I wondered sometimes. There are other children. That helps. That gives you a purpose to continue."

"Did it affect Dr. Gentrey's professional life?"

"You know he was dropped from the media for a time. It was only recently that you occasionally saw him being interviewed again. Here at CAMH and at his practice, he continued as normal. I think the regularity of work helped him for the first several months. After that, he was his ordinary self. Most colleagues were sympathetic. There was a bit of schadenfreude among a few people here. They took some perverse joy in the golden boy being knocked off his perch. That occurs everywhere."

"Thanks, John. I'd better get home. I'll look at the files this evening."

"Let me know what happens." Everson shook and Danny shook hands. "Have a good evening, Danny."

XI

Danny spent early Tuesday morning looking at files and thinking about the process. He and Nadiri had agreed to meet at ten to sort out who to interview. He also called Sam Parkel and they arranged to meet for coffee at four in the afternoon. Nadiri came with her own files and information and Danny gave her the files he received from Everson.

"Check out these three in relation to the ones from the office," Danny said. "I looked at them and we can't go forward with interviews based on them. There's not a strong enough connection to the issue we're concerned with. Dr. Everson agreed with that. I'd like your opinion, too. What do you have?"

"I have three as well. They all show a pattern of violence, though there is only one for which Gentrey wrote that he was personally worried. Gentrey took handwritten notes during sessions. They were mostly records of what was said. But he sometimes put in questions and opinions."

"Who is the person?"

"A male. Peter Ufaron. In his forties. He has psychotic tendencies and is sometimes barely functional. He had sessions twice a week with Gentrey. He has had a series of outbursts. Some, those with his family, never became a public matter. A few others, at work and socially, were public."

"What kind of violence?"

"Usually his fists and wrestling matches. At work, he once sent another employee to the emergency room to get patched up."

"Can I assume he wasn't a cyclist?"

"No evidence that was an issue that mattered to him."

"What's your advice? Do we ask him some questions?"

"I think so. We don't have a lot to go on right now."

"Let's decide that later. I saw Deirdre Upton, the head of the Union of Cyclists. She gave me the names of three cyclists who had violent tendencies. She also reminded me that in any large community there are eccentric and possibly violent people. And the cycling community is very large. Here they are. I want you to check if any of these people sent threatening communications to Gentrey after the incident. Then we'll decide what to do."

"Where are we?"

"We're not very far. We have, in the violent patient from the office, someone to look into. Not yet a suspect. Probably never a suspect. And we have some others you'll look into. I have something nagging at the back of my head, but it hasn't come forward yet. We continue the slog. If nothing turns up, then, as Inspector McIntyre said, we extend the search."

"I'll get on this and get back to you, sir. Can I still take the afternoon to myself?"

"Of course. We'll connect tomorrow."

Sitting at his desk, Danny wondered if they should get to the wider family. He was convinced Gentrey was killed by someone who knew him, someone who had a grudge against him or someone who fit both categories. He would sleep on it and decide tomorrow.

In the late afternoon Danny drove to his appointment with Sam Parkel. They were to meet at the bagel shop near the corner of Spadina and Lonsdale in Forest Hill Village.

The Village, as the locals called it, was a few blocks long, shorter than the Bloor West Village Danny explored the day before. Forest Hill was one of Toronto's wealthier communities and it contained a number of Jewish families and institutions. The Village was a centre, full of restaurants, a small supermarket, coffee shops, a bookstore, six banks, hairdressers and other shops. It reflected the fact that Forest Hill had been a separate jurisdiction from Toronto until 1967, when it joined the larger city. Residents still felt it was special and unique.

Sam lived several blocks north of The Village. When Danny arrived, Sam was waiting in the bagel shop. They went to the assortment of bagels, in bins in the middle of the store, and each picked one out. Then they lined up to wait their turn. Danny took advantage of the opportunity to get some lox and cream cheese on his toasted poppy seed bagel. Sam ordered his 'everything' bagel toasted with butter. When served, they took their bagels and coffee to the tables in the back.

There was plenty of room but Sam noted something immediately, before they sat. "There are tables upstairs, Danny. At this time of day, I doubt anyone will be there. Should we sit there?"

"That's probably wise, Sam."

They went upstairs. Sam was correct. They were alone.

After asking about their families, the two men settled in comfortably with their coffee and afternoon nosh. Danny began, "I'd like to ask you about Dr. Gentrey. And I'd like to ask about CAMH, if you know much about it."

"Shoot."

"Can you tell me any more about Dr. Gentrey than you did on Friday night?"

"You know I liked him and admired his mind and his work. We connected on occasion at various professional events and have had coffee together a few times. When I was trying to get him to come to York, we had several meals, some with colleagues of mine in the department."

Sam continued, "He was a very civilized man, if that's a way of saying that he had character. He was polite, decent. He didn't flaunt his knowledge, as some accuse him of doing. He just knew a lot and was what you could call an enthusiast about learning and research. He probably belonged in the eighteenth century, at a salon in Paris. Was he controversial? Sure. But only in the sense that people who do breakthrough research are controversial. He challenged some models of personality theory. That's always controversial."

"Let's get on to CAMH", said Danny. "Do you know what his role was there?"

"I was at CAMH for several years, before it was called CAMH, until I went to the university. I still do some research with partners at CAMH. And that sometimes requires that I be there. Research in psychology is very collaborative, unlike some other humanistic disciplines, like English or philosophy. In this way, Gentrey was also different. He usually worked solo."

"What was Gentrey's relationship to other professionals at CAMH? If you know?"

"He was respected. Some were a little afraid of him because he often knew more about their specialties than they did. Most liked him because he was a good colleague. There were rumours that Gentrey was someone who might move into one of a few senior positions that are being created in a reorganization after the new CAMH, with its new buildings, has been completed."

"Would the cyclist incident have mattered?"

"It might. CAMH is very sensitive about its image, perhaps even more so than other teaching and medical institutions, which is saying a lot. That's because of the stigma that is still associated with mental illness. It wasn't long ago when it would have been called an insane asylum."

"So, the controversy might have held him back?"

"I don't know, Danny. I can tell you that today it would not be a serious matter in a university appointment, but those are different. I have a distinguished colleague who certainly has been on the border of being taken to court several times as a person who beats up females. He still gets grants, even awards."

"Who could tell me about this reorganization and the new positions?"

"The CEO and head of CAMH is Helen Comstead, a very able person. She'll know who's doing the searches and recommendations to the board."

"I'd like to get in touch with her, Sam."

"Not hard. That's one of the advantages of being the chair of a large major department. They answer the phone when you call. I know Helen. I could give her a call in the morning and let her know you need to see her. If she's not available, I'll leave a message. Or if you prefer, I'm certain that she'll respond to any police request without my introduction."

"I'd like you to make that call. I'll call her later in the morning to get an appointment."

"Consider it done. I'll phone at nine o'clock tomorrow."

"Thanks. This is very helpful."

Danny drove home, thinking he may have opened another avenue. He wondered if this one was the road to the solution.

XII

That Tuesday, Nadiri left the office at twelve-fifteen in the afternoon and drove with anticipation to her apartment in Thornhill.

The apartment was on the fourteenth floor of a sixteen-story building not far from Thornhill Secondary, where she went to high school and many of her enduring friendships began.

Her parents would have preferred her to live with them, as she was a single woman, but they accepted her decision to be independent and gave her some help for the down payment on her condo. Her mother convinced her father to do this when she said, "We need to let her be free to keep her with us." A wise insight into her daughter's temperament.

It was a small one-bedroom place, but as Nadiri often said, it was her haven. She also liked the wonderful view it had looking south to the city and west to the sunset. As she was driving she mused on how important having her own place had become to her. She also thought about herself in the context of what was happening in the wider society, and smiled as she did so, noting in her head her debt to Professor Mandelbaum.

She had invented a term 'solitaries' to describe a whole bunch of people in wealthy industrial societies. There were a large number of people living alone who preferred her kind of living arrangement. They liked being solitary, though they were not lonely at all. Many had full lives and enduring commitments to others, but they needed to be solitary to fulfill their own needs. She was one of them and knew several others. She wondered if her boss was also one of them.

She arrived at her building a bit after noon, parked the car and went upstairs. Her heart quickened when she found the door to the apartment unlocked.

"I'm home," she called as she entered.

"I'm in the kitchen," called a female voice. "I brought some lunch."

Nadiri hung up her coat, went to the kitchen and said, "I've missed you, Fiona. It's been almost two weeks."

"Me, too, Nadiri," answered Fiona as they embraced.

"You look wonderful," Nadiri said.

"I'm fine. Busy. Like you. You look terrific yourself. Some lunch?"

Nadiri played with the buttons on Fiona's blouse. "I want you for lunch. We can eat and talk afterwards."

Fiona smiled, took Nadiri's head in her hands and they kissed.

They never made it to the bedroom. They made love on the rug in the living room and on the couch. Afterwards, they did go to the bedroom, settled themselves entwined under the duvet and dozed for a while.

"That was wonderful," said Fiona as they came back into the world.

"How lucky we are," Nadiri said. "I don't want to think about where I would be if we hadn't found each other."

Fiona Dalett was older than Nadiri, forty-five to Nadiri's thirty-four. She lived nearby, in Markham. She was married to a wealthy developer and had three children, all in elite private schools. In addition to being the vice-chair of her two daughters' school, she was an elected school trustee in Markham. She and her husband were active in local politics and charities and she was on the board of the hospital. She was also being talked about as someone who would be an excellent candidate for the town council. Some even suggested that she might be the next nominee for the Liberal Party for the provincial legislature.

Fiona and Nadiri made a contrast. Fiona was fair, Nadiri dark. Nadiri was three inches taller than the five feet four Fiona and she was lean in contrast to Fiona's curvy body. Fiona's face was rounder than Nadiri's. Her eyes were hazel, Nadiri's almost black with a touch of gray. They had been in a relationship for the last two years. As far as each of them knew, this was their secret.

"How long can you stay?" Nadiri asked.

"Until a bit after three. I have to pick up the kids after school."

They put on robes and went to the kitchen. They got food and plates and, rather than eat at the table, settled themselves in the living room, the food on the coffee table, Fiona on a chair with her legs folded under her body, Nadiri sprawled on her couch.

"Let's not let two weeks go by before we see each other again," Fiona said.

"Absolutely," Nadiri said. "Do you know when you can be free?"

"I'll sort it out later today or tomorrow. I'll call you tomorrow. How busy are you?"

"Very. We have the murder of Dr. Gentrey to deal with; you will have heard of it. And another open case my boss will not let go of."

"Do you still like your new job?"

"I love it. It's exciting. I also like my boss, which matters a lot. He's a very interesting man. Not your ordinary cop."

"Not too interesting, I hope."

Nadiri laughed. "Nothing of that sort. I think he's involved with a woman who's a musician, but I'm not certain. Besides, he's not the kind of guy who would ever get romantically involved with a subordinate. He has a strong sense of what is ethical and is very professional. At the same time, he's able to mentor me and he gives me responsibility. He's tough, but he's not afraid to listen to others."

"Sounds like a good guy. Is he the one we saw on the news about the honour killing?"

"That's him. I found out he also plays the violin like an angel."

"And he quotes Shakespeare. A cop of a different order."

"Yes. A good guy. He's been very kind to me and I really like working for him. What about you?"

"The usual busy mom life. The kids are fine. I'm busy with school stuff and the board of the hospital. I don't know where it will lead. I'm going to have to make some decisions about my public life soon. Andrew is all for me getting involved. I think he thinks it's good for business, and Andrew likes anything that's good for business. I should be grateful. It keeps him busy and I can look after the kids and lead the kind of life that includes this."

"I want to ask you something." Nadiri said. "I need to tell my sister, Afari, that I'm gay and I have a lover. I won't mention your name or say anything that would identity you. I need to get her, my brother-in-law and my parents to stop finding men for me. It's awkward and annoying. And it's unfair to the men they invite to family meals. I'm not talking about coming out. This would be between me and my sister, the person closest to me. As you know, she's taken care of me all our lives. She knows how to keep a secret. She would never do anything that might harm me or any other member of the family."

"This is important to you?" Fiona asked.

"Yes. I've never lied to my sister. I feel that I'm doing so now."

"You've told me, but I'll ask again. This will not go further?"

"Your name, your age, and who you might be is not the issue. I just need to get my family to stop finding men. That part of my life is over. I'll simply tell Afari that I realized I'm gay and I have a lover."

"That's fine with me. I trust you Nadiri."

"You can. I love you, Fiona"

"And I love you. If life were different, we wouldn't need this conversation."

"Yes. But you must never jeopardize your relationship with your children."

"Of course. We understand each other so well." Fiona looked at her watch. "We have about forty-five minutes before I'll need to shower. Shall we try the bed for a change?"

XIII

One more. And then he will finally have done what he thought he should have done years ago. His psychiatrist said he should not live in regrets about the past. The past, the doctor said, could not be undone. He should look forward. Make a life that had some happiness in it.

What the doctor does not know, he thought, is that the past can be undone. You can make up for what happened. You can make those who caused your suffering pay for the past. They say they are sorry and they think that's enough. He wondered what the next one would say.

Again, he went slow. He took pleasure in the anticipation. He liked knowing he was in control of the future while the other had no knowledge that his days were numbered.

Now, he was changing the pattern of his life. He actually went for a hamburger for lunch with some of his coworkers. He went to a bar and had a beer, even though he didn't like beer, with some of the guys in the bowling league. He even worked up enough courage to say hello to his neighbours when he saw them. His psychiatrist praised his determination. He wondered if he would be praised if the doctor learned that he had taken revenge on two of the three people who had destroyed his life.

XIV

Danny got home at six-thirty that Tuesday. He thought about calling Nadiri to get an update, but gave her a little space, even if only for an afternoon and evening. He changed into comfortable clothes, put on some Boccherini, and settled into a relaxed mode.

Gabriella arrived a bit after seven. Danny suggested again that they go to the Danforth for supper. "There's a place I go to occasionally. You might like it. It's small, for a Greek place on the Danforth. Almost a mom and pop restaurant. About ten tables. Very homey and the food is always fine. They should have a table on a Tuesday night. If it were later in the week we'd need a reservation."

They walked the four blocks to the restaurant holding hands. Their conversation was almost domestic as they talked about their day and their families.

It was called Elena's. As they entered the owner/waiter smiled. "Welcome, Detective. I don't see enough of you these days. Only on television."

"Good evening, Constantine. May I introduce Ms. Agostini? Do you have a table for us?"

"For you, always." There were only two tables available. He led them to one in a quiet corner.

After a few minutes, Constantine brought menus, bread and pita, as well as olive oil and balsamic.

"What is Elena cooking tonight?" asked Danny.

"You have to tell me if this is a meat evening or not. Then I'll tell you." Constantine looked at Gabriella. "You know about his eating rules?"

"Oh, yes," Gabriella answered. "I've already prepared a meal for him."

"I think tonight the best thing in the kitchen is some fresh tuna that Elena can grill with Greek olive oil, oregano and some other spices she doesn't even tell me about."

Danny looked at Gabriella. She nodded. "That's excellent. We'll have the tuna her way and whatever salad she prepares. We'll start with some hummus and tzatziki."

"I'll bring a nice bottle of wine," Constantine said.

"You're obviously a regular," observed Gabriella.

"I'm here about twice a month. It's a cozy place, the food is wonderful, and Constantine and Elena are fine people. I like having a local place to go to. In good weather I come more often because I like eating outside."

Constantine appeared with the wine, saying, "This is an excellent Greek white. You can't get it at the LCBO, which knows nothing about Greek wine." He looked at Gabriella. "Maybe even less than they know about Italian wine. It's on the house."

"You know I can't do this, Constantine. Cops don't do on the house."

"To me you are not a cop, Detective. You're a neighbour. I've not seen you for a while. Neighbours like to treat other neighbours. Besides, you're not here alone. Your companion is gracing my establishment with her beauty."

"You're a dangerous man, Constantine," Danny said with a smile. "OK. You win. But only if you'll join us in a toast to the New Year."

"With pleasure." Constantine found a third glass, poured the wine and they clinked glasses. Constantine then brought their hummus and tzatziki, and poured more wine into their glasses.

Danny and Gabriella talked, quietly and attentively. After some time, Danny said, "I don't know why I feel so comfortable, as if we have been doing this for a lot more than a month."

"Me, too. Let's keep doing it and not overanalyze. Gabriella ate some of the tuna and said, "Wow. This woman knows how to cook. Simple, emphasizing the ingredients, not her fancy take on them. Even my Nonna would approve and she was tough."

"Tell Constantine. Nothing would make him happier. They're a very devoted couple."

They ordered dessert and coffee after the main course, and continued talking.

"I've been thinking about us, Danny. In fact, I've been thinking these last few days about little else. I had to remind myself to practice and look at scores. There is something I need to ask. Does Avi know about us?"

"Ruth knows about us, though I didn't go into detail. Avi is smart enough to have figured out something is happening because you were at the Chanukah celebration and I let you stay to help with the cleanup."

"You need to tell him, Danny."

"Of course. I've told Avi about every date I've had. I'm just waiting for a time when we're alone and at ease."

"Soon, Danny. Very soon."

"Yes. You're right."

"When you tell him, he is almost certainly going to ask about whether we intend to have children."

"Really?"

"Danny, I teach boys his age. This happens to Catholics as well. This is a real concern. We've not discussed this, only because the relationship is so new. I want you to tell Avi that we do not intend to have kids. This is a relationship between two mature adults."

"Do you want children?"

"I thought I wanted children a long time ago. I've made a life without children and I'm content to continue that way, at this time in my life."

"Is this because I have Avi?"

"No, that's where I am. I'm fine with it."

"Why do you think Avi will ask about it?"

"He needs to know he remains at the centre of our life. You're a great father. He needs to have you for himself. At fourteen, he does not need what he would regard as a rival."

"Insightful, Gabriella. I'll look after it."

"I need to say one more thing. I do not want to do anything to get in the way of you and Avi. He is part of who you are. Your love for him is wonderful for you both." She paused. "I want you. I want an intimate and meaningful relationship. I think we can be very good for one another. I've not had this feeling before. However, if our relationship in any way hurts what you and Avi have with one another, I'll withdraw. It will totally break my heart, Danny, but I'll get out of the way."

"I get it. You're as sensitive as I thought. Let's keep going as we decided. I'll speak to Avi and reassure him. By the way, I have a key to my place at home for you."

She smiled and reached into her purse. "This is a good sign, Danny.

I made keys for you to the condo. Here they are. The only other person who has keys is Beatrice."

"You're joining Avi and Ruth. Our lives are expanding, my lovely woman. Let's get the bill and test my bedroom."

"What a good idea."

XV

In the morning, Danny met briefly with Nadiri. He then checked with an aide and found out the home address of John Everson. He pushed paper until ten and then called Helen Comstead at CAMH. He was put through immediately.

"Good morning, Sergeant. Sam called and told me you would be in touch. How can we help?"

"Thanks. Good morning to you, Dr. Comstead. I don't want to go into details, at least not over the phone. I'd like to meet with the person who's responsible for the searches you're doing. I understand from Sam that CAMH is reorganizing as a result of the new facility you've finished. Some information about new positions and who is part of the search might be helpful."

"I won't ask you why at this time. I assume this is something you'd like to be done immediately."

"Yes. This is a murder inquiry about one of your own. It has the highest priority."

"A good way of putting it, Sergeant. Could you give me your number? I'll call you back in about ten minutes."

After eight minutes his phone rang. It was CAMH.

Helen Comstead said, "Sergeant, the person who's responsible on a day-to-day basis for the searches is the vice-president for human resources, Martin Jarvis. He's in a meeting at the moment. I spoke with his secretary and arranged for you to meet with him and me at one o'clock today. Is that time alright with you?"

"Excellent. If you're this efficient all the time I'm going to recommend you start organizing the police. Seriously, that's what we need."

"We'll meet in my office. Building B, room six-twenty-seven."

"I'll see you shortly."

Danny arrived at CAMH early, reflecting his eagerness to meet with the two administrators. He walked up Ossington Avenue to look at the street a lot of people were saying had the best group of new restaurants in the city. This week was becoming one where he explored neighbourhoods in his downtime.

Ossington was simultaneously funky and gentrifying. It had health food stores, an organic butcher and what *The Globe and Mail* food columnist said was the best pho in Toronto, in a hole-in-the-wall Vietnamese restaurant. There was an interesting Spanish tapas bar, and several bistros with unique cuisine. All this in the midst of Portuguese shops, including a Churrasqueira advertising itself as a royal place to eat. It was below freezing, but there had yet to be any serious snow and the walk was pleasant.

He turned around, walked back on the other side of the street and arrived at Comstead's office at precisely one o'clock.

Helen Comstead was of medium height, a brunette, dressed with quiet elegance in a pantsuit. While Comstead was a doctor, her colleague, Martin Jarvis, was a hospital administrator who had been at several other major institutions in Ontario.

"Coffee, Sergeant?" asked Comstead.

"If you're having one, I'll join you."

"How can we help?"

"Dr. Comstead, Mr. Jarvis, I'm first going to ask that this conversation be confidential. We're in an ongoing investigation, I'm gathering and analyzing information, and I need to work quietly."

"Absolutely, Sergeant Miller," said Comstead. "We're used to confidentiality." Jarvis agreed.

"Let me tell you where we are," Danny said. "This is a case in which a number of avenues are being explored. What we are doing is casting a big net and then working more or less by elimination. If I can make an analogy it would be like a doctor knowing that someone is very ill but finding it difficult to discover the cause of the illness. Was it from something the patient ate? Was it from the environment? Did it emanate from the liver? The kidneys? So, what the doctor does is test for everything. Then he eliminates what doesn't seem to be the cause. Slowly, he's down to one or two possibilities."

"That's clear, Sergeant."

"My point is this conversation could help to find the murderer.

It could also eliminate people from the net. I don't know. It might be what a colleague calls a 'eureka' moment; it might be a 'let's-keep-going-and-we-can-eliminate-something' moment."

"I understand," Jarvis said. "Now tell us what you need to know to help make better sense of what happened."

"Exactly," Danny said. "What I need to know is what senior positions are part of the search. That's first. Then I want to know who is on the list. Can I assume that there are long short lists, perhaps short short lists by now?"

"Yes," Jarvis said. "Several senior people are retiring, having seen the reconstruction through successfully. As well, the organizational structure is changing because we're a bigger place with a wider and more diverse mission than we had before. Three senior medical positions are in the process of being filled. We're close to deciding on at least two of them. They are two vice-presidents, research and clinical practice, and a physician-in-chief. Do you want me to discuss any other positions? There are a few openings for administrative types like me."

"No, not yet at least. I'm interested in the medical side. Was Dr. Gentrey one of those in consideration?"

"He was," Jarvis said. "He was short-listed for the two vice-presidential positions, along with three other candidates for each."

"I assume you would have decided he was a serious candidate before you short-listed him. The bicycle incident three years ago didn't disqualify him."

"Yes," Comstead responded. "Some on the search committees worried about this. We had lengthy discussions and agreed that he had been found not to be guilty of anything other than being in a bad place at a bad time. We decided not to let that get in his way. Three years had passed. Any negative public relations issues would die down quickly."

"Who else was on the short list with him?"

"They're still on the list," Jarvis said. "We'll be making the final choices next week."

"I need names, Mr. Jarvis. I said this meeting is totally confidential." He looked at Comstead. "I am used to confidentiality, too."

Comstead nodded and looked to Jarvis, who then spoke. "There are three candidates for each. For the research position there are Drs. Louise Chung, Olivia Knapp, and Evan Soberman. For the clinical practice position, there are Drs. Zane Bruder, John Everson and Sara

Feldson."

"If Dr. Gentrey were alive and well, which of these positions do you think he might have been offered?"

Comstead said, "He was most suited for the clinical practice position, though he was such an unusual colleague we thought he could also qualify for the research job. We also have a strong group for the research position, including two outside candidates. Given that—all of this is speculation—we might have gone inside for the clinical practice position. There are also two outside candidates there. Dr. Everson, who you know, is now the only inside person on the list."

Danny relaxed, signalling he was done with getting information. "Thanks. This is very useful. Can I ask you, informally, whether you have any thoughts about who might have wanted to murder Dr. Gentrey?"

Jarvis replied, "I didn't really know him. We had little contact and I haven't gotten deeply involved in his area."

"I knew him well," Comstead said, "and, like many people around here, I had a lot of admiration for his mind and his work. I found him fun. He knew everything inside the box and a lot outside the box. He was an original thinker. There aren't many of those. Some people were frightened by him, but that says more about them than about him. And you don't kill somebody because he causes you to be uncomfortable when he is around. I could speculate more. The profession comes across patients who have violent tendencies. And, of course, it might not be related to his professional life at all."

Danny said, "The net is out in both those directions, doctor. Even further. We've eliminated lots of people. There is still a list."

"I hope Dr. Everson has been helpful," Comstead said. "We all want this solved. I know his family."

"He's been helpful, and so have you. I appreciate your assistance. And it was good coffee. A lot better than we have at the station."

"It's an indulgence of mine, Sergeant," she said. "I'm addicted to good caffeine."

They said their goodbyes and Danny left. He was so deep in reflection that when he got to his car he didn't remember having walked to it.

He took a detour before going back to the station. He drove up Ossington to Harbord, across Harbord to Spadina, and up Spadina to

St. Clair, heading toward Gentrey's office on St. Clair. His destination was Everson's home at 37 Dunvegan Road, a short walk from Gentrey's office. Some instinct told him to take a look at it. He parked a few blocks away, on St. Clair. When he got out of the car he took a toque from the pocket of his anorak and put it on. He then walked across St. Clair to Dunvegan Road. He strolled passed the Everson home slowly, since no one seemed to be around. He saw what he expected to see, walked around the block back to St. Clair, got into the car and drove to the station. At the station, Danny sat quietly at his desk for a time, doodling and writing notes on a pad. He called Everson's office.

Everson was not in, but an administrative assistant answered. Danny asked for an appointment. "It will not take more than ten minutes," he said, "but it's important. As you may know, Dr. Everson has been helping the police as a consultant."

"He's booked for the rest of today and tomorrow," the assistant replied. "How about two days from now at two-thirty?"

"Too late. This is an emergency. When does he start tomorrow?"

"Nine o'clock, as usual."

"Tell him I'll be at his office at a quarter to nine. As I said, it will only take ten minutes. Please call me if this doesn't work for some reason."

Danny then called Nadiri, who was working with other officers on the floor below. "Hold yourself ready. I may need you for a meeting with the Inspector this afternoon."

After that, Danny made another call, this time to McIntyre. He was put through at his insistence. "Sydney, I need to meet with you and Nadiri. This is very important. Are you free?"

"I'll be free in half an hour, Danny. Come then."

When Nadiri and Danny settled in McIntyre's office, Danny said, "I may have solved the Gentrey case. Or I may be totally wrong. I need to test my ideas out on you."

"Go on, Danny," McIntyre said. "No good idea is too wild to pursue. We'll be your sounding-board."

"Let me tell it to you as it came to me. Several things came together and then I pursued the idea further. First, I wondered why the killing was done in his private practice on a Tuesday. Tuesday and Thursday were Gentrey's days at CAMH. What was he doing in his office? Better yet, what was he doing in his office with another person? Could that person have been a private patient who he was seeing in a crisis? That's what I thought it must be. Along the way, as you will see, I came to think it might also be a friend or a colleague. Then there was a coincidence, as Nadiri knows."

She said, "The name of the mother of the woman killed in the bike incident was Marilyn Everson."

"Yes. I casually mentioned it to Everson and he was quick to tell me that Marilyn Everson was his sister. The young woman, Elise Edwards, was his niece. In fact, he was her godfather. He gave some background. Elise was ill, bipolar, and had a long history of mood swings and erratic behaviour. She had attempted suicide six months earlier. He was genuinely sad, both for her and for the parents. I guess what troubled me was he didn't tell me this when we first talked about the profile of Gentrey's killer. He's a professional and knows the importance of disclosure. I don't think he was hiding it, but his implication that it didn't matter in his thinking was bothersome."

"Danny, are you going where I think you're going?" asked McIntyre.

"Yes. But I have to tell you how I got there and then we can talk."

"Keep going."

"I realized a few days ago we might only solve this case by getting into the head of the murderer, by figuring out the motive. You'll ask, as I did to myself, why would Everson wait three years to get retribution? I thought the motive might be more complicated. I then spoke with a person I met at a family dinner. He's the chair of the department of psychology at York. He knew Gentrey well. He also knew enough about CAMH to tell me they were doing searches for three new senior medical positions as a result of a new organizational structure. All this is the result of the new buildings and a larger mission. I digress. What's important are the searches. I discussed them this morning with the head of CAMH, Dr. Helen Comstead, and the head of human resources who is conducting the searches, Martin Jarvis. In confidence, they told me that Gentrey had been on the short list for two of the three. Two vice-presidencies. Research and Clinical Practice. Also, the searches are not finished. The results will be announced shortly. There had been four names on each short list. Now there are three. Everson is on the short list for clinical practice. The other two are outside candidates, which Comstead noted gave Everson an advantage, given the politics of the thing. I don't need to go into that."

"Is all this coincidence or do those facts point to Everson?" McIntyre asked.

"Right. I agree. They point to him. No smoking gun. There is one more matter. I found out Everson's home address. It's on Dunvegan Road, a short walk across St. Clair from Gentrey's office. A little over an hour ago I took a stroll on Dunvegan. Nice house. Tasteful plants in the front. Lots of rocks in the front garden, about the size of the instrument that killed Gentrey."

Danny sat back. The three of them were silent for a full minute. Nadiri broke the spell. "If it was Everson, that explains why we're getting nowhere with the patients and the cyclists."

"Yes," McIntyre said. "I'm very surprised, but getting nowhere with the others doesn't make it Everson. Still, Danny, you give pause for thought. What do you think we should do?"

"I've given it lots of thought. I'm really not rushing into this. I realized that we didn't ask Everson, who was a colleague of ours in collaboration and consultation, the most important question."

"What's that, sir?" Nadiri asked.

"Where were you between five and eight on the evening that Gentrey was killed? I made an appointment with Everson at eight forty five tomorrow morning. Nadiri, I'd like you to come along. I intend to ask the question. By the way, Everson is my height, about six feet. And he's right-handed."

"So you think that the motive may be more complicated than revenge for his niece?" McIntyre asked.

"John Everson is a complex and bright person," Danny answered. "It may be a compound motive rather than a singular one. I had to invent the term compound motive, but it makes sense to me."

"Well, we can't do anything until you ask him the question. If he doesn't have an alibi, Danny, you may be a genius. If he does have one, I'll credit you with a fine and active imagination."

"I don't mind being wrong. The point is we have to pursue this avenue."

"I agree. Call me as soon as you leave Everson's in the morning."

"I'm not finished, ma'am. I think we should talk about what to do if there's no sound alibi. Everson's no fool. I don't want him destroying any evidence if he did it. I think that up until now he believes he's not a suspect. He is, after all, on our side. After tomorrow morning, that could change."

"I see what you're saying," McIntyre said. "Fair enough. Prepare the affidavit necessary to get the necessary warrants tomorrow morning to search his house and his office. I assume you think there might be evidence in his briefcase or in his jacket or something of that sort."

"Yes. We have Gentrey's DNA. If there's blood on anything then we might have our smoking gun. Also, we need to look at the rocks in the front garden. It's a perfect place to replant the weapon, if that was it. I hope there are no rocks in the back garden. The forensics people will be angry enough at me without that added to it. I also hope it doesn't snow tonight. Now, of course, we can detain him if he doesn't have an alibi, but I don't want the egg on our faces if he didn't do it. And if he tries to run he would implicate himself. If anything, I think he'll get his lawyer immediately. So, if he has no alibi, we need to search his house and his clothes as soon as possible after I see him."

"I hear you, Danny. I'm not yet convinced it's Everson. Nonetheless, we can justify a search in the interests of either finding that you're correct or eliminating him from concern. If necessary, you'll have your warrant an hour after you call. Let's start the process."

Danny filled out the affidavit. Then he and Nadiri left and returned to their office. She asked, "Do you seriously think it's him, sir?"

"Yes. I'm off, Nadiri. Time for a bite to eat and then some music with friends. Tomorrow morning will be interesting."

XVI

Nadiri drove the two of them to CAMH. They arrived at Everson's office at eight forty and took a seat in the waiting room. Everson himself appeared at eight forty-five and invited them into his office. Danny introduced Nadiri and thanked Everson for seeing them.

"My administrative assistant said it was an emergency," Everson said. "How can I help you?"

"I told her it was an emergency to get here. She was putting me off for two days and I didn't want this to wait. As I told her, it will only take a few minutes."

"Fair enough."

"I have a question to ask you. It's the result of my own negligence. I forgot to ask you the question we ask everybody involved."

"What would that be?" Everson asked.

"It is the simplest question we ask and I need to ask it of you. Where were you between five and eight on the Tuesday evening the Dr. Gentrey was killed?"

"Seriously, Danny? I'm supposed to be one of the good guys. I'm helping you and I've helped the police in the past."

"Seriously. I need to get your answer and get the question out of the way."

"Let me look in my diary."

Everson paged through a diary on his desk and then said. "I was here until about five-thirty. I had a patient here until five and then I cleared up some paper and left. I went home and I was at home the whole evening."

"Was anyone else at home with you?"

"Not that evening. My wife is an economist with the Royal Bank and she was in Ottawa for some meetings with the government. Our son has his own apartment in town."

"Did you call anyone? Did anyone call you at home?"

"Not that I remember. My wife and I did speak at about nine that night. If you're asking whether I have an iron-clad alibi, the answer is no."

"I have to ask, John. There are questions you must ask in your professional life. Mine too."

"I understand."

Danny rose. "I'll let you get on with your day. And Officer Rahimi and I will get on with trying to identify the murderer. We'll be in touch."

"Let me know what you find. Especially if it's someone related to CAMH."

"Will do."

Danny and Nadiri were silent as they left the building and walked to the car. It was parked on Fennings Street, a quiet side street. When they were seated, Nahiri spoke first. "No alibi, sir. If he did it, he's a good actor."

"Yes, Nadiri. He's a contained man. Don't drive yet.

Danny then called McIntyre, who was waiting impatiently. "Sydney, he claims to have been at home from roughly six that evening. No one else was home. No one called him at home and he didn't call anyone. The hours from about six to nine are unaccounted for."

They spoke further, McIntyre wanting a report on the actual conversation. When Danny finished, she said, "What do you think?"

"We should get the warrants and get to work. Fast. I think Everson is figuring out what he should do. Once he learns of the warrants, he'll call his lawyer."

"I must admit, Danny, there is a piece of me wondering if we're pushing this too fast."

"It's all we have, Sydney. We can explain why we're doing it. If we don't do it, that also requires an explanation."

"We'll go ahead. I've already informed the head of homicide and he has informed the chief. They said we should make the decision and they'll support it. I'll make the arrangement for the warrants as soon as we get off the phone."

"Good. Nadiri and I will be coming back to the station. See you soon."

Nadiri started the car and drove north to Dundas. "Are you going out on a limb, sir?"

"Perhaps, Nadiri. I don't think so, but others might. There's enough here to support the search, as far as I'm concerned."

"If it's worth anything, sir, I agree with you."

"I'm pleased you agree. I thought you did. If you didn't you probably would have told me privately."

"I would have. I'm a rookie at this and don't always trust my judgment. I still second-guess myself."

"So do I, Nadiri. So do I. I wish these sorts of things were clearer than they are these days. In our world there always seems to be a bit of fog."

When they arrived at the station, they went directly to McIntyre's office.

"We're moving," she said. "The forensics people are ready. All I need is the signature from the justice of the peace. I should have it soon."

Until now we pursued several of those avenues at once. Now we'll wait to see what this one yields."

"Yes. Either we have it done or we slog on," McIntyre responded. "I've experienced this kind of thing before, as you have. Nadiri, the anticipation can drive you around the bend. It's like waiting for a jury to come in with a verdict."

"I agree," said Danny. "I think I'm just going to go to the community centre and see if I can get a partner for a squash game. It'll be a good way to deal with the energy that is bottled up. I'll be back around lunchtime."

"Good," said McIntyre. "Nothing will happen for a while. Enjoy the break."

XVII

The dénouement came quickly, almost as an anti-climax to the tension in the air. At four o'clock that afternoon, McIntyre appeared in Danny's and Nadiri's office. They looked up at her in anticipation.

"It looks like you were right, Danny. The searchers found traces of blood in the pocket of a beat up old leather jacket that was hanging in the hall closet. It's being tested at this moment. They also found a rock. Not in the garden, but, strangely enough, on the desk in Everson's study at home. He was using it as a paperweight. It has traces of blood, and skin, too. It's been sent to the lab as first priority."

She sat down. The three reacted as if they were pricked balloons. They needed a moment to get back to normal.

"Where do we go from here?" Danny asked.

"I think we wait for the results. There's no danger of Everson leaving. He's too smart for that, and we have some people watching his house."

The results of the tests arrived two days later, on Saturday. They were clear. Gentrey's DNA was found on the rock. The blood on the rock and in the coat matched Gentrey's blood group. Everson was arrested that day, charged with first-degree murder, and jailed. After Everson's arrest, Danny and McIntyre talked in her office.

She asked, "What I don't get is why he put the rock on the desk. Why not get rid of it?"

"I think we would need a psychiatrist to answer that. Did he think he was invulnerable? Did he, somewhere in his inner being, want to be caught? Did he want to show how clever he was? There are those three and a hundred other questions. If there's a trial, we'll learn more."

"I want to apologize for doubting you. Danny."

"You shouldn't, Sydney. We're colleagues. We need to test ideas on one another and we need to be honest with one another. Over the five years we've worked together, I've questioned some of your decisions. Often wrongly. We need one another's honesty. I'd like to think I'm right a reasonable percentage of the time. But I'm also wrong sometimes."

"A good attitude, Danny. Not always taken by all of our colleagues. You won't like to hear this, but we'll need to have another dreaded press conference. This is not as big as the Nizamani murder. But a prominent person killing another prominent person is big news. I've spoken with the communications people and the chief. We'll just give facts. If there is a trial more will come out. Still, the press needs a chance to ask questions, even if we can't answer some of them. In the next hour there will be a press release. Tomorrow morning we'll have the conference."

"I have to make some phone calls to people who helped with our investigation, Sydney. To Louise Eamons, Deirdre Upton, Helen Comstead and later tonight from home to a guy named Sam Parkel. I'll see you in the morning."

Though it was a Sunday, the press conference was well-attended. The arrest came as a surprise to everyone, and it was important news.

McIntyre began with a long statement giving the bare facts, elaborating on the short press release. As she was ending she said, "I want people to know that this case would not have been solved without the hard work and professionalism of Detective Sergeant Daniel Miller. He led the team and he found the solution. In these last few weeks the city owes him a big thanks for his work."

Danny shook his head and would have given anything but his violin for the floor to open and swallow him. He stood and took the microphone.

"Inspector McIntyre is kind. I led a team of detectives, street constables and others, all of whom worked hard to get this done. This is like a hockey game. One person can't win alone. You need the hard work of others. If you'll permit me to follow my analogy, there were a lot of people who have earned assists and praise for their slogging in the corners in this instance. I'm grateful to them."

"Sergeant, what led you to Dr. Everson?" asked *The Globe and Mail* reporter.

"There were a lot of coincidences. Finally, too much piled up and we had to follow through. I want to add that this was a case where we had a lot of possibilities. I told someone there were many avenues that could lead to a solution, not one. We worked hard on all of them simultaneously. One paid off."

"Do you think the bicycle incident had anything to do with it?" asked the reporter from *The Star*.

"I think, as Inspector McIntyre said, it was part of the mix. I don't think it's possible to go further than that with what we know at this time. Perhaps if there is a trial, more will come out."

The Global TV correspondent followed up, "Do you think there will be a trial? He certainly has a good lawyer."

"I don't know. Probably. There is always a presumption of innocence and the crown will need to prove its case in a court of law. I shouldn't speculate. Our job is to find the murderer, as I said about the Nizamani case. Then, the courts and the justice system take over. For what happens from now, you'll have to ask the crown attorney and Dr. Everson's lawyer for more information."

He recognized the CBC reporter, Rosalie Daniel. "Sergeant, what was the motive? Yes, he did it. Can you tell us why he did it?"

"I've thought a lot about that. I have yet to come up with a clear answer. Why rational people do irrational things is sometimes beyond me. I think the motive is a complicated one. Something that can't be fit into a short sentence. Dr. Everson is a complex individual, just like everyone else. I'm not going to shrink the shrink. We'll learn more as time passes."

"Is this another case for Shakespeare, Sergeant?" asked the reporter from *The Sun*.

"I think there are very few, if any, people who understood who we are better than William Shakespeare. However, there were a few who might be in his class. I think, if I had one person to go to, I'd pick Sigmund Freud for this one."

There were some laughs, of recognition, not of amusement.

Rosalie then asked, "How does it feel to be so successful Sergeant? You've solved two major murders in a short period of time."

"First, I have not solved them. The homicide squad did. Second, I'm not always successful. There's still the murder of James Frawley on my desk. It's been there a long time, too long."

Rosalie persisted, "When does that become a cold case?"

"When they bury me, Rosalie. It's on my mind."

McIntyre intervened, as she had done in the previous press conference. "Thanks, everyone. If we get more information, we'll see you again."

When Danny went back with Sydney to her office Danny said, "I think you're going to tell me, Sydney, to take a bit of a break. I could probably use it. Let me give you your own advice. Even inspectors need a break."

"You're right, Danny. If you heed my advice, I promise I'll do so too."

"Good. We'll both be better off for it. I missed my weekly squash game this morning, but I may yet have time to have a bagel with my friends. I'm off."

XVIII

That Sunday night, Danny had arranged to have Avi come for dinner and sleep over. He would drive him to school the next morning before going to work. He made a Chinese stir-fry, beef and vegetables in black bean sauce, accompanied by fried rice. It was something he knew Avi liked and was unlikely to be served by Rachel or Ruth.

They had some father-son talk, about school, Avi's basketball team, Danny's work, and plans for the next week.

As they were having fruit for dessert, Danny said, "You know I tell you about my dating and stuff like that. I need to let you know that Gabriella and I are entering into a relationship. This is the first serious relationship I've had since your mother, and I really don't have a sense of where it will go."

"I figured that out on Chanukah, Dad. You looked at her differently from the way you look at other people."

"Do you have any concerns?"

"Aunt Ruth spoke to me about it. We had a good talk. She said that while she had some questions—you know, about the Jewish matter—she wanted you to be happy, and it was clear to her that you were very happy being with Gabriella. She called you a feiner mensch and said you would do what was right."

"Did she really use the term feiner mensch?"

"She did. I know what a mensch is. You and mom have told me often enough that you want me to grow up to be a mensch—a good and kind and caring person. What's a feiner mensch?"

"It was a term your grandmother, my mother, used. She used it very rarely—maybe for four or five people, including my dad, who, I would add, was a feiner mensch. I never heard it used by anyone else, so it may be a term that comes from the Carpathians, where our family lived. It means someone who is not only a mensch, but has the special quality of being outstanding, someone who can be relied upon at all times to be kind, empathetic, someone who goes out of his way to be a mensch. Your Aunt Ruth is my example of that kind of person. We often disagree but she is always there."

"Well, she said that about you. She said you sometimes drove her crazy, but it didn't matter because she loved you and you were a feiner mensch."

"I'm honoured. It's a lot better than any medal."

"I see that, dad. About you and Gabriella. What do you mean that you're in a relationship?"

"We have a commitment to one another. We care for one another. We look after one another. We are loyal to one another."

"Are you going to get married?"

"It hasn't come up. I don't think so. We've both been married. The ceremony doesn't seem important. Also, at this time, we won't be living together."

"How old is Gabriella?"

"Thirty-four."

"Do you think you'll have children?"

'Bless you, Gabriella,' Danny thought. He leaned forward to emphasize his next remarks. "No. We will not have children. She is happy in her life and I do not want any other children. Avi, my son, I have all the children I want in you. My first commitment is to you. You are my guy forever. In order for your mother and your step-father to be happy they needed to have children and you have lovely half-sisters. I do not want any child but you."

They were both very moved. They rarely talked like this since they rarely needed to do so. But this was important. Avi broke the silence. "She seems like a nice person, dad."

"She is a nice person, Avi. Better than nice. The two of you will get to know one another over the next several months. Let your relationship develop as it happens."

They turned on the television. The Raptors game had already started. They settled on the couch and Avi snuggled familiarly into Danny's shoulder, which gave Danny enormous pleasure. Occasionally, they commented on what was happening.

Just before halftime, Avi said, "Dad?"

"Yes, Avi."

"I also think you're a feiner mensch, and I want you to be happy."

PART IV

I

Danny and McIntyre took some time off, as did Nadiri. Not much, but McIntyre spared both Danny and Nadiri a new murder case. For the next few weeks, she said, they needed to write their reports, and would also be assigned to some violent crimes.

Late one afternoon in the week after the Gentrey case was solved, Danny went to the local LCBO on the Danforth to pick up some wine, both for his home and for when he ate at Gabriella's. As he was deciding on a vintage burgundy, he heard his name called. He turned around and saw Howard Mandelbaum in jeans and a sweatshirt.

"Good to see you. Do you live around here, too?"

"A few blocks west."

"I'm several blocks east."

"Do you have time for a coffee?" Mandelbaum asked. "There's a Timothy's a few blocks away at Carrot Common."

"Sure. I'm alone this evening. Let me have five minutes to choose the right wine."

"Good. I'll call my wife to let her know I'll be along later."

After they left the liquor store, they walked quickly to Timothy's. It was January in Toronto. The snow had come. Everyone outside was so bundled up they looked like the Michelin Man, and all who walked into the wind had their shoulders hunched and heads down.

They got their coffees and found a table.

"I'm glad we met," said Danny. "I had made a mental note to give you a call. I've been taking some time off these last few days."

"From what I can tell, you've earned it. I'm the reverse. The new semester has started and now we drag through the winter in academe."

"Well, please don't murder anybody. We're busy enough."

"Don't worry. I think it was Henry Kissinger who said professors spend a lot of time, energy and intelligence arguing over very little. We only murder one another in British mystery novels. How is Nadiri doing?"

"Just fine. You pegged her correctly. I'm glad she wound up with me rather than in your department."

"I'm not. But that's just knowing what an asset she can be."

"She was especially fine in the Nizamani case, as you know. Her sensibility to the context and willingness to be totally engaged made a difference."

"You know, Danny, someone once defined a sociologist as an academic who gets a large grant from the Canada Council to find the whereabouts of the local whorehouse."

Danny laughed. "I didn't put it like that, but that's what I thought as well, as a guy who majored in political science. You and Nadiri have managed to convince me otherwise. I guess you might say that people think that a detective is a guy who takes five days to figure out who shot whom when there are ten witnesses to the event."

"Well, you've been giving your profession a good name lately. The Gentrey murder can't have been easy to deal with."

"No, it wasn't. That's one of the reasons I made a note to call you. I need to speak about it with someone who knows it's confidential."

"Of course. Like you, I suspect, I'm good with secrets. Let me try this out on you. When you said at the press conference you weren't going to shrink the shrink—a nice way of putting it by the way—you didn't tell the whole truth."

"Was it that obvious?"

"Not at all. You told the truth in that you said you weren't going to do it. However, I can't see how you solved the murder without having done it."

"You're correct. This required a different method from the Nizamani case. I spent a lot of time trying to get into the head of the killer. Not only Everson's, others' too."

"What led you to Everson? Sydney basically told the public that you solved it. More or less by yourself."

"Let's not get into that. It bothers me. What led me to Everson? A combination of things. Several inconsistencies. And the way he behaved about some matters. That opened it up. Before this occurred, I thought the only way to solve a case was to understand the motive of the murderer. It wasn't sociology this time, it was psychology. So—I would never say this at a press conference, maybe in my memoirs before I die—I had to imagine myself into the heads of several people. Everson started to give me some answers."

"You wouldn't speculate in public about the motive. What do you think it was?"

"Very complicated. Everson is a complex person. I think it was a combination of three things, all on the list of sins. First of all, he was angry about the death of his goddaughter and he carried that anger with him for a long time. Not only was he angry, but he had to work in the same place as the person he held responsible for her death."ü

Danny took a sip of coffee. "The second sin is envy. Like many of his colleagues, he envied Gentrey's mind, his learning, his earlier public life. He resented the man because he was one of those people—Northrop Frye is the best Canadian example—who was bigger than their specialty. He even felt threatened by it because Everson thought very well of himself."

"And number three?"

"The third sin was ambition. This has not come out at all, Howard, and it may never come out at the trial. Everson thought Gentrey stood in the way of his advancing to a much more major position at CAMH. As a very wise person said about human nature, 'men rise from one ambition to another: first, they seek to secure themselves against attack, and then they attack others.'"

"Wise, surely. Who said it?"

"Machiavelli."

"I think one of your strengths, Danny, is not to be wedded to a single methodology. Many in my field and elsewhere fit the events into their chosen methodology. I like to choose the right methodology to deal with circumstances."

"That works better, Howard. I like to think outside the box. Boxes can be useful, but they can also be very limiting. Thanks for listening. I needed to bounce all this off someone."

"It fits for me. Well done. Of course, we'll never know for certain. But your ideas got to the solution. By the way, you got it wrong again."

Danny smiled. "What did I get wrong this time? Do you have another Greek myth for me to look up?"

"Not a Greek myth. Do you know the name Dupin?"

"I've heard of it. Where from?"

"He's the first modern fictional detective. Before Sherlock Holmes. He was created by Edgar Allan Poe. The first, and most famous, of the Dupin stories is *The Murders in the Rue Morgue*, which you can get online. In it, Dupin challenges the methods of the police. He does it by discussing how to get into the mind of the murderer. So, yes, Freud would be useful, but it's Poe who I would have cited as the thinker best suited to understand Everson."

"I'll read it. Tell me, Howard, are you always a professor?"

"Are you always a cop?"

"Touché. Answer a question with a question. A very Jewish thing. I'll read it. I'm glad we bumped into one another."

"I am too. Let's keep it up occasionally."

"Good idea."

II

Nadiri arranged to have an evening with her sister during the down time that week. "Come to my place," she said. "I rarely get the chance to cook for you. I need to have a talk with my big sister."

When Afari arrived, the two talked about family as Nadiri prepared their supper in the kitchen. They sat down to a frittata with Iranian caviar, and a green salad with olive oil, lemon and lots of garlic.

"You do this well," Afari said. "Do you cook a lot?"

"Very little. I live mainly on simple food. About once a month I'll have two or three girlfriends for dinner and then I get to practice."

After they finished, Nadiri made tea and served bamieh, a doughy sweet from a local Iranian bakery.

"Now, Nadiri, why are we having this meal?"

"You know me so well, Afari. I have something I need to speak with you about. I haven't talked about this with anyone else. I don't even know how to talk about it. I need you to know, and I need you to keep a secret."

"We've had many secrets between us, Nadiri. They go back to our childhood."

"I know. I trust you entirely. You've always looked after me. I am grateful to have an older sister like you."

"What is it, my dear?"

"I'll tell you a story. Interrupt at any time."

Afari could tell Nadiri had rehearsed this several times. It was that important. And Nadiri knew Afari was a fine listener, the best one in her world.

"As you know, since I was eighteen, I dated a number of men. Some were from our background and some were others, mainly from the university. Those of our background were often introduced to me by the family.

"There were a few who seemed to suit me better than the others. In some cases—you know them—we dated—or whatever the right word is—for several months. And, of course, our parents and others wondered if it would result in marriage. More than that, in some cases they hoped it would end in marriage.

"Over the years, I had sex with three men. I mean we went to bed, not just teenaged fooling around. With these men, I experienced sexual relations a number of times."

Afari nodded. "Of course. You were a grown woman in her twenties. In this culture, something like that might happen."

"Oh, Afari, I had some guilt at first. But not really. We are a worldly family. The problem wasn't guilt. The problem was that I did not have the ecstasy that is supposed to be associated with sex. It was flat. To be frank, I enjoyed pleasuring myself more than I did with these men. I wondered about it. A lot. And I hoped that someone would come along with whom I could have that joy and with whom I wanted to live."

"It didn't happen?"

"No, you're wrong. It happened. One day about eight years ago I was at a gathering of women at my friend Amelia's house. You know her well. I was sitting next to someone I had not met before. Her name was Jessica Rogan. She seemed a wild spirit. Full of life, with extraordinary energy. Curious. Attractive. We were at a table in the dining room. Towards the end of the evening I felt a hand on my thigh. I turned; she smiled and gave a brief nod. I was supposed to find this disgusting. Afari, it was electric. It was amazing. I'll never forget that moment.

"She gave me her telephone number before we left. We were lovers for six months. I spent most of that time waiting for our next meeting. Often, we didn't even talk. She left me after that six months and moved on to someone else. I learned this was a pattern for someone wild and restless.

"It changed me forever, Afari. I've been disappointing our parents—and perhaps you—by ignoring the men introduced to me. That is the reason. I'm gay. I'm lesbian. That is my nature."

By this time, Nadiri had tears in her eyes and on her cheeks. This was the first time she ever talked about this with anyone but Jessica and Fiona.

Afari reached across the table and took Nadiri's hand. She rose, went to Nadiri and led her to the couch, where she took her in her arms as Nadiri wept. Nadiri folded into her sister as much as she could.

After a while, they sat up. Afari went to the kitchen to get some water for Nadiri. She asked, "Would you like some wine? I noticed a bottle in the fridge." Nadiri nodded. Afari uncorked the wine bottle and poured two glasses. The two women sat across from one another, Nadiri on the couch and Afari in what Nadiri thought of as Fiona's chair.

Afari said, "I'm not totally surprised. I thought this might be the case. I wondered if you were gay and were suppressing it, even denying it. It makes no difference at all to me. I love you as you are. I have loved you as you are since you were born."

"You're wonderful. This means everything to me."

Afari added, "You're not finished with your story."

"You're correct. I'm not finished. I have a lover. A woman I adore and who makes me happy. For reasons I don't want to talk about, it's necessary for our relationship to be secret. I'm certain you're the only person who knows there's a relationship. We've been together for two years. If circumstances were different perhaps we would live together. That's not possible."

"You say she makes you happy."

"Wonderfully. Afari, we don't just make love. We talk about who we are. We exchange confidences. We can be silent and it is so comfortable."

"Good. Being happy is good. Stay happy."

"Your acceptance is so important to me."

"You have it. Now, I suppose I should stop inviting men over to dinner."

"Please. Enough. I do feel for them. I don't like this kind of misunderstanding."

"I agree. Do you want me to try to talk with Mother and Father?"

"What can you say? Those poor men they court for me."

"I'll think of something. After all, you're thirty five. I can claim that you've decided to be single. Perhaps you're a career woman."

"I am a career woman. I also have a wonderful lover. And the best older sister in the world."

"Now let me tell you about our vacation plans for the summer," said Afari.

They ended the evening as it began, with family matters.

As she was leaving, Afari said, "We should do this again sometime. It's good for both of us." Nadiri simply hugged her. This was one of those moments in life when words were insufficient.

III

Gabriella and Danny had no fixed routine and were happy to keep it that way. Danny's schedule was always flexible. He could be working day and night all week or he could have gaps even in mid-week when he could look after his personal life. And a phone call could always come.

Gabriela had the rhythm of the school year at St. Mike's and at the Conservatory. That meant she could be free in the mid-afternoon, or be busy until ten in the evening with rehearsals. It depended on the time of the year.

They both had the Wednesday evening sessions of the Bloor Street Chamber Group.

The result was they would have at least one mid-week meal together, at a local restaurant, usually Elena's, which was becoming 'their' place, or at one of their homes, and they would spend time together on the weekend. They both liked the theatre and films in addition to music and would at the last minute sometimes decide to attend a play or a movie. Sometimes, they walked and talked. Often, they stayed at one of their places and streamed a film or TV episode. At Gabriella's suggestion, they began reading aloud to one another. They both marvelled at how much richer life had become with each other.

McIntyre assigned several cases to Danny and Nadiri, none murders. The most interesting was one that had as part of it the issue of Orthodox Jewish divorce. A very religious man who was refusing to give his estranged wife a *get* was assaulted by two thugs. At first, Danny thought the wife's family was responsible. But it turned out that, in addition to manipulating the *get* to obtain more money from his wife's family, the man was also embezzling funds from his business. His partners, also part of the ultra-Orthodox community, took matters into their own hands, not trusting the courts.

Gabriella and Danny sometimes talked shop with one another. The divorce issue interested Gabriella because of her own history and complications with the canon law of Roman Catholicism. It was yet another example, Danny said, of the conflict between tradition and the civil code that binds us.

They talked about the future as well. "I'd like to travel, Danny," she said on one of their walks. "I travelled alone once and hated it. It needs sharing and the insight of another soul. Have you done any travelling?"

"I've been to Israel twice. Two summers in my teens. It was a very spiritual experience. Not religious at all, yet very spiritual. It rooted me in my past and my identity. And Israel is beautiful. Every corner of it has a big history, every stone matters, both for me and for you and for Muslims. On the second trip, we had a bonus. We stopped off in Paris for three days. Rachel and I went to London on our honeymoon. And I got sent to Venice for three days for what was described as an international police conference but was really a short vacation."

"What about Canada?"

"The family took trips to Ottawa, Montreal and Quebec City. I've also been to Vancouver, Halifax and Regina on professional conferences and things like that. Two summers we rented cottages for a few weeks in Jackson's Point. That's about it. How about you? Have you been to Italy?"

"Twice. When I was eight and then when I was fourteen. We visited our family, those who remained in the village we came from, Taurano, in the south. There are aunts, uncles, lots of cousins. We got to Rome and Naples as well. Two years ago the choir went abroad and sang in Rome, once for the pope. Scott and I honeymooned in Mexico for two weeks. I travelled alone to England three years ago. I stayed in London for five days and then rented a car and went to Stonehenge and Devon and Cornwall. It was a weird experience. I kept talking to an invisible companion. By the fourth day I was desperate to share my experiences. England was beautiful, London was exciting and had great music and theatre. But I will never travel that way again.

"And I've been all over Canada" she said, "Mainly because of the choir and the youth orchestra. The only province I've missed is PEI."

"Would you like to go back to Italy?" Danny asked.

"Yes. I'd like to visit the little village, but I'd also like to spend time in Florence and Venice. I have a big bucket list. Paris, the south of France, Spain, Scandinavia, Latin America. And more. I'm open to a lot."

"Let's think about it," Danny said. "Between both our schedules we'll need a lot of lead time to plan getting time off together."

"What about March break? We could take a week in some place like Costa Rica or Martinique."

"If we do it, it'll be a last-minute thing. I'll have to check with Sydney and, of course, I might be in the middle of an important case."

"That's good, Danny. Let's think about this short term and long term. Of course, we are both very comfortable, but neither of us makes big bucks, so we'll have to budget as well."

"How about putting some money each month in a joint account devoted solely to travel?"

"Let's do it."

IV

The pause for Danny and Nadiri ended on the Tuesday of the first week of February. At ten o'clock in the morning McIntyre asked them to meet with her in her office.

"We have a new murder. I learned about it a half-hour ago. At about nine this morning the body of a man was discovered in his place of work, a jewellery wholesaler. The place is in Lawrence Plaza, at Bathurst and Lawrence. That's what I know. It's yours."

Danny and Nadiri immediately went to the car and Nadiri drove north to the plaza. When they arrived, there were the usual local police cordoning off the area and keeping people away from the scene.

The plaza had many shops and Danny knew it well. Its most iconic place was the United Bakers, a dairy restaurant beloved by many in the Jewish community, where you could get many of the foods served in Jewish homes and some terrific soup. The plaza also had a boys' clothing store where many in the community bought clothes for children for holidays and bar mitzvahs. There were these and much more, including the usual bank and drug store.

The jewellery shop was in four rooms on the second floor of one of the buildings. They took the stairs and went up to view the scene before the forensics people arrived.

The business consisted of a large display area and three rooms at the back. The body was in one of them with various jewellery-making tools scattered around. They walked carefully and examined it with their eyes without messing up the scene.

He was a man in his forties, with a short beard, dressed in a white shirt with no tie, a black vest that was unbuttoned and black trousers. He had greying hair. The *yarmulke*, which was pinned to his hair with a clip, was askew.

The body was lying on its back. There were several knife wounds in his stomach and that was likely the cause of death. There were also some wounds around the eyes of the body, which also bled.

By this time, the forensics people had arrived. Hugh O'Brien was in charge. He quickly greeted Danny and Nadiri and he and his team got to work while Danny and Nadiri went downstairs.

Danny had encountered one of the young officers holding back the public, Honeker, during an earlier case. Danny went up to him and said, "Good morning, Officer. We meet again."

"Yes, sir."

"Do we have anything? Has anybody come forward to give some information? This mall is a busy one."

"Nothing so far, sir. We're just getting organized. Do you want us to do anything?"

"Let me hear from forensics first and then we'll see. I think we may need to start questioning people soon. I'll let you know. Where is the person who found the body?"

"He's around the corner, in a car with another officer."

They went around the corner, and introduced themselves to the officer. Danny entered the car to talk with the man who had found the body.

He, too, had a beard and was dressed in a white shirt, black vest and black pants. He had a hat on his head, tilted back, revealing a yarmulke underneath it. He was about sixty, older than his colleague, and he was rocking back and forth as if in prayer, or in shock.

His name was Chaim Noyer. "I am the owner of the business," he said. "I came in about eight-thirty and found Yitzchak as you saw him. I checked if there was a pulse. Nothing. I called 911."

"What is Yitzchak's full name?" Danny asked.

Noyer looked up and surveyed Danny's face. Danny realized this was probably because he pronounced Yitzchak correctly and easily, the guttural 'ch' sound being very difficult for native English speakers.

"Yitzchak Fogelman. He had worked for me for many years, about fifteen. He is a person who designs jewellery and cuts diamonds. A very skilled person."

"Do you have any thoughts, Mr. Noyer?"

"I don't know what to think. He is a normal man. Married. One child. He is observant. I don't know of any enemies who would do this."

"Was anything missing? Were you robbed?"

"Forgive me. I didn't look. I called 911 and went outside to bring people to the body. I said a prayer. Nothing seemed out of order in the display room. I'll have to go in again and look to be certain."

"You've been helpful, sir. Could you stay around for a while? I need to go up to the scene and I'll ask you to come and have a look around."

"Where am I going to go? Who will inform the family?"

"We'll look after that shortly." Turning to the officer, Danny said, "Check if Mr. Noyer would like some water or tea or whatever. If you bring food or drink, check with Mr. Noyer where you can go get it. He has certain religious rules he observes."

Noyer nodded. Now he knew.

Danny phoned McIntyre and told her what he had found. "Sydney, this is a busy place. We will need some officers to do the survey of all the shops and offices. Nadiri can organize this. She's done this before."

"I'll get you some help. And yes, I know who you like and I'll try to get them on the team. Call me after you talk to Hugh."

After some time, O'Brien came downstairs. He took Danny and Nadiri aside. "It is as it appears. He was killed by several knife thrusts. I'll know how many when I do the autopsy. He was facing his assailant, who used his right hand."

"Two things, Hugh. First, time of death."

"Not long ago. It's now a bit after eleven. Probably between four and six hours ago. I need to confirm that before it is official. I know your second question, I think. I don't know what to make about the wounds around the eyes. They had nothing to do with his death. I'm pretty certain they occurred after the stomach wounds."

"Thanks, Hugh. We'll go up and do our thing."

"I'll let you know the time of the autopsy. Maybe later today. Possibly tomorrow morning."

Danny and Nadiri went upstairs to the jewellery business. The forensics people were waiting. Danny asked them to empty Fogelman's pockets. They put the items in bags and then took the body out of the building to the morgue.

In his pockets, Fogelman had a wallet, with the usual driver's license, health card, credit cards and some cash. Danny made a note of his home address and telephone number. There was some small change, a ballpoint pen and keys. As well, there was a miniature book in Hebrew, which Danny recognized as the daily prayer book found in most Orthodox synagogues, with an appendix of the five books of Moses.

The room where Fogelman was murdered was one with tools and machines, and a small desk in a corner. Danny recognized a jewellery making machine, a stone polishing machine, various bits and drills, and two eye loupes. Everything was in order, though clearly Fogelman was working on polishing a diamond ring that was on the counter.

Another room served as a storeroom and the third small room was an office. Danny told Nadiri to keep looking while he went downstairs to bring up Chaim Noyer. Noyer looked around the display room at

Danny's request. "Sergeant," he said, "at first glance I don't see anything missing. I'll look again later today, when I am more composed. I'll let you know if anything is gone."

"Mr. Noyer, as promised, I'll be going to report to the family. Do you know about Mr. Fogelman's private life? Is there anyone I might call to meet me there to aid the family?"

"We belonged to different shuls, Sergeant. We would sometimes daven in the same place near here if we stayed late. I know that he belonged to the Kollel and that his rabbi is Rav Aharon Goldstein. He's the man to call."

"I know Rav Goldstein," Danny answered. "I will get to him as soon as I can. Thanks, Mr. Noyer. I'll get back to you in a day or two as we hunt for the murderer."

He managed to reach Aaron through the Kollel, pulling him out of a class. "Aaron, it's Danny. I'm calling, I am sorry to say, in my professional capacity. One of the people in your community, Yitzchak Fogelman, has been murdered. I don't have time to go into the details now. It was at his place of work. My colleague and I are driving at this moment to his house to inform his family. I knew you would want to know immediately."

Aaron gasped and said, "OK. No questions now. I'll be going over and I'll inform my wife Aviva, who I'm sure will be there as soon as possible."

Fogelman's home was a short distance north of the plaza, a small bungalow off Bathurst Street two blocks from the Kollel. Aaron arrived at the same time as their car. The two men shook hands and Danny introduced Nadiri.

"Do you lead or do I?" Danny asked.

"I don't know anything. It would be better if you did so."

They rang the bell. The door was answered by a middle-aged woman dressed modestly in dark clothes in the custom of the Orthodox. Her hair was covered with a kerchief. She knew the Rabbi and already was distraught. The combination of the police and the Rabbi could not be good. Mrs. Fogelman, with a kind of iron discipline, invited them in and took them to a small living room. When they settled, she began. "Did anything happen to Avrom?"

"No," Aaron answered. "It's not Avrom. Your son is fine. It's Yitzchak."

"What happened?"

Aaron turned to Danny, who said, "Mrs. Fogelman, I am deeply sorry. Your husband was murdered a few hours ago at his place of work."

She crumbled, as if she no longer any bones to hold her up. Skin without a skeleton. Aaron moved to sit near her while she cried quietly and seemed to be shattered. He put out a hand to Danny and Nadiri, indicating they should just let her express her emotions. The doorbell rang. Danny answered. It was Aviva Goldstein. They knew one another, but neither talked. Aviva went into the living room and sat beside Chava Fogelman and held her, rocking back and forth.

After a time, Mrs. Fogelman asked what had happened. Danny told what little he knew of the story. Aviva had told Chava she and Aharon knew Sergeant Miller and he could be trusted.

"What will happen?" she asked.

"We will do everything in our power to catch the murderer. That's my job."

"Es vet mir gornisht helfen ," Mrs. Fogelman said. He is gone to the oylem haba . He can't be brought back."

"No, he can't," Danny replied. "But we are a people who believe in justice. And we can find justice for your husband."

Danny and Nadiri rose to leave, knowing that Mrs. Fogelman had the support she would need. Aaron accompanied them outside. They stopped to talk.

"Danny, I will need to know more, if there is more to know," Aaron said. "Let's talk in a day or two."

"Of course, Aaron."

"Is this possibly an act of anti-Semitism?" Aaron asked.

"At the moment, no. Not a sign of it, Aaron. Just a terrible killing."

"OK. I'm glad you're on the case."

"I'm sorry. I wish I had no work"

"We are, as they say, Danny, crooked timber."

"Yes, Aaron. As Ruth said a few weeks ago at a Shabbos dinner, we've been expelled from the garden. I'll do what I can to get the body released quickly."

"I didn't ask. I know you will. Call me when you have a chance."

"I will. I need more information from you in any case. Goodbye, Aaron."

Aaron said, "Danny, Officer Rahimi, may we meet again in happy circumstances."

"Amen, Aaron," Danny said as he got into the car.

V

Danny attended the autopsy at four o'clock. Meanwhile, a team was at the plaza, interviewing as many people as possible, hoping to get a lead. Tomorrow, in the afternoon, Yitzchak Fogelman would be buried in Mount Sinai Memorial Park on Wilson. Danny made appointments to meet with Chaim Noyer and Aaron the next morning. He would find a time, somehow, to visit privately with Chava Fogelman in the next several days. After the funeral, she would be sitting shiva for a week, but he could rely on Aaron to sort out the theological complications.

As the autopsy progressed Hugh O'Brien became more specific. He told Danny there had been three knife wounds. The knife had been about eighteen centimetres long. "It could have been an ordinary kitchen tool," O'Brien said. "It wasn't as sharp as the knives of professional killers." In examining the eyes, O'Brien concluded that the wounds were made with a different instrument. "I'm going to send one of my people to examine the tools. The killer could have made these with one of the bits or drills. If so, he placed the instrument back where it belonged. Let's see if we can find it. The time of death is between six and eight this morning."

"Very useful, Hugh," Danny said. "Can we turn the body over to the family soon? You know the rules for religious Jews."

"Of course, Danny. I also know religious Jews bury their dead. No cremations permitted. I very much doubt we will need another look in any case. What we get today is what we can get."

"I'll call Rabbi Goldstein and let him know."

When Danny returned to the office, Nadiri was still there. "I'm going over the reports, sir. So far the interviews have not revealed anyone who was a witness. Was the time of death very early, as Dr. O'Brien speculated?"

"Yes. Between six and eight. We'll have to find out from Noyer about Fogelman's work habits."

"Can I ask how you know Rabbi Goldstein?"

"Of course. We were boyhood friends and classmates. Also, my father often went to the Kollel, a place where the sacred texts are studied. Rabbi Goldstein heads the Kollel. At a very young age for that sort of thing. He is still a good guy, as I have told him, despite his religious preoccupations."

"He seemed that way. He and his wife were very kind with Mrs. Fogelman."

The next morning, Danny met with Chaim Noyer, at the plaza, even though the jewellery shop was still sealed. He took Noyer up to the display room to have another look, and then they went to the kosher Second Cup coffee shop in the mall to talk.

"There is nothing missing, Sergeant," said Noyer. "If there is, it is minor. Even I can figure out that it was not a robbery."

"Tell me what you know about Yitzchak Fogelman."

"He was a quiet man, not someone who pushed himself forward. He worked for me for fifteen years and he was as reliable as anyone I know. Never missed a day. He liked to get to work early and leave early. I think this had something to do with looking after his son. I'm not sure. I think his wife had some duties with looking after her parents."

"Did it matter that he came in early?"

"No. He was a designer and a diamond specialist. He did his job well. So it didn't matter if he wanted unusual hours. He usually arrived a bit before six, after davening with a very early minyan near here. He was a fine craftsman, Sergeant. Very good at two specialties. About ten years ago he was offered a job in New York, where the trade is centered, by one of my distributors. He could have made a lot more money. He chose to stay in Toronto. He will be impossible to replace with one person."

"Any enemies? Anyone who had a grievance?"

"None I know of. I don't know a lot about his home life. It seemed fine. He talked warmly about his wife and son. He was centered at home, in work and at the Kollel. As I think you know, for people like us that makes for a full life."

"Yes. Did any of your clients like to come in early to speak with Mr. Fogelman?"

"It would be very unusual. He sometimes did work with clients on the design of a piece of jewellery. He did a lot of custom work. As far as I know, he had no early appointments yesterday. Yet he buzzed someone in. It's not something that was ordinary."

"Mr. Noyer, thank you for your help. I may need to talk with you again as we proceed."

"A bad business, Sergeant. It has shaken me up."

The two exited the café and Danny went to his car to drive to the Kollel to meet with Aaron Goldstein.

They found a quiet corner. "How is Mrs. Fogelman?" asked Danny.

"Terrible. About what you would expect. She has some family with her and they will remain throughout the shiva. Maybe longer."

"Tell me about Yitzchak Fogelman. I just spoke with his boss, Chaim Noyer, and now I'd like to hear from you. Noyer said the Kollel was an important part of Fogelman's life."

"It was. Using the past tense is lousy, Danny. It was. He joined the Kollel when he was nineteen, then making a commitment to Chassidic life. He davened here, usually in the afternoons and of course on Shabbos. He studied here. He and his wife's friends came from here. He also taught a class to young people, boys about fourteen and fifteen, just after bar mitzvah. It was a study of the commentaries of Rashi on certain portions of the Torah."

"Any problems? Any controversies?"

"None that I know of. He was a quiet person, not one of those who pushed himself forward. There were the usual discussions and disagreements about texts, about interpretations of the law, but you don't kill someone because they have a different view about a page in the Talmud."

"Noyer said that he was regular, very reliable."

"Yes. I can recall him missing one class, when he was ill, in all these years. What are you asking?"

"I'm not certain. It's often useful to get into the head of the victim. Was he obsessively regular?"

"Interesting. I never thought of it like that. He was always on time. Now that I think of it, he was prompt. But that kind of habit is appreciated. He wasn't a leader, but the community valued him and Chava, and they made contributions that were important to our daily life."

"I'm looking for any eccentricities, Aaron. He seems almost too normal."

"There are normal people in our world, Danny. Not everyone is as odd as you."

"Of course. Although not everyone would think that a normal Chassid is normal."

"Let's not go there, at least not now."

"I'll want to speak with Mrs. Fogelman. It's not crucial at this time. Could you organize a moment for me in the next few days?"

"I'll sort it out." They rose, shook hands, and Danny left.

When Danny returned from the office, there was a message to call Hugh O'Brien. When Danny called, O'Brien said, "The mess around Fogelman's eyes was made by one of the tools in the shop, a screwdriver. The killer first killed Fogelman, then took the screwdriver and did his business. Then he must have returned the tool to its place."

"Useful. Thanks, Hugh."

Danny spent the rest of the day looking at interview reports from the officers who were coordinated by Nadiri. He wondered which method was appropriate to solving this killing.

VI

He was exhilarated. He could jump for joy. He told himself to be calm. He remembered the poster—'Keep Calm and Carry On.' That was what he needed to do. He had to appear normal. He had to take deep breaths.

However, he had just completed his task. The past was erased. He took years away from those who had robbed him of years of happiness. He took revenge on those fingers, those lips, those eyes. The task was done.

This was the first task he had fully completed in more than two decades and it gave him great satisfaction. The anticipation was exciting. A day later, the taste of the act was still in his body.

He would look to the future. He was learning to be organized. He planned the acts and carried out his plan. He could do anything now.

VII

That evening, Danny went to the chamber group, anxious to get lost in the music of the seventeenth and eighteenth centuries, and delighted as usual to be playing with such good musicians.

Several people in the group knew that Danny and Gabriella were dating, though none knew how far the relationship had travelled in a short time. They didn't gossip. They were here for the music and the pleasure of playing with colleagues. Gabriella and Danny, without ever talking about it, behaved as colleagues, Gabriella in charge as the conductor.

It was a short ride home from the rehearsal and, when they were close to Gabrialla's place, Danny said, "Could I come up for a minute? I have something pleasant to tell you."

"Of course."

They went upstairs. Gabriella reached into the fridge and took out a corked bottle of white wine. "There is enough for each of us," she said, and poured the wine.

They settled in the living room and Danny said, "I spoke with Avi about us. You were right—he did ask about children, among other things. We had a good talk. We owe Ruth on this one. She had already talked with him and indicated she was content. That mattered. I'm certain they also spoke about the matter of religion issue because Avi didn't raise it as a problem."

"Your sister is a terrific person. She has strong values and opinions, all good ones, and she lets others be themselves."

"I'm lucky. Anyway, without getting into a repeat of the conversation, Avi indicated he would be OK. It was especially important I told him he was all the children I wanted and you and I were in a different kind of relationship. I will tell you that he was really mature. He told me that he wanted me to be happy."

"A fine big sister and a great kid. You are lucky."

"And a great lover on top of that. Now, my sweet woman, we both could use some rest. I'm on my way."

They embraced and Danny left as Gabriella said with a smile, "Drive carefully."

VIII

The next day Danny took the small Fogelman file and put it on one side of his desk. He then pulled out the large Frawley file and put it on the other side. He looked at one, then the other, then the one and then, again, the other. He made some notes on a pad. He thought some more and went to see Sydney McIntyre.

"Any news?" asked McIntyre.

"Nothing much. We're interviewing people. We don't have a suspect … Sydney, I want to try a long shot. First, I'd like to see if the Fogelman killing and the Frawley killing have any relationships. Also, I'd like to look at the Michaelson file."

"Danny, do you have any cause for believing the Michaelson murder had anything at all in common with either Fogelman or Frawley?"

"No. I've never even seen a document from the file. I want to look."

McIntyre sighed. "You know what will happen?"

"I do know what will happen. When Ed Morgan learns I have the file he'll go nuts. He'll regard it as an insult. He'll make your life miserable."

"Exactly."

"Sydney, has Morgan gotten anywhere with the file since he took it on?"

"No. It's as mysterious as Frawley's killing."

"So. Let's say I was taking a test to be an inspector. My hottest detective asks to look at a file that no one has gotten anywhere with. He thinks it may, an outside chance at best, have a relationship to other killings. He has been successful in the past. The detective in charge of the file is, at best, barely competent. He's also a pain in the ass. He'll be hopelessly awful about it. What do I do?"

McIntyre smiled. "You do have a way of persuading me. You win. I'll handle Morgan. I'll get the file to your office shortly."

Danny looked at reports from Nadiri's team until the Michaelson file arrived. Then he first worked through the file systemically. For the second reading, he took his time over several items.

McIntyre was out of the office in the afternoon. When she returned, she knocked on the door and poked her head into Danny's office. "Anything?"

WILD JUSTICE

"One small thing. No, half a small thing. But enough to get me to ask if I can follow up on all three files while still working on the Fogelman murder."

McIntyre raised her eyebrows.

"In each of the murders there was a follow-up to the killing. For Frawley, there were his broken fingers. For Fogelman there are the wounds around the eyes. And for Michaelson, he too was stabbed. Then the killer used the knife to make cuts to his lips. For each there seemed to be a statement made. Granted, it is not the same statement, but it could be interesting. Also, though this is not clear, the last two killings were done in a similar manner. With an ordinary knife, about the same size. The first murder, Frawley, we think was spontaneous. The second and third were premeditated."

"After the Gentrey case, I won't ask if you are pushing this too far. What do you want to do with your half a small thing?"

"I want your permission to continue to handle the Michaelson file. You can make a copy for me. Morgan can do whatever he does with the case and I'll do my thing."

"Yes and no, Danny. Yes, you can continue to look at the Michaelson file. No, Morgan will not be handling it at the same time. I think it is bad policy, and bad policing, to have two teams working parallel on the same case. I'll let Morgan know. I'll take the heat. As you say, that's why I get the big bucks. Be prepared for some heat of your own. Morgan won't let this rest with me."

"Good. I'll let you know what is happening. If nothing comes of it, I'll give you back the Michaelson file."

Danny arranged for Nadiri to meet with him first thing the next morning. He outlined what he had found. Then he said, "I still think the key to the Frawley case lies in his past. Perhaps the same holds true for Fogelman and Michaelson. Yes, they are as different as Catholics, Protestants and Jews, as different as teachers, law consultants and jewellers, as different as a bachelor, a gay married man and a heterosexual married man. I realize that. But I want to know about their pasts.

"Here is what I am asking you to do. I want you and whoever you need—Taegan, Connor and others if necessary—to make a chart of the history of each of the three men. Do it, say, by year. When they were born, where they lived, where they went to school, what they did with their families, how and where they spent their summers—for example, I would bet that Fogelman spent one or more summers in Israel—where they worked, who they married or didn't marry, what organizations they belonged to and spent time in—clearly, Opus Dei for Frawley, and the Kollel for Fogelman, etcetera. Record it clearly."

"What are you looking for, sir?"

"Anything. I don't yet want to say we are looking for this or that. I want us to approach it with a clear head. Let's let it tell us what it can tell us. Just get the data. Then we'll build a story. If there is a story. And of course," Danny smiled as he said it, "I want it by this afternoon."

"I get the message, sir. You'll have it as fast as we can do it."

IX

Nadiri worked hard that day, calling in support and assigning tasks. Taegan oversaw Michaelson and Connor was in charge of Fogelman. She recruited Ted Honeker, who Danny had mentioned, as part of the team, to look at Frawley. Each of them was teamed with another constable. "Everybody reports to me," she said. "Be comprehensive, but go quickly. Sergeant Miller wants this as fast as possible. I want daily reports." They nodded in agreement. It didn't need to be said that they would be working that weekend.

That Friday evening, Nadiri went out to eat. It was the second Friday of the month, which meant that she and her friends woul for dinner. There were ten women, all from the same graduating class at Thornhill Secondary. Most were married, a majority had careers, some had children. They had been doing this since they graduated from university. If necessary they turned into a support group, helping one another through family, personal and career crises, providing a safe place to talk about important matters. Some dinners were serious. Some were just very happy occasions, occasionally raucous, where good friends let down their hair. All were nurturing.

This month they had chosen a place in Bayview Village, south of Thornhill, near the corner of Sheppard and Bayview. It was called Openings and had a menu with both Asian and American cuisine. Julia, who recommended it, said they had wonderful floats, which sealed their making the booking.

When Nadiri arrived a little after seven, three women were already at the table. They ordered drinks and by the time they arrived four more women were seated.

They chatted about their lives, asked after their families and settled into a warm familiarity. After they ordered their meals, Maya Notondu, an executive at the Royal Bank, took the centre.

"I have a problem," said Maya, and the rest of the table gave her their attention. "My sister has been going out with this guy who works in my section of the bank. He seemed nice, told her he was serious, and took a loan from her to, he said, tide him over for a few months because he was in arrears on his student loan payment."

There were sighs and nods at the table from the others. They knew this scenario.

Maya continued, "He turns out to be a jerk."

"No kidding," Celia Rogdanovivi said.

"That's not the problem I want to talk about. Yes, my sister soon learned he was bedding other women. And then they broke it off. He told her he understood the loan was a gift."

"Here is the issue. I have some power over this guy. I have power in making decisions about his promotions and raises. How do I behave?"

"Well, you behave professionally," said Nadiri. "You … what's the word?"

"Recuse," Celia replied.

Nadiri continued, "You recuse yourself from anything to do with him if you can't put the incident out of your mind."

"No," said Celia. "You get revenge. You screw up his career if you have the opportunity. He lied. He screwed your sister. That makes him fair game."

"Now you have it," said Maya. That's the quandary. He did lie. He is a dishonest person. He certainly should not be in charge of other people's money. But Nadiri made a point. How do I behave as a banker, as an executive?"

As the conversation was proceeding, Barsha Gupta, who was married with three children, and had a degree in English literature, took out her tablet, something which drove Nadiri crazy. She looked up revenge and then said, "As you probably all know, Gandhi said, 'An eye for an eye would make the whole world blind.'"

Patricia Brown, who worked for the Ministry of Finance at Queen's

Park, intervened, on Celia's side. "Robert Kennedy said, 'Don't get mad, get even.'"

Mariana Lopez, who just received tenure in the philosophy department at York, broke in. "Let's take this on another level. Let's try to depersonalize it."

"Yes, Professor," said Maya, and they all laughed.

"Seriously," said Mariana. "Nadiri, one of those cases you were involved with had revenge as part of its motive. Do you guys remember the Nizamani case, about honour killing? In the end, Mrs. Nizamani killed her husband, a kind of revenge for what he did to her and their daughter. Was that justified?"

Consulting her tablet, Barsha said, "According to Francis Bacon 'revenge is a kind of wild justice, which the more man's nature runs to, the more ought law to weed it out.'"

Nadiri said, "Yet there was enormous sympathy for Mrs. Nizamani. My latest case, the one where Dr. Everson killed Dr. Gentrey, also had an element of revenge, but no one thinks it was right. What's the difference?"

"I think," Patty said, "people felt Mrs. Nizamani had justice on her side. I think we felt she did what the law could not do."

"Bacon would say," Mariana said, "revenge is never justified, because it puts the law in the hands of individual will and not in the civilized community."

Barsha said, "You're right. There's another Bacon quotation on the site. 'In taking revenge, a man is but even with his enemy; but in passing over it, he is superior ...' And then there's Byron. 'Sweet is revenge.' He gets to the idea it satisfies something inside of us."

"It does," Nadiri said. "Who at this table hasn't had a revenge fantasy? The problem Maya has is whether she's justified in moving away from her professional standards in this case."

"You've got it, Nadiri," Celia said. "I wonder whether it's justified. There's a line from Juvenal, 'revenge is always the delight of a mean spirit, of a weak and petty mind.' The point is, and you're doing this Maya, you don't rush into it. You need to think seriously about revenge and its consequences."

"I'd like to get back at him for what he did to my sister. I'm not certain using my power in the bank is the right way to do it. Thanks. Maybe the question is what is the best way. I'll have to be creative.

Maybe it will do if I somehow make public the fact he's a liar and he cheats people out of money."

"A little Ashley Madison, maybe," said Mariana.

"Could be," Maya said.

"Maybe Bacon and Gandhi and Kennedy and Juvenal can be reconciled. Good luck, Maya," added Mariana.

The conversation moved on to other things, sometimes taking in the whole table, sometimes going one-on-one.

They left the restaurant after ten o'clock, all feeling the pleasure of having been with good friends with whom you could be yourself.

On the drive home, Nadiri thought how important these Fridays were. She also knew that she would be ruminating on the discussion about revenge and Maya's predicament for some time to come.

X

On Sunday afternoon Danny went to the Kollel, where Aaron had arranged for several people to be interviewed. He learned very little he didn't already know. No one knew of anyone who thought of Fogelman as an enemy. He was not beloved, but he was liked and respected. As one said, "He seemed to have lived a righteous life. Who would do this?"

In the early evening, Aaron accompanied him to the Fogelman home, where Chava and Avrom Fogelman were sitting shiva. Few people were there at that time—they would assemble in an hour for the evening prayers. Danny got to speak quietly with Chava. He was told Fogelman was a good husband and father, he lived according to the dictates of his faith and was a student of the sacred texts.

Nadiri was already at the station, in the room they had set up to be devoted to the experiment in tying together the three cases. He was about to go down to inquire on the progress of the team when Ed Morgan appeared at his door.

"Good morning, Ed," said Danny.

"Good morning, my ass," replied Morgan. "Who do you think you are? You go on television, you're some shitty hotshot, and you take my case."

"See the inspector, Ed. She gave me the file."

"Sure. As if you didn't ask for it. You people have no respect for anyone else. You do whatever you want. You think your money can get you anything you want."

Danny was tempted to ask who 'you people' were, but he realized the answer might mean he would be spending the morning writing reports about workplace harassment.

"Ed, ask the inspector. She gave me the file."

"You don't even have the guts to admit what you did. Stand up like a man."

"Ed, ask the Inspector. I have work to do and I am going to do it."

He stepped around Morgan to get out of the office, making certain they did not touch. He heard "fuck you, you son-of-a-bitch" as he walked away.

When he got to Nadiri, they sat down with some coffee.

"Where are we?" he asked.

"Not bad for a weekend. We have a lot on Frawley because of your research. We're getting there slowly with the others. Let me tell you that the three guys worked this weekend. Little time off. On their own. There were no orders from me."

"I really appreciate that. When do you think we can have something to compare the three lives? Even if it's not complete."

"Late tomorrow. Perhaps Wednesday morning. I'm pushing to get as much as we can to do a comprehensive job by Friday. It sounds simple, but it's not. Imagine doing it for someone you don't know."

"Sounds good. Get me dates and places of birth, schools and jobs when you have them."

"That's not hard. I'll have that to you today. It's filling in the little things. As you said, what clubs did they join, where did they and their families go on vacations? Finding out things like that takes time."

Danny took the three files to read them again, asking questions. 'Back to avenues,' he thought. Which avenue will yield the important link? School? Hobbies? Neighbourhoods? Employment? Common interests? He spent the rest of the day trying to work out what was the route.

Waiting is hard when you are investigating three murders that might be related. Activity gives you the belief, and sometimes the illusion, that you are working it out. But Danny knew he had to wait. It made the next few days longer than they should have been.

He practiced his music more than usual. He picked up two squash games, on Tuesday and Thursday mornings. He got a call on Thursday around one in the afternoon, which finally ended the pause.

It was from Aaron. "Danny, I'm calling because a matter has come to my attention that might be relevant to Yitzchak Fogelman's murder. I'd like to talk with you about it this afternoon."

"Can you tell me what it is? I'll come as soon as I hang up the phone, but what should I be thinking about?"

"I think it would be better if you came with a fresh mind. I don't want to be secretive. You just need to hear all of it for yourself."

"I'm on my way to the Kollel."

When Danny arrived, he was greeted by Aaron and brought into his study in a small back room. Inside, there were two young men, about fifteen, a touch older than Avi. They were dressed in the manner of the Orthodox—white shirts open at the neck, black pants and shoes, wearing the ritual fringes to fulfill a Biblical commandment, their hair in side curls above the ears, yarmulkes on their heads.

The boys stood up when Danny entered. Aaron introduced them as Yankel Birnbaum and Binyamin Helfgott. Danny shook hands with the young men and took the vacant seat facing them as Aaron went behind his desk.

Aaron began in Hebrew, to make the two teenagers more comfortable and show that Danny was someone who understood their life.

"Detective Miller," he said, "these two young men have been with the Kollel most of their lives. They attend the Torah Academy Collegiate and study here. In discussing the murder of our friend Yitzchak Fogelman this morning, they asked to see me privately. I think you need to hear what they said."

He looked to the boys. "Please tell Detective Miller what you told me. This is between us alone."

Binyamin started. "We told the Rav that Mr. Fogelman would touch us while he was teaching the class on Rashi."

Danny knew how the teaching would have been done. There would have been eight, perhaps ten, students in the class, sitting at tables for two or more. The teacher would have no lectern. Rather, the group would read some passages and then discuss their meaning. The teacher would sometimes wander around the room. It was a kind of teaching that relied on knowing the text. The teacher would sometimes stop behind a pupil and point to a word or a passage for emphasis. Sometimes, a class might begin with students being asked to read some passages. In that case the teacher would wander the room and answer individual questions by again going to the student and using the text.

Danny looked at Aaron, the look asking which one of them should follow up.

Aaron took the lead. "When you say touching, where did he touch you?"

Binyamin answered again. "He would touch our face and our back. Sometimes our chest. It wasn't a touch. His hand would go up, and down. I don't know how to describe it. It was like a mother touching a baby. It was as if he couldn't keep his hands away from us."

"Yankel?" Aaron asked.

"Rav Goldstein, we're not the only ones. When we were leaving the class, he would pat our behinds." The young man blushed as he said this.

"When you say you were not the only ones, what do you mean?"

"He touched most of us. All the students know this. We were told by the older students this would happen."

"Why did you not tell me this before?" Aaron asked.

"We were afraid. We thought that we might be punished for lashon hara, for saying bad things about a teacher."

Aaron then nodded to Danny.

"Yankel, Binyaman, what did you think about this?"

"We didn't know what to think, Detective," said Binyamin. "Was this normal? He was our teacher. A good teacher. He was a respected member of the Kollel, a devout person. What should we think?"

"I understand. Why did you speak with Rav Goldstein now?"

Yankel spoke. "He asked about anything that might contribute to solving the murder. This morning he asked about anything that might have been abnormal."

"You were correct in telling your Rav," Danny said. "I want you to know two things. Your comments here will be confidential for now. They will only be made public in a manner that will not involve you personally. Second, this is very useful information that will contribute to finding the criminal and bring justice to the Fogelman family."

Aaron asked the young men to leave. After they exited, Aaron asked

WILD JUSTICE

Danny, "How important is this?"

"It could be very important. I'm investigating the Fogelman murder in two ways. By itself and in relation to two others. It fits some of the theories I have going around in my head about the relationship, but I don't have all the facts yet. The facts must fit the theory or the theory goes out the window. I'm sad about this, but I'm not totally surprised. I'm pleased it's come to light. It helps. All this is between us, Aaron."

"Let me know when you have more certainty, Danny. Right now, I have some work to do with Yitzchak Fogelman's students."

They exchanged some small talk about their families, shook hands and Danny left. He was aching to see what Nadiri's team would report tomorrow morning.

At nine o'clock the next morning, in addition to Danny and Nadiri, there were four other people at the meeting—McIntyre, Taegan, Connor and Ted Honeker. McIntyre and Danny had discussed his thinking and they realized this might be a very important moment in considering the three murders.

They met in the larger office downstairs, which had become Nadiri's centre. She had three big charts on the front wall, next to one another, detailing the lives of Frawley, Michaelson and Fogelman. They all spent a few moments looking them over.

"What do we have?" Danny asked.

"Not a lot, sir," Nadiri said. "There are a few overlapping points. They were born within one and a half years of each other. They were sent by their parents to schools with religious affiliations, Frawley went to a separate school, Michaelson went to a private school with an Anglican affiliation, and Fogelman went to a Hebrew day school.

"Their summers were different until they were about seventeen. At that time, they all were at Camp Unity, which was an interfaith camp sponsored by the Frederick family foundation. Frawley and Fogelman were junior counsellors, and Michaelson was a swimming instructor.

"Michaelson and Frawley went to U of T. Frawley did science and theology; Michaelson did politics and law. Fogelman went to Israel to study at a religious school for two years. Then he trained in the jewellery business. Their lives seem to have diverged after that. We could find nothing to indicate they had any contact after the camp."

They all discussed what this might mean without getting far. Danny then asked, "Did they overlap at the camp?"

"Michaelson spent two years there," said Nadiri. "Frawley and Fogelman spent one year. They were together in the summer for that year."

"Then that's where we will concentrate our investigation," Danny said. "At least for now."

"What are you thinking, Danny?" McIntyre asked.

"I'm trying to get into the head of the killer. Yesterday I learned something about Fogelman that fit a theory I've been fooling around with." Danny then recounted his conversation with the two students at the Kollel.

Taegan asked, "So it might be related to the sexual orientation of the victims?"

"It's not as clear as I would like it to be, Taegan. Frawley is very complicated. But maybe his sexual feelings were sublimated into his religion. I don't want to overdue this armchair psychology. However, his self-mortification and deep religious feelings could be understood as a kind of ecstasy. Not my word. I'm stealing it from a book."

Connor came into the conversation. "I don't want to seem disrespectful, sir, but isn't this pushing his beliefs very far. I don't think Pope Francis' faith is a substitute for sex."

"Good point, Connor. I don't want to push this any further than makes sense. However, I'm not alone on this. This is an insight many psychologists have. There is a famous line by Freud I recently read in looking at the psychology texts. He once said, 'sometimes a cigar is just a cigar.' I agree. But sometimes it's not."

"What are you suggesting, Danny?" Sydney asked. "I don't get where you are going."

"Well," said Danny. "The first point is that we have gotten nowhere investigating the three murders separately. Then there is the idea that all three might be linked, that there is a single murderer. Further, I sense the key to all these murders lies in the past. There is also the fact that not only were the three men killed, the last two in the same manner, but that the killer left a message after each killing—broken fingers, scoring on the lips, wounds around the eyes. There was plenty of opportunity to rob something, but nothing was robbed. Put those together. Yes, it's a big set of assumptions. If any one of them ends up being wrong, then it's all wrong. There is nothing else to go by, Sydney. To answer your question, I am suggesting the link may be that camp.

Whatever happened there."

"If it is one murderer," Nadiri said, "then you're saying he had a grievance against these men and killed them over twenty years later."

"I don't know if the grievance was real or just in the mind of the murderer. Yes, he thinks he has a grievance. He is getting even."

Nadiri could not help but recall the conversation with her friends at dinner three days earlier. Was this also about revenge?

Danny continued. "I don't think this is your classic serial killer. He is killing for a reason. The reason may be in his head, but he is killing particular people."

"If that is the case," Sydney said, "then we don't know when it will stop. He could have more people on his list."

"Yes, we don't know," Danny said. "Nadiri, where is the camp?"

"It no longer exists. It was in Muskoka. Lake Edison, which is not far from Haliburton. We found that it closed a few years after the three were there together. It was purchased by someone who kept it as a summer camp without the interfaith thing. It's actually a well-known camp for kids."

"Do they have the records of the interfaith camp?"

"That's how we found who did what at the camp. The new people kept the records. We were lucky. They had used a computer. Really terrible by today's standards, but Taegan figured it out."

"Here's what I would like to do. A long shot, by the way. I'd like to get the names of the campers. Did you find out anything about the camp?"

Taegan responded, "It was for kids between twelve and fourteen. The idea was to get kids of different faiths and backgrounds together, learn about one another. This would make for understanding and respect. There were some scholarships."

"How many kids?"

"Almost two hundred," replied Taegan replied. "Precisely, one hundred ninety-six."

"All boys?"

"No. Half and half."

"That helps. Where did the kids come from?"

"All over the country."

"That helps too."

"Let me try this on you," Danny continued. "I'd like to find the names and whatever else you can get of the boys. For a first round I think we should concentrate on boys from the GTA. Burlington in the west, up to Newmarket, and out to Oshawa in the east."

"Then?" Sydney asked.

"We find out where they are, what they are doing today. We eliminate some, some get on a list of possibilities. We are especially interested in loners. We grind it out, eliminating as we go along. In the best scenario, we'll have a list of suspects. It may be fifteen people on the first list. It may be five. We keep going until we find him."

"It's an immense amount of work, Danny," Sydney said. "I'll go along with it because we've not found any other leads. Also, because there may be a fourth and fifth killing coming and, if this works, we can prevent those. Give me an hour. I'll need to clear it with the brass."

"As you say, it's all we have." Danny turned to Nadiri and her team. "I'll bet you didn't think that doing detective work meant doing deep research into lives. As the inspector sometimes says, slogging gets it done."

"Well, then," Nadiri replied, "we slog."

"I need to stress this," Sydney said. "Time is not on our side. We need to move as quickly as possible."

Four "yes ma'ams" ended the meeting.

XI

He was deeply puzzled. Life had turned flat only a few days after the exhilaration of having finished his task. He should be joyful, happy. Instead, he was brooding, depressed, feeling life had no meaning again.

His psychiatrist said that his feeling down was just par for normal life. You can't always be up, he said, and you won't always be down. Let it ride.

Of course, he couldn't tell his psychiatrist why he had been up, why he had found meaning in what had otherwise been a meaningless life. Now, he realized he had no great task to look forward to. There was no anticipation of doing the thing that had eluded him for over two decades.

Now, there was only his life to look forward to. Yesterday he took a long walk on the boardwalk, hoping that The Beach would do its magic as it had done several times for him over the last few months. It did not happen.

He thought a lot about this. He wondered if he needed a goal beyond just working and living. Perhaps he should think about what else he could do to make the world a more just place. He would look on the computer for cases of child abuse. Maybe he was meant to do more than get retribution for himself.

XII

Danny spent Saturday working with Nadiri's team. They made some progress. Out of the one hundred and ten boys who were at the camp that year, thirty-six came from the Toronto area. One had been killed in a car accident six years ago. Six were not living in the Toronto area. After narrowing it down to twenty-nine, they made three lists. The A list would be those who fit the possibility. Bs fit the possibility but did not fit the profile. Cs were highly unlikely. By Saturday night there were three on the A list, two on B and four on C.

They kept going on Sunday, working half the day. Danny was confident they would be nearly finished by late Monday.

On Sunday evening Danny was having dinner for six at his house. However, he wasn't doing the cooking. Gabriella had asked that she cook for him and Avi. It expanded to include Avi's best friend Jordan and his cousins Deborah and Leo.

Gabriella arrived mid-afternoon with bags of groceries. She took over the kitchen and Danny played dishwasher and sous-chef. They talked some more about travelling together and agreed that if Danny could manage it they would try for a last-minute trip to someplace warm and remote during the school's March break. As well, they fantasized about going to Italy, combining a visit to Gabriella's relatives in Taurano with Florence, Venice and the Abruzzi, places they had both always wanted to go.

The young people came around five-thirty. They helped set the table and there was talk about school, what people were reading, and some family gossip. A little after six, they sat down to eat.

Gabriella first brought in a huge platter of the antipasto she had made for Danny along with some homemade focaccia studded with olives. They helped themselves, asking about Italian food in general.

"Italians are sensual people, like the French," Gabriella said. "Food is enormously important in the culture and as part of our identity. Eating is not just about food. It is about family, about gathering together, about nurturing. The country lives on pasta and tomato sauce. And each family has its own tomato sauce recipe."

"That's like us," said Deborah. "You were here for the latke party. Uncle Danny's latkes are different from my mother's, even though they learned how to make them in the same kitchen. You're right, Gabriella. A Shabbos dinner isn't simply about eating. It is an important family and cultural matter."

"Holidays have taste and smells," said Jordan as he helped himself to more salami and peppers. "I like the idea that we celebrate a lot of holidays at home, not only in shul. And we invite others."

Avi asked, "Do you know if there is a special Jewish cuisine in Italy?"

"I don't know a lot about it. I will tell you, though, I looked up a number of Italian kosher restaurants to get ideas for this meal. There are a bunch of kosher restaurants in Rome, at least one in Venice and one in Milan. And there's a kosher Italian restaurant in Toronto, many in New York, at least three in Brooklyn. Some serve only fish and dairy, some have meat. All serve real Italian food."

They were finishing the antipasto. Gabriella congratulated herself that she prepared this meal for six as if there were to be eight at the table. She taught young men and she knew that they had unbelievable appetites.

She and Danny cleaned the table. Then, she announced, "The next course in Italian meals, primo, is usually pasta. So that's what we will do." She and Danny went into the kitchen and they brought out a huge bowl of fettuccini in a veal and tomato sauce. She dished out plates for everyone.

"This is fabulous," Leo said. "I've never had pasta like this. Did you make everything?"

"Yes, Leo. From scratch. Like many young Italian women, I learned to cook from my Nonna, which is the Italian name for Bubbie. She would be very cross with me today—she is not alive anymore, but I still talk to her sometimes, especially in the kitchen—if I didn't make the pasta or if I used sauce from a bottle bought at the grocery store. As in your tradition, a lot of the family connections revolve around the kitchen."

Avi held out his plate, which he had devoured. "As they say in *Oliver Twist*, Gabriella, 'more, please.'"

"With pleasure, Avi. Anyone else?" Jordan and Leo passed their plates.

As he was finishing his second portion, Avi said, "You know we played St. Michael's College basketball two weeks ago. We're in the same league, which includes eight religious schools. We beat you guys. By eight points."

"I heard about that. Our team is not at the top this year, somewhere in the middle. Our senior boys know about your school and tell me that you play hard but fair."

"That's the best way," Jordan said. "We have some talent, but we need to maximize it with effort. Both schools seem to have kids who are competitive, who do what they do in a strong way."

"I only know you four and few others from Maimonides, but I've thought that you are not much different from my students at St. Mike's. That's a compliment. What I mean is that you're serious about your studies, you strive to do well, you value education, and you have a respect for your tradition and your community. As well, you all do two kinds of studies. My students are in a separate school doing the Ontario curriculum and they do sacred music on top of that. You do the same secular curriculum and then study your sacred texts and history."

"I never thought of it like that," Deborah said.

"I think, as human beings, you have a lot in common. Many of my students come to be lay leaders in the Catholic community. I'll bet that happens with Maimonides students as well. People in education in the Catholic community have a lot of respect for Maimonides. They say that it does a lot of what we want to do."

"But it is Catholic," Jordan said. "It's different from us. Catholics believe in the divinity of Jesus."

"I'm not going to stop this conversation, but I am asking for a pause. I promise I'll continue after I cook our next dish, secondo. I won't forget where we are, but now I need to fix your main course."

Everyone helped to clear the dishes and Gabriella and Danny stayed in the kitchen. After fifteen minutes, Danny herded the young people back to the table. Gabriella came in with another platter, on it this time was a course of sea bass in lemon and garlic sauce.

They were in gastronomic heaven. Leo summed it up, "This is probably the best fish dish I have ever had." There was agreement around the table.

"Thanks, everyone. I know that you know from your own homes how good it is to prepare a fine meal for great people that they enjoy. It makes me happy.

"Now, I said I would continue our conversation. Yes, Jordan, many Catholics believe in the divinity of Jesus."

"Many?" Avi asked. "I thought all Catholics believe in Jesus as the son of God."

"Do all Jews believe in the God of the Old Testament? Many do, but not all. There are a lot of Catholics who relate to the tradition and values, especially in Canada and the US. Also in Latin-America, where some have said that you can't be a good Catholic unless you help those suffering and the poor. It's called liberation theology, and a lot of people in Rome don't like it."

"We have a concept called tikkun olam, which means to try to heal the world," said Deborah. "I think that sometimes matters more to me than prayer."

"We have something like that," Gabriella said. "It's called bearing witness. To me, it means you practice your values in your daily life. You are a good Catholic if you help the poor, if you are a kind person, if you try to make a difference when you encounter others. It is a kind of social belief. It says that you are being Catholic when you practice Catholic values, not simply by going to mass. Frankly, it's a bit radical. But I'll bet Pope Francis could handle it."

"Are you saying that there are many ways of being Catholic?" asked Avi.

"Your father told me Judaism is a big house with lots of rooms. There are many ways of being Jewish, not one. It's the same, as far as I'm concerned—and I'm not at all alone in this— in Catholicism. I identify as a Catholic, and all of you identify as Jews. But I am a certain kind of Catholic, one who, I hope, bears witness. What was your Hebrew term? Tikan olam?"

"Tikkun olam," corrected Danny.

"I don't want to talk too much," Gabriella continued. "But I'd like to think that doing music for others contributes to tikkun olam; studying important books does so; catching murderers does so. There are lots of ways to contribute to making the world a better place. In the end, Avi,

I'm a member of the human race. It sounds corny, but all that is human is important. I don't think that Jews have a monopoly on goodness, and I certainly don't think that Catholicism—which has done some very bad things in the past—has that monopoly. Sorry, end of speech."

Leo said, "I've never heard this kind of thing before."

Danny said, "Leo, my own opinion is that there is one big problem with schools like Maimonides and St. Michael's Choir School. I don't know how to solve it. The schools are very fine and they do their job. But the young people in the schools don't encounter the wider world as much as they should. The Catholic kids are around other Catholic kids and teachers and the Cathedral all the time. Same for the Jewish kids.

"I'll put it another way, though I hope this doesn't come too close to home. Jewish history is filled with our suffering, especially the Holocaust. Yes, we have suffered. But other people also have suffered. We need to know about that and help both others and ourselves. The horrible situation now with refugees from the Middle East, though they are not Jewish, is something that matters. Tikkun olam for me includes that."

"I didn't have any friends who weren't Jewish until my second year in university," Deborah said.

"And Deborah, you are a fine and good person," Danny said. "I think we need to think about others as well as ourselves."

"You may be right, Mr. Miller," Jordan said. "I'm going to do some thinking."

The conversation moved on to other matters as the young people asked Gabriella about the curriculum and requirements of her unique school.

When they finished the fish course, Gabriella spoke with a twinkle in her eye and a lilt in her voice. "If we were at an Italian wedding, people, or if we were in Naples on a Sunday, I would now follow with a meat course."

Avi said, "Not even I could manage that and I love food."

"I'll spare you. Let's clean the table and I'll bring in some pareve ice cream. With blueberries."

It was a lengthy meal, ending after three hours at the table. The young people soon left, all thanking Gabriella and Danny for the evening.

Gabriella said, as they were cleaning up, "Really, they are terrific kids. And I meant it when I said they are not all that different from the boys I teach."

"I'm with you on this. That's what makes us a little different in our Catholicism and Jewishness."

"More than a little, Danny."

"Probably. Let's just go on being who we are. I like the concept of bearing witness. What's on tomorrow for you?"

"I start late, a bit after ten. But I go late. After school, we have rehearsal at the Conservatory."

"I start late too, but I'm hoping we'll get on the road to a big breakthrough later in the day. If so, we'll be focusing in on a murderer. Hopefully by the end of the week."

XIII

When Danny got into the office the next day he went into Sydney McIntyre's office to brief her on what would be happening. He then went downstairs to the case room to work with Nadiri and her team. It was four in the afternoon when they finished. The A, B and C lists were compiled. They taped the A List on the board. It was:

Mauro Bosco, 38, Cook and dishwasher at Lefty's Diner on Roncesvalles

Saul Finkelman, 39, Biker for SendQuick Courier Service

Juan Gomez, 38, Cleaner for Business Cleaning Service in downtown Toronto

Alan Hanson, 39, Occasional worker for Atlas Roofing Company

Roger Jameson, 39, Clerk in the storage area of the downtown Store of Home and Office Supplies Ltd.

James Ryan Murray, 38, Clerk in Marrano's Italian Market on Christie Street

Paul Reeseman 38, Cashier for Metro Supermarket Store at Eglinton Avenue and Yonge Street

Michael Williams, 39, Itinerant worker. Most often a

delivery person on a truck for Meals for a Week Caterers

"We have our first job," Danny said. "We have the home addresses for all of these men. We need to interview them and find out what we can. Of course, they need to supply alibis. The Fogelman murder occurred only six days ago and they should be able to remember where they were between six and eight that morning. Frawley was killed months ago, and Michaelson more than a month ago, so they may be fuzzy about knowing their whereabouts at the time of those murders."

"How deep do we go, sir?" asked Honeker. "I've never done this before."

"Don't push too hard. Remember, seven of these men are innocent. Maybe all of them are innocent. They're persons of interest until we erase them from the list. They're not suspected murderers until we have more. If we can't knock them off the list after the first conversation we have with them, we can go further the second time around."

Danny looked around. "I think I'd like to begin this evening. I'd like to see at least one of them at home, if he is in, and get going. I have a sense that time is important. Are you up to working this evening for a while? You've been here all weekend."

Two nods, one "yes" and one "let's do it" answered his question.

"Alright. There are five of us. I'll team with Connor, and Nadiri and Taegan will be the second team. Ted, you are off until Wednesday morning. Go home and see your family, take a pause. Sometimes that even helps a case. Connor, you get off Wednesday. Taegan, you are off Thursday.

"Connor and I will try to see Mauro Bosco, the first name on the list, this evening. Nadiri and Taegan, you try to see Saul Finkelman, the second name. We'll meet tomorrow morning here at nine to talk about it and maybe move on to some of the others."

They nodded. It was four-thirty. "Connor, let's leave here at six. We'll get to Bosco's apartment in the Roncesvalles area at about six thirty. Hopefully, he'll be at home."

"We'll do the same, Taegan," Nadiri said.

"Everybody get something to eat. Ted, take a break. You others, call your families to remind them you are still in the world."

Nadiri accompanied Danny as they walked up to their office. "I think it may work, sir," she said.

"You have more faith in my thinking than some others, Nadiri."

"I remember you said your theory was based on some premises. If one was wrong it all went up in smoke … That's not what you actually said."

"Close enough, Nadiri."

"I went over the premises in my mind. I've thought a lot about them. I think they are more likely to work than not to work. That's why I said I think we are on to something."

"We'll know soon."

"By the way, sir, do you think I could have Thursday afternoon off? I could use it, but I don't want to ask if it gets in the way of the investigation."

"It's yours, Nadiri. You've been working around the clock. Remind me tomorrow. Now I'll take a short walk before I see Mauro Bosco."

Connor also liked to drive. They chatted as they drove to the west end, to an apartment in the Junction neighbourhood on the west end not far from Bosco's job on Roncesvalles.

"Do you mind if I do any questioning, sir?" Connor asked.

"No, but let me start, and signal me when you want to join in."

"What are we looking for specifically?"

"Several things. I just want to get a feel of his personality. Then it would be useful if he had a clear alibi for one of the murders, if not all of them. If we need to go further, then we will see if he catches himself."

"What do you mean?"

"He probably won't know much, if anything, about the three men. If he knows too much, then I'll wonder."

They arrived at the Junction, parked the car and walked the block and a half to Bosco's address. He had an apartment on Dundas West, in an old three-story building. The neighbourhood was gentrifying, but still had some of the qualities of an old area that had been passed over. While walking to the apartment, they passed a new trendy fish restaurant, and a shoemaker and a corner store that had seen better days. A few buildings had been renovated and they seemed to be the trend. Danny wondered how long someone like Mauro Bosco would be living here. He both welcomed the changes and regretted some of their consequences at the same time. The first floor of Bosco's address was a speciality bakery, calling itself a boulangerie, with two small apartments above it. Bosco's was the top one.

They rang the bell downstairs. It was answered by a male voice. They identified themselves and went up.

Bosco was waiting for them at the top of the stairs, his apartment door was open behind him. He seemed puzzled.

"Mr. Bosco," Danny said, "we need to have a conversation with you. We are in the middle of an investigation and we think you might be able to help us. As far as we are concerned, you have done nothing wrong."

"Sergeant, I live a quiet life. I didn't do anything wrong."

They were still in the hall. "Mr. Bosco. We don't think you did anything wrong. We need to get some information. That's all."

Bosco, discombobulated, invited them in. The apartment was small and neat. Bosco had just had his supper and there was the odour of tomato sauce coming from the tiny kitchen.

He nervously said, "The only cops I see are the ones who come to the diner where I work. We have regulars. They know me."

They sat down, Danny and Connor facing Bosco. Connor signalled to Danny, who nodded.

"Mr. Bosco," Connor said, "I'm one of those cops who might go to Lefty's if I was assigned to that station. As far as we are concerned you are a good citizen. We just need some information for a case we are handling. It's like doing jury duty, something we all do."

"Sorry. I had some troubles fifteen years ago. I've been clean since then. I don't want to go back to that."

"That won't happen, Mr. Bosco," Danny said. "Now, can we ask you some questions?"

"Sure, Officer."

Bosco remembered the camp, but not much else about it. The names of Frawley and Fogelman didn't register. He did remember Michaelson after they gave him his first name. "Oh, yeah," he said, "Eddie. He was at the lake. A nice guy. Funny."

When they asked him if anything about the camp seemed unusual, Bosco couldn't recall anything out of the ordinary, with one exception. "There were some weird interfaith prayers. At least, a lot of us thought they were weird."

Finally, he had an alibi for the Fogelman murder, or one that was close enough to being foolproof. "If it was a Thursday," he said, "then I was at Lefty's by six thirty, when I start. I'm off Sunday and Monday.

We open at seven and I help do the prep. Two other guys, the brothers who own the place, were there too."

They thanked Bosco and left. They told him he had been helpful and they wouldn't need to see him again. In the car, Connor said, "It looks like we can cross him off, sir."

"Unquestionably," Danny answered. "We'll check the alibi with the owners, but I'm with you. Highly unlikely. Let's get some sleep, and we'll meet in the morning."

Danny, Nadiri, Taegan and Connor gathered to discuss the case at nine on Tuesday morning.

Nadiri reported that Finkelman was somewhat eccentric. "He belongs to the cyclist culture I investigated in the Gentrey case. In addition to his being a bike courier to make a living, he goes on bike trips with others on the weekend. They do an easy hundred kilometres a day, winding up in a pub or a café where they meet other cyclists. His small apartment is filled with trophies."

She looked at Taegan, "We didn't get a sense he had a grievance." Taegan nodded. "He remembered the camp. He said he found it strange because some of the people there were what he called 'over-religious'. He liked the summer he was there. Frawley was one of his counsellors, and he used him as an example of what he meant as 'over-religious'. He didn't remember the other two."

Taegan continued, "We got a sense he took drugs, occasionally. He has a form. He was arrested twenty years ago on a drug charge, as we noted on the chart. He got a suspended sentence. Nothing since then."

"Any alibis?" Danny asked.

"Kind of an alibi for the Fogelman murder," Nadiri said. "Half an alibi. He says he reported to work at eight o'clock that day, maybe a few minutes earlier. SendQuick Courier has its offices downtown, around Dundas and Jarvis. So, if he was there a little before eight, he could have murdered Fogelman and ridden downtown. He also claims he usually meets a neighbour, a Sally Reynolds, when he goes downstairs. She leaves for work at the same time, about seven-fifteen. If that checks out for last week and work checks out, he is clean. We'll do the checking today, but it seems to us, unless he is a great actor, he had nothing to do with it."

Danny reported on Bosco, recounting his recollections and alibi. "This morning I called the diner where he works. One of his bosses told me he is very regular. He hasn't missed coming by six-thirty for at least a month. So his alibi checks out."

"Six to go," Danny said. "You take Hanson and Murray. Their workplaces are not far from one another. Connor and I will work downtown on Gomez and Jameson."

"Just one thing," he added. "I know you know this, but I'll say it anyway. If you go to their workplaces, be careful not to embarrass them. Let their employers know we're questioning them for information, not because they're thought to be guilty of anything. Only one is guilty. We think."

Nadiri said, "We'll go with care."

Connor and Danny drove first to the offices of Business Cleaning Services, near Queen and Beverley. When they spoke to the supervisor who was present, he told them Gomez worked at night, after businesses were closed. Gomez was on a shift that looked after a piece of PATH, the underground downtown mall. He worked overnight from nine to six.

"He's got to be sleeping now," said the supervisor. "Our workers are part of the night side of the city. There are lots of us, though the day workers take us for granted."

"Let's let Gomez get some sleep." Danny said to Connor as they walked back to the car. "We can go to see Jameson now and then go to Gomez's address near Kensington Market later in the day."

They arrived at the office supplies store at Yonge and Marlborough at ten forty-five. They entered the large store, and made themselves known to a clerk. They were taken to an office in the rear to the manager, Peter Mosconi.

Danny explained to Mosconi why they were there. "We are in the middle of a very serious case. We think your employee, Roger Jameson, might be able to help us. We're not sure, but we're covering all the bases. I don't want this to look bad for Mr. Jameson. Time is important, so we have come to ask some questions."

"Thanks, Sergeant. Roger has been doing better work in the last few months. He has had some troubles, but he seems to be over them."

"Can we do this privately, Mr. Mosconi?"

"Sure. Use this office. The whole place is wide open. This is one of the few private spaces. If you come with me, I'll find Roger."

Mosconi found Jameson in the large storage room where they kept inventory to be placed on the shelves as things got sold. He was loading a trolley with some boxes.

Jameson was dressed neatly in clothing that was somewhat frayed. Like Bosco before him, he was thrown by the presence of the detectives. They explained they just needed some information. The four of them walked to Mosconi's office.

Danny had a sudden flash of memory. 'I think I've seen him before,' he thought.

They settled in Mosconi's office, Danny behind the desk, Jameson and Connor in the two chairs facing him. Jameson sat down and gathered himself, his right foot going up and down in a kind of persistent tic. Danny knew. He had seen Jameson in the waiting room at CAMH when he first went to see Everson.

Danny started as he had with Bosco. "Mr. Jameson, we don't think you've done anything wrong. We need to have a conversation with you about a case we are investigating. You may be able to help."

Jameson looked nervous, understandably. "We're just looking for some information."

"I don't know anything," Jameson said. "I live alone. I don't have much of a social life."

"What we are asking about goes back to your teens. Do you remember your summer at Camp Unity?"

The tic became even more pronounced. It also began more slowly in his left leg.

"What about it?"

"Tell me about that summer."

"It was an interfaith camp. I got a scholarship from the United Church we attended."

"Do you remember any of the other campers? Do you remember any of the counsellors?"

"Which ones?"

"Do you remember young men your age like Mauro Bosco, Juan Gomez, James Ryan Murray, Michael Williams?"

"I remember Bosco. Italian. Catholic. He was a good swimmer. Murray was in my bunk."

"Do you remember your counsellors?"

There was a very long pause. Danny let the silence do its work.

Finally, Jameson answered, "I remember a Jewish guy. A strange name. Yitz something. He became a jeweller. I remember Jim, Jim Frawley, another Catholic. He became a teacher."

"That's very useful. Thanks, Mr. Jameson. Do you remember a swimming instructor?"

More silence. "Yeah. Eddie. Eddie Michaelson. He became a lawyer. He married a man."

"Do you know what happened to Mauro Bosco or James Ryan Murray afterwards?"

"No. We lost touch."

Connor was wide-eyed, trying not to stare at Jameson. Danny said, "Mr. Jameson, do you know where you were last Tuesday early in the morning?"

"How early?"

"When do you get to work, Mr. Jameson?"

"Nine."

"Where were you last Tuesday morning between six and eight?"

Jameson answered immediately and with certainty, "I was home, in my new apartment near The Beach."

"Do you live with anyone?"

"I told you I live alone."

"Can anyone vouch for you being at home between six and eight last Tuesday morning?"

He got annoyed. "I told you. I live alone. Why are you doing this to me?"

Danny was certain. He nodded to Connor. "Mr. Jameson, I am arresting you for the murder of Yitzchak Fogelman. We will continue this interview at the police station."

Jameson was so distraught he just collapsed and said nothing.

Connor was already calling for a police car to come to take Jameson to the station. They sat silently until the car came. One of the officers appeared at the office. The three escorted Jameson to the waiting car.

XIV

That afternoon, there was a buzz in the station. Rarely, if ever, had anyone seen three murders solved at once. Nadiri and Taegan were called back from their interviews. Taegan notified Honeker.

Jameson was put into a cell, and provided lunch and the opportunity to call a lawyer. The full interview was scheduled for three, conducted by Danny, assisted by Nadiri. McIntyre, two other sergeants, and Taegan, Connor and Honeker were given the opportunity to watch the interview through the two-way mirror and to be available for consultation.

In the interview room, Danny welcomed Jameson and introduced Nadiri. He had had three water bottles placed on the table. He turned on the tape, performed the ritual of stating the time, date and who was present, and then spoke.

"Mr. Jameson, I know you've been informed you could have a lawyer. You said that was not necessary. Is that correct?"

"Lawyers and I don't get along. They have not helped me."

"You are waiving your right to a lawyer?"

"Yeah."

"Mr. Jameson, not only do you have the right to call a lawyer, but we can arrange for a lawyer from legal aid if you cannot afford a lawyer. Many people find a lawyer very useful in these circumstances."

"I'm tired. I don't want a lawyer."

Danny pulled his chair back, crossed his legs and was silent for a good twenty seconds. Then, very quietly, said, "Mr. Jameson, you have a story. I'd like you to tell me your story."

"Why should I tell you?"

"Because," Danny said softly, "we need to understand why you have done what you did. I know you did it for a reason. You did not murder those three men because you are a violent person."

McIntyre and the two sergeants, behind the mirror, were wondering what was happening. This was an unusual way of handling someone who was to be charged with three murders, something more appropriate to a session with a psychiatrist than to a murder investigation. The three young constables simply thought it normal.

"I have a story."

"I know you do, Mr. Jameson. Please tell us your story."

"I had a reason."

"What was your reason, sir?"

"Those three wrecked my life. They did things that destroyed me. They robbed me of over twenty years."

"What did they do?"

More silence. Danny didn't move. Nadiri followed his lead. Then the floodgate opened, and Jameson started to tell his story.

"It was in the camp when I was thirteen years old. They were older. Jimmy was a counsellor in my bunk. Yitz was a counsellor in the next bunk. Eddie was on the water. At first it was Jimmy at night. He came to my bed in the middle of the night and touched me here." He pointed to his genitals.

There was a pause. Danny asked, "Did he do anything else?"

"Yeah. After a while he woke me in the dark and took me outside. Yitz and Eddie were waiting. They undressed me and had sex with me. Usually two of them did it and one watched. The guy who watched jerked off. They treated me like I was a sex doll."

"Were you the only one who they abused?"

"No. There were a few others. I don't remember all the names. One was a kid named Juan, another was named Paul."

"Do you think they traumatized you?"

"They wrecked my life. I'm a school dropout and a former druggie. I couldn't hold a job for long until now."

"Have you had help from doctors?"

"I've seen many shrinks. I have one now, a nice guy. Some of them would give me drugs. A couple of the drugs became addictions."

"Why did you kill those three now, more than twenty years later?"

"I was getting better. I wanted a future. My shrink—other shrinks too—said my problem was in my past. I wanted to do what I didn't do for twenty years. I wanted to act. I wanted those bastards to know what they did. They were living normal lives and I was a person barely hanging on."

"When you went to see James Frawley, Jimmy, did you want to harm him?"

"I went to tell him what he did. I wanted him to feel bad, maybe to apologize. He told me to get out. He talked about God a lot and how he was close to Jesus. He said he was a good man, following in Jesus' footsteps. He made me feel it was my fault, that he had nothing to do with it."

"What did you do?"

"I took the chair apart and hit him. I beat him. I left him bleeding. I wiped everything, and I left."

"Not yet, Mr. Jameson. You did something else before you left."

"I broke his fingers. I broke the fingers he used to abuse me, to rape me. I broke the fingers that went up my ass."

"Did you feel any guilt the next morning?"

"No. I felt terrific. He had robbed me of twenty years and now I robbed him of a future."

"Just a bit more before we break, Mr. Jameson."

Again, Danny sat back. Again, he spoke softly.

"Why did you mutilate Eddie and Yitz after you killed them with your knife?"

"They liked to use their mouths on me. Eddie most of all. They liked to look and jerk off. Yitz most of all."

"I'd like to break for a short time, Mr. Jameson. Can we bring you a sandwich or coffee?"

"Yeah. A sandwich and coffee would be good."

Danny stopped the tape, signalled to Nadiri to stay and he went out of the room. He took a deep breath as the door was closing.

He held up his hand, indicating he wanted to talk first. "Get him something to eat and a coffee."

"Connor is on his way, sir," Taegan said.

"It really is a sad story," Danny said. "I know he was a patient at CAMH. I saw him there once when I went to see Everson. He has an analyst. We should get in touch. We should have our psychiatrist talk with him. He'll need a lawyer and he has no money. Get one from the list. A good one. This will be a complex case."

"I agree with your suggestions, Danny," McIntyre said. "He does have a story. A very, very sad one."

One of the other sergeants, Rob Quincey, asked, "Where do you go from here, Danny?"

"We'll finish the questioning. As we were speaking, I assume you got people to search Jameson's apartment."

"Correct," McIntyre said. "They're on their way."

"I'll take a cup of coffee too, if possible." Taegan pulled out his phone to call Connor.

The sandwich and coffees arrived. They gave Jameson time to eat and then put the tape back on.

The rest of the interview yielded no surprises. Danny emphasized that the first killing was spontaneous, and he had Jameson go through the abuse in more detail. Jameson said he used a knife from his kitchen on the other two men. Near the end he asked Jameson what he hoped to gain from the murders.

"I wanted a future," he said. "I wanted a life…I'm not good with words, Sergeant." He stumbled and muttered something to himself. Then he continued, "I had nothing for all this time. I wanted something. I thought if I could act, then I could … I don't have the words … lose the past."

A little before seven, they finished. Danny said, "Thanks, Mr. Jameson. I am formally charging you with the murders of James Frawley, Edward Michaelson, and Yitzchak Fogelman. You will be detained. You will need a lawyer. If you do not have one the court will find one for you."

He announced the time and stopped the tape. Jameson exited first, into the care of two guards who would escort him to his cell.

All of them—Danny, Nadiri, McIntyre, the two sergeants and the three constables—met in the case room afterwards over some pizza and drinks.

"Well, folks, we did it," McIntyre said. "Three murders solved and handed to the courts. Danny, as is becoming usual, great work."

"This time, really, it is not me. This was the team. Nadiri, Taegan, Connor and Ted deserve lots of credit. They worked very hard. They worked smart. I want to see that in their files. I mean it."

"Seems fair to me," Quincey said. "Good job, Danny and team."

"What do you think about Jameson?" asked the other sergeant, Gamal Kumar.

Danny looked around, suggesting someone else talk first.

Nadiri entered the conversation. "He is, strangely, somewhat sympathetic. I don't mean he's like Mrs. Nizamani, for whom I have great sympathy. I mean he seems very vulnerable from what had happened to him a long time ago."

"Yes," McIntyre said, "as we said before, this isn't your typical serial killer. He really isn't a serial killer at all."

"Do you think he would have stopped with those three?" Connor asked.

Danny spoke. "I don't know. I'm trying to get into his head. Did the killings give meaning to what he felt was a meaningless life? The last one occurred a week ago. Would he have continued, with some sort of rationale, because if he stopped he was back into his earlier life? Happily, we'll never know."

McIntyre looked around. The team was totally spent. "Time to go home and get some rest, people. You've been living here for too long. I'll look after the paperwork as much as I can. Danny, I'll need a report but it can wait a few days. We'll get out a press release tomorrow morning. I don't know if we need a press conference. We'll see the reaction from the media and the communications people upstairs. Some very detailed follow-ups to tomorrow's release might do."

Danny drove home in deep reflection. When he got in the door he undressed and put on a robe. He went to the kitchen and got a glass of wine, then went into the living room where he put on Bach's cello suites and sat and contemplated late into the night.

XVI

Danny took most of the next day off. He wanted to walk and not be cold, something impossible in Toronto in February. He settled for a walk to Elena's, where he had a salad for lunch and a coffee with Constantine. He needed a little bit of normal life. He practiced his violin most of the rest of the day, though the case was still on his mind.

In the evening there was the pleasure of the Bloor Street Chamber Group, where they began a new work, the first two movements of Handel's Concerto Grosso in D Major (Opus 6, no. 5), popularly known as St. Cecilia's Concerto. Danny and Gabriella had fallen into the habit of driving the short distance home together in Danny's car. On the way to the car, parked on St. George Street, Gabriella said, "I got a very nice phone call today."

"From who?"

"From your sister. We had a long conversation and we arranged to have tea tomorrow afternoon downtown, near my school."

"I'm supposed to be good at questioning people. I don't know if I should ask."

"She was lovely. She told me that the kids had nothing but praise for my cooking, and asked about recipes. She said Deborah was especially moved by the conversation at the table. And, of course, she mentioned some guy we both know."

"Ruth is doing what she does better than anyone I know. She just jumps in and decides what makes sense and does it."

"I'm grateful she took the initiative. I'm looking forward to tomorrow. She's a person I would like to get to know."

When they got settled in the car, Danny said, "I didn't go into the station today. I'm weary. This case took a lot out of me."

"Tell me a little about it, if you feel like talking. If not, it can wait. It has to affect you emotionally."

"It does. I'll talk about it on the weekend. You'll see the press release report in tomorrow morning's newspaper. Right now, I wanted to tell you I did call McIntyre about a personal matter. Vacation time. I have March break off. If you want to go somewhere, I'm all in."

"I'd really like a week on the beach with you in March. Let's see what we can find. It's late, you know."

"Let's look on Saturday. Who knows?"

The next day Nadiri took her half-day in the afternoon. When she returned to her apartment from the station, the door was locked. She entered and waited with excitement.

Ten minutes later, Fiona entered. They embraced and started to talk.

"I don't know what to do, my sweet. Let me tell you my dilemma."

Nadiri got two glasses of wine and went to the couch. Fiona settled in her chair.

She continued, "I've been offered two public positions. One is from a group of people who want me to stand for Markham City Council in the election in October. The other is from the premier. She asked me to meet with her. She wants me to head the Liberal Party in the riding—Albert Montanegre, the long-standing president of the riding association, is retiring—and then, in the next election, probably a few years from now, be the Liberal candidate for the provincial legislature. She was very flattering, though, of course, that's part of the arm-twisting."

"What's the problem?" asked Nadiri. "You deserve both. You want to make a difference. Your kids will be very proud of you."

"The problem is I have to decide if I want my life to change in a way that makes it very public. The problem is that I'm in love with you. I can't keep going without you in my life on a regular basis."

I love you too. Sometimes I live for our meetings."

Nadiri continued, "We would go on as we are now. Nothing need change. The premier who made the offer is openly gay, has a partner who appears on her side, and was elected after coming out. People in this province don't care much about this anymore."

"If that were all, it would be easy. But I will be under greater public scrutiny than ever before. You've said I can't risk losing my children. Andrew would divorce me if he found out about us, about me."

"You will have to decide. I will support whatever you choose and will do whatever is needed to keep us going."

"What would you do?"

"I don't know. I'm not familiar with the public life. I work almost anonymously. I know my boss, Daniel Miller, hates being a public person, but does it as part of the job. I can't help you decide. I can only say I'll support your decision."

Fiona sighed. "I don't know. I have some time. I'll think some more about it and perhaps we'll have another conversation."

"I have something else I want to say, something totally wild, Nadiri."

"Wild is fine with me," Nadiri replied, smiling.

"I'd like to try to figure out if we could go away someplace together for a week or so. I want to walk in the street with you. I want to sit in a restaurant. I want to hold your hand in public."

"Fiona, I would give anything for that. How do you imagine it can be done?"

"I am the problem. You can go anywhere. I thought I might let my old friend Daphne in on our secret. Tell her I had a lover, a male she will assume, and I wanted her to pretend she and I were going away for a girl's holiday. She would cover for me. Then you and I could meet somewhere far away—in England, on Vancouver Island, anywhere."

"I love it. But it's very risky for you."

"Maybe. I'll try to keep it simple. Not make it too complicated. Would you think about it?"

"It would be wonderful, heavenly. Let's talk some more how it might be done."

"Oh, I didn't tell you," Nadiri continued. "I spoke to my sister about being gay. She was so good to me I just wept."

"Good. You need her."

"Now, lunch or bed?" asked Nadiri.

"We can always have lunch, don't you think?"

XVII

The following Friday afternoon, Danny drove to the Feldman house with great anticipation. Ruth had called him earlier in the week and told him she was inviting Gabriella for Friday night dinner. "It's not only me, Danny. The kids really took to her. Including Avi. They suggested we return the favour."

Danny told Ruth he was delighted. Gabriella asked him about the ritual and the blessings and he briefed her on them. He also did a transliteration of some of the Hebrew songs they would sing at the table before the meal, which Gabriella memorized.

When Danny arrived, Ruth called out, "We're in the kitchen." She and Gabriella were wearing aprons and were doing the cooking.

"I'm learning a lot," Gabriella said.

"There's not much to learn," Ruth said. "Her Nonna did a good job. Now I know why the kids loved the meal at your house."

Gabriella and Danny told Ruth they would be going to Martinique for March break. "Avi told me," she said. "You know it's hard to keep anything secret in this family. Good for you. Enjoy."

It was a warm evening. The Grossmans were guests as well as Elie and Lotty Marcus. Elie Marcus was the *chazzan*, the cantor of the synagogue. He was trained not only in Jewish sacred music but also had a graduate degree in composition from Columbia University. Ruth seated him next to Gabriella and they had a long exchange about the sacred music they both performed.

In retrospect Danny remembered that night as one of the most warm and important nights of his life. Avi gave Gabriella a hug, Ruth praised her and took her in hand, and even Irwin was gallant. And Gabriella knocked everybody over when she joined in the singing. What he thought would be a tense evening turned into a very relaxed, joyful one. Again, he thought, Ruth was taking care of him.

At the end of the evening, Ruth, Deborah, Gabriella, Danny and Avi were in the kitchen, cleaning up. Deborah asked Gabriella more about her world and about its many rooms. Avi suggested Gabriella come to Maimonides to work with the choir there. "I would like that," said Gabriella, "but I don't want to step on anyone's toes. Ask the principal and the choir director. If it's OK with them, then it's fine with me. It's their show. I'll help them as much as I can."

As they were finishing, Gabriella turned quietly to Danny. "Excuse me, Sergeant Miller. I wonder if I can get a ride home."

"You took the TTC?"

"Yes."

"Well, Maestra Agostini, I'd be delighted. Not only will I drive you to your place. I think, in the interests of safety of course, I should escort you into your apartment."

"I wouldn't have it any other way."

EPILOGUE

A week later Danny was summoned to meet with the new chief of police.

He and John Kingston didn't know each other well, but from what Danny had seen, he liked Kingston. He seemed highly competent, fair and direct.

He entered the large office and the two men shook hands. Kingston, the first black chief of the Toronto Police Service, was a bit taller and wider than Danny. He had a face that was almost regal, proportioned and strong. He was a serious person, though he smiled easily and if you didn't know that, the wrinkles on his face would have told you it was so. He came up through the ranks and had been on the force for thirty years.

He asked Danny to sit, suggested coffee, which he poured from a carafe on a sideboard, and settled down.

"It's good to see you again, Danny. I think we last met when I stopped in to see Sydney about a case you were on. About a year ago, before they put me in this very nice office I make certain to leave several times a week."

"Congratulations, sir. It's no secret you were a popular choice."

"We'll see what that means when I have my first conflict with the union. In this office, when we're alone, please call me John. I prefer to think of us as colleagues working for the same goals. Let me congratulate you. I don't think I can remember a time when a detective did what you managed to accomplish these last few months. Three major cases. Five murders. You worked in the best professional manner."

"Thanks, John. You know how it works. I had a lot of help. Especially from some bright and committed young people."

"You did. I know that. But I've read the reports, and those murders would not have been solved without you. You were the difference. I admire your ability to choose different methods for different cases. Not everyone can do that. Not everyone thinks of doing that. There will be some commendations coming to you."

Kingston continued, "I asked you here to make a proposal, Danny, though I'm very happy to have had the opportunity to offer thanks for your work."

"A proposal?"

"Yes. I take it you know there are some inspector positions open. And you're smart enough to know you would be considered. Well, I'd like you to be a homicide detective inspector, the position formerly held by your boss, Sydney McIntyre. You were number one on nearly everyone's list. You were number one on my list."

"I'm surprised. Before we go further, what does this mean for Sydney? Is there a problem? I certainly don't see one. She does a fine job."

"The reverse. Sydney asked to be moved when it would be convenient. She'd like to get experience in other areas. I agree it would be good for her and for the force. So, there's an opening in Major Crimes. Sydney will fill it. You'll take over Homicide."

"I won't tell you I haven't given a promotion some thought. I will tell you I never considered that it would be moving up where I am."

"Any problems?"

"Yes and no. I like my work. It drives me crazy sometimes, like the Nizamani case, but I can do some good. I like being out in the community. Let me try it this way. I don't know how you conceive the job. There must be a job description in some bureaucrat's file. I would be less tied to my desk than Sydney was. I would supervise, sure. But I would occasionally get out and actively investigate a case. The balance would be different. John, if it's a desk job alone, you have the wrong guy."

"I appreciate your frankness. Let's make a deal, our own arrangement. You do the job for, say, about a year. Do it your way. Then, let's meet and ask if that's working. If it's working then keep doing it that way. If it needs some adjustment that we agree on, then that happens. I wouldn't make this arrangement with everyone, you know. You have a reputation for being straight and I see by the way you work that you can adjust to circumstances."

"That's an offer that's hard to turn down," Danny said. "Not everybody will be happy. When someone mentioned to me a month or two ago that I might be considered for an Inspector's job, I told them one of my father's maxims; by the way, he was another guy who worked his way up through his firm. He told me to never accept a job that hasn't been offered to me. Another maxim of his was, 'If somebody makes an offer, even if it looks perfect, sleep on it.'"

"Smart man," Kingston said.

"How long can I sleep on it?"

"I need an answer by next week."

"You'll have it sooner than that. I'll talk to the family and I'll sleep on it."

Continue reading for a preview of the next Danny Miller investigation.

SOCIAL JUSTICE

The five friends met every six weeks or so to discuss their common undertaking.
 Two years ago they formed a club in which they pledged secrecy. They brought it into being after a discussion about how their work sometimes seemed to be in opposition to their values, contradicting the reasons they went to law school, where they met. They had entered the legal profession to do some good, and now, after a few years as associates in several downtown Toronto law firms, they found themselves working for the owners and executives of wealthy companies, helping to make them even wealthier. They regularly took part in meetings representing corporations and individuals where the lowest number discussed regarding a sale or a merger was in the area of half a billion dollars. Their job was to help their clients make profitable deals and avoid taxes. They realized, in practicing their profession, they were expected to be blind to issues of social justice.
 It rankled. They met over coffee and the occasional beer to discuss what had happened. As one of the two women in the group said, "We have been seduced by a good salary and the idea that success means being made a partner in the firm." Someone else noted they now needed their paycheques to keep up the lifestyle they unthinkingly bought into: the house in Leslieville or Roncesvalles or the outer part of The

Beach or west of The Annex; the private school they wanted their children to attend; the holidays in the Caribbean or Europe.

"We've become what we wanted to reform when we entered Osgoode fourteen years ago," said a third member. "We've been co-opted."

They pondered what they might do to reclaim some of what they now believed was their lost authenticity.

The five of them—two women and three men—acted. They would single out individuals who they believed were greedy, those who were abusing other people and society. These people hired lawyers like them to manipulate the law. It was time to mete out some justice.

They went slowly, to not call attention to themselves. The first 'claim to justice,' as they styled their actions, was an anonymous leak to *The Globe and Mail*. They revealed how Robert Werner, a major corporate raider, bought up companies, made lots of money, and destroyed thousands of jobs in Canada.

They didn't do anything to impact Werner's wealth. He remains one of the richest people in the country, an international figure. However, they hit him where it hurt—his reputation. Negotiations with the University of British Columbia to name its business school in his honour—it would have cost him a mere forty million dollars over ten years—came to a halt. He was asked quietly to leave the board of Mount Sinai Hospital after his term was over. He no longer appeared on lists of major philanthropists. He was a moneyman, and now he and his money were tainted.

After this, they waited. And then they got bolder. Their second act was to rob the house of another billionaire, Michael Lubente. He was an investor who made some of his fortune by being the silent partner and major shareholder of a nationwide chain of companies that offered payday loans at exorbitant rates to people who could not go to the banks for support. When the robbery of millions of dollars in jewels was reported, they made certain the media knew how the money to buy the precious gems was acquired. The gems themselves were in safe deposit boxes, where the friends expected them to remain forever.

Lubente appealed to the public for sympathy. Instead, the reaction he got was one of disdain and he too ceased being a public model of rectitude.

Their third act was another robbery. This time they arranged to steal a very prestigious and valuable collection of Degas sculptures of horses and ballerinas from a home in Forest Hill. The owner was one of Toronto's great braggarts, Everson Echoiman, the head of a hedge fund that claimed to make money quickly and easily for those who had the wit to invest. He had been taken to court a year earlier, accused of operating a small Ponzi scheme, just big enough to outdo his competitors by three-quarters of a percentage point. He was no Bernie Madoff, who was obvious in his deception. Rather, Echoiman cleverly managed the books to make it appear legal. The judge declared that, while Echoiman was on the margin of legality, and while he had deceived many, there was enough doubt in the evidence to find him not guilty. The judge, going over the usual line, said he wished Canada had the Scottish verdict of not proven, which would at least mean the double jeopardy rule could not be invoked in a future prosecution.

By day, the five friends worked for law firms that had prestige and might, and they made some of their money defending people like Werner and Lubente, manipulating the law in their favour. After work, they lived their lives as up-and-coming lawyers. And they also plotted to do what they thought was just in the face of the wealthy using the law for their own gain. They had little worry they were doing wrong. The organizer of the robbery said, "If we get caught, none of us could afford to hire the very firms we work for. Only the wealthy have access to the best minds in the law."

After the robbery, they went quiet for a while. Then they would act again to redress the injustice of the system. And to do something to assuage their consciences.

ACKNOWLEDGEMENTS

I'd like to thank my excellent readers, who read this work as it was evolving: Fran Cohen, Martin Sable and Lisa Haberman. They all were encouraging to a neophyte novelist and all helped make this a better book.

Mike O'Connor and the students in Writing 4004 at York University were very helpful and creative. It was a great pleasure working with them.

Finally, to Jan Rehner, who was my guide and my listener, and who asked all the right questions, my profound thanks for all she contributed and for those two important words.

ABOUT THE AUTHOR

Arthur Haberman is a retired professor of history and humanities. He lives in Toronto and loves the city and its people.